Darkness in Dixie

Book 4 in the Clarence Duval Series

Also by Rob Bauer

Fiction

My Australian Adventure

The World Traveler

The Buffalo Soldier

The Long Way Home

Nonfiction

Outside the Lines of Gilded Age Baseball: Alcohol, Fitness, and Cheating in 1880s Baseball

Outside the Lines of Gilded Age Baseball: Gambling, Umpires, and Racism in 1880s Baseball

Outside the Lines of Gilded Age Baseball: The Origins of the 1890 Players League

Outside the Lines of Gilded Age Baseball: The Finances of 1880s Baseball

Darkness in Dixie

Book 4 in the Clarence Duval Series

Rob Bauer

Although some of the people who appear in this story were real people, this is a work of fiction. My portrayal of each character is fictional, and so are the events I've written about.

This is a work of historical fiction. Names, characters, places, and incidents are the product of the author's imagination or are used fictitiously. Use of actual historical events, authentic texts, and names is of public access and public domain.

For any inquiries regarding this book, please contact Rob at robbauerbooks@gmail.com.

No part of this book may be reproduced in any form or by any electronic or mechanical means, including information storage and retrieval systems, without written permission from the author, except for the use of brief quotations in a book review.

I dedicate this book to all those whose lives were blighted and destroyed by racism but have been forgotten by history.

The world needs to hear your stories.

Author's Note on Language

One of the difficult things about writing historical fiction featuring African Americans is the use of racist language. Words that are painfully demeaning today were, sadly, commonplace usage in the era when this story is set. I've chosen to keep these words for the sake of historical accuracy. I mean no offense to any of my readers.

Contents

1

Pfeffer's Letter

Clarence Duval stares at the envelope Sally Healy handed him a few minutes ago. He runs his dark index finger along the short edge of the paper, ready to unseal the letter, but then stops and sets it on the bed again, staring intently at the return address. He still can't believe he's gotten mail from Fred Pfeffer, his old tormentor from so many years ago. Clarence continues looking at his name printed in black ink on the outside, as if just staring long enough will reveal some clue about what's inside.

In his second-story guestroom, the midday sunlight cascades through the glass window, making the white cotton sheets covering Clarence's bed shine brilliantly. To the right of the bed rests the small, varnished cherrywood dresser, although Clarence only needs one drawer to hold his spare clothes.

Sitting on the edge of his bed, Clarence bites his lip, half in curiosity and half in fear of what he'll find if he opens the piece of mail. He reaches for the envelope once more, holding his breath while he lifts it from the radiantly white sheets. Eyes closed, his right index finger extends toward the corner, sliding under the lip of the envelope and tearing open one edge.

"Aaay!" Clarence jumps up as if bitten by some invisible insect, the half-opened letter falling from his hand to the floor. It's only a soft knock at the door, he realizes. Sally Healy pokes her head into Clarence's room.

"Are you all right, my dear?" she asks Clarence in her lilting voice, the English carrying a hint of an Irish brogue. "Have you opened your mail from yesterday yet?"

"I'm sorry, Sally. Nothing's the matter. You just took me by surprise as I was about to open the envelope." Gingerly, Clarence retrieves it from where it's fallen.

"Your hand's shaking, Clarence. I didn't know mail could be so terrifying," she teases with a kindly smile, her strawberry-red hair resting on her shoulders.

"Usually, you're right."

"Can I ask who the letter's from? I didn't look when I saw it had your name on it because it came yesterday, and I was busy getting the house ready for you."

"An old teammate of John's. Fred Pfeffer. Do you know him?"

"John talks about him a wee bit, yes. I believe they correspond for news about baseball."

Clarence sighs. "That would explain how Pfeffer knew to send a letter to me here. John must've told him I was visiting soon." Clarence realizes he's been holding his breath whenever Sally speaks. He lets it out slowly.

"Clarence, you're still shaking. Whatever's the matter?"

"Pfeffer gave me a hard time on the baseball trip back in '89. A really hard time. I never thought I'd hear from him again. I don't know if I should open the letter or not."

"Well, whatever you do, I expect John home from his job at any moment, and he's anxious to talk to you, so don't dally."

Clarence gives Sally his best smile as she turns and walks back downstairs. "Right. I'll be along in a minute," he says to her retreating figure.

Again, he bites his lip while holding Pfeffer's message. At the same time, Clarence realizes his heartbeat is racing. *Funny how life can be*, he thinks to himself. *I spent months with the Buffalo Soldiers and faced danger daily. I was scared at times, but I never froze.*

Now, here I am, in the safest place I know, and I'm frightened of opening a piece of mail.

Finally, Clarence snatches up the envelope and tears open the top the rest of the way. That done, he carefully extracts the message and unfolds the cream-colored stationery. Pfeffer writes in a strong, clear hand. The pen strokes flow in a beautiful cursive script that Clarence envies for its graceful lines. He reads,

Clarence Duval,

Well, boy, I'm sure it's a shock to see a letter from old Fred. I surprised myself by writing it, but here's why I did it. For one thing, I hear John Healy had to leave the St. Louis police force. I'm sorry to hear it. Wish him the best for me at whatever he plans to do instead.

There's another thing, though. You see, boy, a few days ago someone showed up at my door in Louisville. How this nigger boy found me, I'll never know, but he knew who I was and claimed to know you. Said you two were in the cavalry together. I didn't believe him because I know you aren't brave enough for soldiering, but he seemed to know a lot about you, so I figured that maybe he did know you, but the cavalry part was just a lie to get my attention. This boy said his name was Lincoln Washington. It's no surprise that colored

3

folks would name their son after that nigger-loving president, I guess. Anyway, that's what this boy told me.

Here's what else he told me. Said he lived in Nashville but was in Louisville to visit family. I guess the niggers have their tribes still. Said he'd heard of me because you mentioned you and I went around the world together, and he knew that I lived in Louisville. He asked if I'd help send a message to you, since he couldn't write very well and wasn't sure where you lived. I didn't want to but decided I should out of Christian duty.

Well, here's his message. This nigger boy told me he'd met your father. In Alabama. The boy told me he was just out of the cavalry in Montana, and on his way home, a flood washed out some track on his train ride to Nashville. So, he had to detour through Alabama. On the way, in a town named Athens, he got off to stretch his legs at the rail station and saw a man about fifty years old who looked like you. Washington asked this old nigger who he was, just out of curiosity, and this boy said his name was William Duval and that he *had a son named Clarence whom he hadn't seen in about fifteen years.*

There you have it. Your papa is alive in Alabama. I don't know if you want to go look for him, after he abandoned you and all, but still, I'm sure you know all too well that that's how niggers are. This boy, Washington, also said your papa didn't look very healthy. Said he moved real slow and walked bent over, almost like a hunchback. I don't care what you do, of course, but I told that boy I'd write to you with his news, so I have.

Give John my best. He was always one of the squarest, whitest men I knew while playing ball.

Fred Pfeffer

Clarence just stares at the letter, mouth open, eyebrows arching, thoughts spinning. His father is alive. Of course, he must go see him. To learn why the man abandoned him, if nothing else.

Before Clarence can think of anything more, he hears the front door open downstairs and John Healy's voice carries through the house. Setting Pfeffer's note on the cherrywood dresser, he stands and takes a deep breath, followed by two more deep breaths. He'll think of what to do about Pfeffer's revelation in a few hours. For now, it's time for Clarence to meet John and get ready for the homecoming party in Clarence's honor later that evening.

2

Clarence's Second Acting Career

"Clarence, my friend, it's been a while. Sit down, and let's hear your news," John Healy says while embracing Clarence in a hug. John hangs his black winter overcoat and top hat on a peg near the kitchen door and then motions for Clarence to sit at the kitchen table.

It's a nicer table, Clarence realizes, than when he last saw Healy in the spring of 1898, polished to a shine beneath the electric lights in Healy's kitchen. The chairs are new, too. Healy's bought sturdy wood chairs with plush cushions and seat backs. They have an embroidered floral pattern featuring bright red and yellow roses on a white background.

"I just got back in town today, John," Clarence says as he sips the cup of coffee Sally sets in front of him. He still doesn't care much for coffee but of course decides not to say anything to Sally. "Where's Mary?"

"Oh, she's at school for another fifteen minutes or so, and then she'll walk home. She'll be overjoyed to see you, I'm sure, but I thought maybe we could talk a bit first and then start your homecoming party when she and her siblings get here. I was hoping to beat you home myself."

"I've only been here an hour or so. Your house is nicer than I remember. Quite a bit of new furniture. And the glass window here in the kitchen? So beautiful and broad. I'll bet Sally can see the whole street while she's cooking."

Sally turns and gives Clarence another of her beautiful smiles while the light streams through the window, making her hair glow just a touch and reflecting off her cheeks.

"The hardware business has been good lately, Clarence. St. Louis is a growing town," John says while easing into a chair slowly.

Did I just notice his arms shaking, or did I imagine that? Clarence wonders to himself as John sits down.

"Where should I start?" he asks John.

"At the beginning, of course."

"You know, John, you barely have an accent anymore. If we went back to Ireland to visit your aunt and uncle today, they'd hardly understand you."

"They would, too."

"I'm not so sure."

"I'd just have to remind them that dinner's at hawft pawst foive," Healy bellows in a thick Irish brogue. Both men give deep, hearty laughs, remembering the old times when they circled the world together in 1888 and 1889.

"Okay, you've got me there," Clarence admits. "Let me guess, the people coming over for tonight's party will arrive at hawft pawst foive too, won't they?"

"Can you believe that was a full ten years ago, Clarence, when we met my relatives in Ireland?"

"No. It's hard to imagine a decade can go by so fast. We saw your aunt and uncle in 1889, and now it's 1899. The new century isn't far away. I'm glad you haven't lost touch with your family's home, though, John."

"How can I forget my heritage? I'll always be a son of the Emerald Isle," John reminds him. "Tell me, though, Clarence, how was your second go at acting? I'm a bit surprised you even tried it again, considering how your first tour with Jarbeau ended."

"Well, it wasn't like I was getting anywhere here in St. Louis now, was I? I'll always be grateful that you took me in and let me stay here for a while, but a man must make his own way at some point. Even though I can read and write as well as most men, if not better, there just aren't many jobs in this city for colored people who are good at those things, no matter how educated that person is."

"You know you'll never wear out your welcome at our home, Clarence. With what you went through just getting Mary here, I'm in your debt for life, even if you never do another thing for me to the end of your days."

"Thank you, John, but you have three kids of your own. Four, counting Mary. Plus, your lovely wife. I won't be a burden on you."

When Clarence says this, Sally, who's been carving up some chicken for Clarence's party, turns and flashes a polite smile to the young man with the brown eyes and close-cropped, frizzy hair. Clarence smells the cornbread baking in the oven.

Sally Healy is tall for a woman and has long, lustrous hair, but is rather quiet. She and John married late in 1889, following the baseball season. John met Sally in Washington, D. C., where he'd pitched for most of that year, and they'd wed in October. The couple already had their three children when Clarence and Mary Healy arrived in St. Louis from Montana in August of 1896 but have not added any more since then. Sally is a kindly woman and superb cook, even though Clarence has never quite taken to her Irish love for corned beef and cabbage.

"You're no burden, Clarence," John insists. "Like I just told you, life's been good to me. Between what I saved from my pitching career and what I've made in business here in St. Louis, the family is in good condition. We can always spare a bit to help out a friend."

"Besides the new furniture, I see you've installed electric lights since I was here last year. No more gas lighting."

"Indeed. Electric lights are far safer. And brighter, too. All I need to do is flip a switch installed in the wall, and the lights come on. Gotta keep up with the times, I suppose. I've even started stocking electric light bulbs at my hardware store where I'm a partner. More and more people are putting them in their homes. It's certainly the coming thing."

"A few of the hotels we stayed in had them, too, John."

"Like I said, the coming thing. No more gas explosions like the one that almost buried us alive beneath the streets of San Francisco." Both men have a burst of laughter at the memory.

"I think I'm still choking on the smell from the smoke in that opium den we had to pass through to escape the tunnels," Clarence tells him.

"Those people were so out of their minds, the whole building could have crashed down on their heads, and I'm not sure any of them would have noticed," Healy answers while nodding in agreement, the chuckles dying away slowly.

"And the Chinese temple we saw certainly didn't have this nice floral wallpaper you've put up. Did you pick it out, Sally?"

"We both did. John was a wee bit skeptical at first. White wallpaper with flowers didn't seem gentlemanly enough for him but I told him it would lighten up the kitchen."

"She was right, of course. Which is another thing that hasn't changed since you left to try acting a second time," John says, patting Sally gently on the back when she walks by to mix more cornbread.

The two men share another laugh, and then Clarence rubs his cheek and gets a more thoughtful look. "Well, what can I say about my second tour as an actor? Bert Williams and George Walker organized our troupe."

"Both are colored gentlemen, correct?"

"Yes. They are both singers and actors."

"How did you meet up with them and convince them to take you on, Clarence?"

"Williams began touring all the way back in '86 with a group known as Lew Johnson's Minstrels. When I acted with Miss Jarbeau, we crossed paths with them a few times. Somehow, Williams remembered me, so when I wrote to him inquiring about joining their show, he wrote back that they needed a new cast member and agreed to give me a shot."

9

"What was the name of their acting company again?"

"They bill themselves as 'Two Real Coons' and call their most popular act *The Gold Bug*."

"What happens in the show, and what do you do?" Sally asks Clarence, her interest perking up while she prepares some potatoes at the counter.

"Williams plays a character known as Jim Crow. He's down on his luck, not too bright, and a little clumsy, but he has a good heart. Walker portrays an urban dandy named Zip Coon. He's an arrogant man of middling means who always wants to sucker Jim into joining his plans to make easy money. Both Walker and Williams play music on the banjo, they sing, and they try to entertain the audience with acting and jokes. I sang a bit and played some of the minor characters in their act. I also played a drum major and went by the name of "Lord Barnie," if you can believe it. The songs have titles like 'I Don't Care if Yo' Neber Comes Back' and 'Quityerkiddin.'"

"I thought those companies hired white men and had them put on blackface," John interjects.

"Most do. Walker and Williams, though, they want to show the audience that colored people can act, too, so they have both white and colored people in their performance."

"Does it bother you that you worked with white folks pretending to be colored, Clarence?"

"Sometimes it does. They aren't the greatest actors. If they were, they wouldn't be working with a troupe owned by two colored men."

John laughs a bit, but then says, "I didn't mean it that way. Does it bother you? The blackface part of it?"

"Well, remember back on the train, way back in '88, when you paid me to paint up Tom Daly with blackface?"

Healy's grin nearly spans his entire face while he slaps his thigh. "I knew you'd remember that. Tom Daly. I never thought he'd make it as a ballplayer after our tour, especially after Spalding released him at the end. But there he is, still going strong today and playing good ball for Brooklyn. He finally grew up. I apologize, though. I interrupted you."

"I was a little ashamed when you told me to do that. The only reason I did it was because I didn't have many friends and didn't want you to get mad at me. There's still a bit of shame today, too. I wish colored performers could make money acting some other way, but no white acting companies will hire us. Walker and Williams try to alter public perceptions as best they can, but I doubt the whites who watch their shows really notice the irony in some of their jokes and character portrayals. They just see colored actors playing the coon act." Clarence gives out a long sigh.

"I might have thought the same, until I got to know you. It was partly chance that brought our lives together, but I'm glad it did."

Clarence gives a quick smile. "Being in the Buffalo Soldiers in Montana was similar. We had many good soldiers in our regiment. Brave lads. Most of them better and braver than me. But it didn't matter. The regiment had no colored officers. We got about the hardest job the Army could give us, rounding up those people and taking them six hundred miles to Canada. A few of the men told me they were in the Buffalo Soldiers to prove themselves and prove what colored people can do, but I don't think anyone watches or notices. I don't know how that will ever change, either."

"It may, Clarence, it may. Fifty years ago, we Irish were in almost the same spot. The Irish were never slaves like colored people were, but when so many of us came to the United States during the Potato Famine, people here hated us. Things are better now, at least some of the time. Some folks still hold prejudice against the Irish, especially since so many of us are Catholics, but it's better. Maybe the day will come when colored people get better treatment in this country."

"I don't know if I have enough patience to find out, John."

"What do you mean?"

"Sometimes, I think about living somewhere else. Another country."

"Where?"

"Not sure. It's just a thought. But, then again, going to Montana was just a thought, too. I have no definite plans. Maybe it's time to trust to luck again."

"What about Elizabeth, Clarence? The young lady you met in New York whom you wrote me about? You wrote that she fancies you."

"Oh, her. That's one time my luck failed me. She only thinks of herself. Wanted me to stay in New York and move to her papa's place in Harlem. Elizabeth always went on about how she'd be a leading lady on the stage one day. It's all she ever talked about, but she didn't have much talent. When she said to choose between living with her and coming back here to stay with you for a while, it wasn't a hard choice. No one at your house suffers from delusions of grandeur, except when it comes to freeing Ireland."

Everyone, including Sally, laughs long and hard at this. She gives Clarence a pat on the shoulder as she walks by to drop some potatoes in a boiling pot.

Clarence continues. "Anyway, it was time for a break from Walker and Williams, too. I'm happy they gave me a chance, but I don't think the stage will take me anywhere meaningful. The road is a hard life at times. Especially when we tour the South, and everything is segregated."

"It does appeal to your love of travel, though, right?"

"I suppose, but I've had enough of dreams of greatness for now. I'm looking for something solid and steady, but Walker and Williams, like I said, they think they have big plans. They're even working on a new act right now, and they want to call it *Sons of Ham*. They say it'll be big, but you know entertainers. They always say that."

Another smile from Healy as he replies, "Just like ballplayers. Every year, ballplayers say they're in the pink of condition and about to play the best ball of their lives."

At this comment, Clarence looks across the table at John Healy. Something's different. He's sure of it. Healy always was on the thin side—even on the Spalding Tour, he was thin. John stands six feet tall or thereabouts, but when Clarence left to join Walker and Williams last year, John looked like he weighed around one hundred-sixty pounds. Now, however, his shirt sleeves hang loosely on his arms, his cheeks look drawn, and he appears at least twenty pounds lighter. *That can't be healthy. I wonder if something's wrong? Something's got to be wrong.* Clarence thinks to himself.

John, however, has already moved on in his thoughts. "So, I got your letter from Chicago last September. What happened when you met Al Spalding at West Side Park?"

"I didn't know what to expect when I got his invitation, to be honest. I was more nervous going to meet Spalding in his office than I've ever been when performing on stage if you can believe it. Spalding treated me royally, though. He showed me the renovations to the ballpark, took me to the team's clubhouse, and told all the players who I was and how I traveled the world on his tour. No mention of marching or dancing, either."

"I'm still amazed he found you, but that was a nice gesture on his part. I hear that Jimmy Ryan is the only member of our tour still playing in Chicago. Did you meet him, too, Clarence?"

"That's right. Ryan's the only one left. We shook hands. He didn't say too much. Ryan didn't look angry, or mad, or upset like I thought he might. I suppose seeing me brought back some memories for him, but hard to say if they were fond ones at the good times on the tour, or sad ones that it was so long ago and now all those friends are gone."

"Some of them literally. You know about Jimmy Fogarty, of course."

"Yeah, sure do, John. I used to keep his obituary with me because it talked about how he made his friends bury him in my old bandleader hat. I lost the obituary, though, when the vigilantes

13

almost killed me in that cabin on the Milk River. I don't suppose I'll ever find another copy of it now."

"Ned Williamson's dead, too. He died in '94."

"You mentioned that to me once, John, but never told me how it happened."

"Well, he got hurt in Paris on our tour, which I'm sure you remember, and wasn't ever the same after that. His drinking came back, and his weight got the better of him. He went to Hot Springs, in Arkansas, hoping that the spring waters there would help him, but they didn't. Not enough, anyway."

"Why go all the way to Arkansas?"

"Spalding and Anson took the White Stockings to Hot Springs to train all the way back in 1886. Ned thought the waters there were wonderful, so he decided to give them another try in hope they might heal him. His obituary said that liver problems killed him. His wife Nellie was by his side the entire time."

"I remember her, too. You weren't there, John, but she fainted in the streets of Colombo after that cobra bit me. I feel bad for her. She was flighty, but Nellie was the only woman who went on the tour who ever spoke much to me. And she helped MacMillan give me reading lessons. I know that a person can't control everything that happens in life, but she deserved better than that."

"And you know about Ed Crane?"

"Again, just that he died in 1896. Just a month or two after I got here with Mary, wasn't it?"

"It's a sad story, Clarence. He, too, started drinking. Hard and steady. He met his end in a Rochester hotel. A bellboy found him on the floor with a bottle of chloral hydrate nearby."

"Do you have any idea what happened to Patrick?"

"I don't. I suppose he must have died at some point, but I never heard anything about Ed's pet monkey after we returned to America."

Clarence shakes his head sadly. "So, we've lost three men from our tour. Some are still going strong, however. Ned Hanlon is a manager now, I read in the papers, and his Baltimore teams have done very well. Tom Burns is a manager, too, in Chicago, even though they've changed their name again. They call themselves the Orphans now, of all things. I don't think it's in my honor, however."

Both men laugh at the irony, although this time John's laugh seems to lack gusto, almost like the conversation so far has tired him out.

Then John continues, "I'm sure it was a relief for you that Anson retired from the game after '97, and you didn't have to see him in Chicago."

Clarence pauses, looks at the kitchen's polished hardwood floor for a moment, and then says, slowly, "Yeah, I suppose it was. I asked Spalding why Anson wasn't there, though. He told me Anson made some unfortunate remarks about his teammates in the papers, and Chicago finally decided to let him go. Although Al phrased it that Anson finally decided to retire from the game."

"Just like Spalding. Always the diplomat. Yeah, Anson told the *Chicago Inter Ocean* that his team was a bunch of loafing drunkards, and that was it. Anson was right in his characterization, however, from what I've heard, even if he could've shown more tact. The team only won fifty-nine games, after all. But, that's always been his way, blunt and straightforward. He could still play ball, though, you know? Anson was forty-five years old by then, and he still hit .285 and drove in more runs than anyone on the team except for Ryan and Bill Lange. No one in baseball history has more hits than he does."

Clarence looks down again.

"Why are you so quiet about Anson? Did something happen I don't know about?"

"I saw him, John. Last year."

"Really? Doing what?"

"We finally have something in common."

"Please tell, Clarence."

"He decided to give Broadway a try. He was in a show called *A Runaway Colt* where he played himself teaching a young ballplayer, named Manley Manners, of all things, how to play ball."

"I never heard about that. Was he any good?"

"Depends on whom you ask. But I saw a piece of his stationery. It claimed he was 'A better actor than any ballplayer. A better ballplayer than any actor.' Typical Anson, I guess you'd say."

"That doesn't surprise me at all, Clarence. He never lacked for self-promotion. Why are you so quiet about it, though?"

"He walked right by me once. No farther away than you and I are right now. Didn't even notice me. I considered introducing myself but couldn't bring myself to say anything. I wonder if he's the same as he always was when it comes to hating colored people? Part of me wanted to know, but it proved the lesser part of me when the chance came. He still scares me a bit, even after all these years, I guess."

"Clarence!"

A young girl's excited shout fills the kitchen when Mary Healy bursts through the door. Her long black hair trailing out behind her ever so slightly, she runs and gives Clarence a leaping hug when he stands to greet her. When she does, muddy snow falls from her feet onto the polished wooden floor, the snow courtesy of a late winter cold spell.

She's panting and out of breath, her cheeks flushed. "Uncle John said you were going to be here today!"

After a moment Clarence sets her back on the floor. She's growing up, and a bit heavier than she was during their Montana adventures.

"Mary, why aren't you with your brother and sisters like you're supposed to be?" John asks the lithe, thirteen-year-old girl with the tan complexion, bright eyes, and gorgeous smile.

"I ran home! I wanted to see Clarence because he's been gone so long."

"Wow, you've grown a lot since last spring, Mary," Clarence tells her. "I told you one day you'd grow up big like a bear, didn't I?"

"I like brown bears but not grizzly bears," she declares matter-of-factly.

Clarence looks over at John, who shrugs his shoulders. Again, Clarence can't help but notice the sagging shirt. It doesn't look natural.

"We studied bears in school," Mary explains after a moment. "Our teacher said grizzly bears are big, evil beasts that eat people and that we should kill them all. So, I don't like grizzly bears now."

Three younger children enter the kitchen next, also out of breath from running to keep up with Mary. The oldest of the trio, a boy of about eight, hugs Sally when she bends down to give him a kiss. Then, he hands her today's mail. While Clarence gets hugs from all the children, she sifts through the small stack, setting one piece aside on the kitchen counter.

"Clarence, there's another letter here for you," she says with a note of mild surprise in her lilting brogue. She extends her hand and passes him the letter in its plain legal envelope.

One of John's two daughters draped around his neck, Clarence looks it over, sees his name printed neatly on the outside, and notes the return address. The top line reads "John Montgomery Ward." That's a surprise. But, Mary's here right now and wants to talk, so he pockets the letter. It can wait.

When doing so, however, Clarence looks over at John Healy again while John greets his children. John's pants are clearly too big for him. His belt, cinched to the last notch, makes Healy look like he needs a trip to see his tailor, while his skin looks almost leathery. He starts to pick up his youngest child, a girl who is about five, but then drops down on one knee to give her a hug instead.

This can't be right, Clarence thinks. John is only thirty-two, and besides co-owning a St. Louis hardware establishment also serves on its police force. Or did. Reading Pfeffer's letter was the first time

Clarence had heard John wasn't with the police any longer. John hadn't mentioned it to him in their correspondence. Or anything else about his health. Clarence resolves to ask Sally about it as soon as he has the chance.

Soon after, however, his "welcome home" party begins. Most who come are friends whom Clarence met when he and Mary Healy first came to stay with John in 1896. Even during the party, though, Healy looks wan in Clarence's eyes. Although his smile shines through his bushy mustache and his eyes retain their old intensity, John moves slower than normal and sits down often.

"Sally, how is John? He doesn't look the same as I remember," Clarence says to Sally while the party continues.

"I don't know what the matter is, Clarence," she replies softly. "He always says he's okay and that things will pass, but he's not as energetic as he was a few months ago."

"I've noticed he's hardly touched any food at the party."

"Yes, he doesn't eat much these days. I know you can see he's lost weight. He complains of fevers and headaches often, too. I'm worried."

"When did he quit his job with the St. Louis police? I always found it curious he took a job with the police, given his anarchist views."

"He said he became a policeman to treat everyone with justice, not just the bourgeoisie. But, Clarence, he left that job several months ago. He didn't tell you?"

"No. I didn't find out until this afternoon."

"That's strange. He works as a clerk now, for the city government, in addition to co-owning the hardware store, but he says he's not sure how long that will last."

"I just hope he pulls out of it soon."

"What did the second letter say that you got today, if I may ask? Was it as hard to open as the first?" Sally inquires with her soft smile, trying to change the subject to something happier.

"Don't know. Haven't opened it yet. It's on the dresser upstairs by my bed. I'll let you know tomorrow if it's anything important."

3

Another Goodbye

On the frosty morning of March 18, 1899, a Saturday, the people file into St. Teresa's Church on Bacon Street in St. Louis to say their last goodbyes to John Healy.

Clarence Duval sits in the second row of pews, gazing down at his feet. He has on his only suit, a black jacket with a dark blue tie, dark slacks, and brown leather shoes. Clarence used most of his savings from his dramatic performances with Walker and Williams to buy the suit, but he doesn't mind the expense. John saved his life once, after all, when Clarence fell into a gold mine shaft in Australia and has been his best friend over the past decade. It is the least he can do to honor John's memory.

In the pew in front of him, Sally sits stoically in her black mourning dress, a dark veil draped over her face. Clarence knows that after watching her husband of nearly ten years die slowly over the past several months, the day is no shock to her. Still, he knows that made the pain no less easy to bear when the end came on Thursday. Clarence woke up to Sally crying by herself in the kitchen and knew immediately that John was dead. Today, Sally puts her arm around her only son while he alternates between open crying and sniffling.

Clarence looks at Mary Healy, sitting to Sally's right. She's sniffling, too. Although, technically, she is John's niece rather than his daughter, she's lived with the Healys since her father Thomas died in a mining cave-in in Butte, Montana, and Mary's mother committed suicide out of depression. That was when Clarence helped Mary get to St. Louis, and John took Mary in and raised her as his daughter for what little of his life remained. Now, for the third time in her young life, Mary must deal with the shock of losing a parent.

Many other people enter St. Teresa's, but Clarence doesn't really look at who they are. The crowd is a large one—John lived in St. Louis most of his life and had many friends.

Clarence, Sally, Mary, and the others rise when the casket enters the rear of the church. Clarence doesn't need, or want, to look at John's thin, wasted body within. He'd rather remember the John Healy he knew in their days in Ireland, the one with the intense look in his eyes and the burning, unyielding, patriotic desire to see Ireland free. The fiery anarchist John Healy who stormed and railed against the injustice of governments and the oppression of the English.

The pallbearers set the casket down after a moment, and the robed priest of St. Teresa's drapes the pall over the casket, sprinkles it with holy water, and offers a prayer. At the same time, Clarence smells incense burning throughout the church. Then, the pallbearers pick the casket up again and move it to the front of the church.

Clarence recognizes six of the eight men carrying the casket. John Ward and Ned Hanlon are there. So is John Tener. He also spots three other ballplayers, Bill Joyce, Joe Quinn, and Lew Whistler, whom Clarence met through John because all three live in St. Louis. Ward, Hanlon, and Tener, Clarence's companions from the world tour, are ten years older now, and none play major league baseball anymore. After not seeing them for a decade, Clarence can see age creeping into the faces of these men who'd been in the prime of life in his memory. Their faces have more lines now than Clarence remembers. John Ward climbed the Pyramid of Cheops and then climbed down in less than ten minutes once. Although he looks healthy, Clarence doubts if he could do that today. He doesn't recognize the last two pallbearers, who are in the uniform of the St. Louis Police Department.

The service is a traditional Catholic one, meaning the priest speaks in Latin much of the time. Clarence attended this type of service once before, back in Montana at the funeral of John's brother Thomas, so it is sadly familiar. The priest had led a recitation of the Rosary the night before, but because Clarence is not Catholic, he had not attended. Sally told him that John requested the priest read the Litany of the Saints as well, which tends to go on for some time, another good reason to save his goodbyes for today.

After the casket arrives at the front of the church, draped in white cloth vestments, and the eight pallbearers take their seats, the priest prays again on John's behalf, and some Bible readings follow. Ecclesiastes, chapter three, verses one through fifteen from the Old Testament. Acts, chapter ten, verses thirty-four through forty-three from the New Testament. The Gospel verse is from John, chapter six, verses thirty-five to forty. Mary asked to read some of the verses, but the Father informed her that only priests spoke during the funeral service. *She's getting so good at reading*, Clarence thinks to himself. *She's a natural at school. I hope she has the chance to stay with it.*

The Funeral Mass continues, the Latin incomprehensible to Clarence, of course, and after the closing prayers, the casket returns to the rear of St. Teresa's, where the priest Commends the body. Again, Clarence smells incense while the service concludes. A final song, "Ave Maria," plays on the church organ as John Healy's body leaves the sanctuary, and then everyone repairs to the parish hall.

The church is quite modest, Clarence thinks, compared to some other Catholic churches he's seen. Although the carpets in the hall are new and plush, the ceiling is much lower, for one thing, and the church has but a few of the stained-glass windows one usually finds in a Catholic church. The sanctuary has two side altars, one dedicated to St. Joseph and the other to the Virgin Mary. He'd asked Sally about the humble condition of the church yesterday, and she told him that when the church's Irish parishioners arrived earlier in the century, they'd been too poor to sustain anything nicer. Now, however, a new St. Teresa's is under construction just a short distance away, on the corner of Grand and Market. Sally told Clarence the new church would have multiple stories, two towers flanking the entrance, marble floors, and a beautiful new sanctuary with five altars and two rows of columns supporting the roof.

Clarence is about to sit down with his coffee when John Ward motions him over. Ward stands in a circle with some of the other pallbearers, including Hanlon, Tener, Joyce, and Quinn. Although Clarence detects a hint of gray in his mustache and his hair has thinned ever so slightly, John Ward still stands tall and erect. Clarence soon discovers Ward's handshake has lost none of its firmness, either, nor his tongue its facility with the English language.

Ward speaks first. "It looks like my letter finally caught up with you, Clarence. I sent it to Walker and Williams in New York, but apparently, you'd left their employ by the time it arrived and are a thespian no longer. I heard from Bill here that Healy was not doing well, and I wanted to get you the message because I know the two of you were close. John wrote me once and told me about you, your military and humanitarian adventures in Montana, and how you brought Mary to stay with him. I've got to say, it looks like you never lost your good luck or your daring."

"Thank you, Mr. Ward," Clarence replies, meeting Ward's grasp with a firm shake of his own.

"I think you can call me John now, Clarence. You've certainly earned the right to call anyone here by their first name. I'm just sad that you returned to St. Louis before my letter found you and you had to see John's decline with your own eyes before I could warn you."

"What did he die of?" Ned Hanlon asks the group. Hanlon, too, shows his years a bit. He and Ward appear about the same age, forty or thereabouts, although Hanlon's handlebar mustache remains as full and well-manicured as Clarence remembers. He also remembers that, when in Australia, Hanlon showed the slightest hint of a paunch, and now the paunch is more pronounced.

"The doctor said he had tuberculosis," Clarence informs the group. "There must be more than one type of tuberculosis, though, because my friend Gabriel died of the same thing, but he didn't have all the same symptoms."

"Damn," Hanlon says. "It's the same disease that killed Jim Fogarty right after our tour. I think it got the old pitcher and infielder Charlie Ferguson, too, back in 1888. Ferguson was really something out on the ball field."

"I believe it was typhoid fever that killed Ferguson," Ward puts in. "But you're right, Ned. If he had only lived, people today would sing Ferguson's praises as one of baseball's greatest players, maybe even better than Mike Kelly, Cap Anson, or Billy Hamilton."

Bill Joyce speaks next. He's a large, clean-shaven man who always wears a smile. To Clarence, it appears he can't be much past thirty, except that Joyce's hair is quite gray. He says, "I owe my career to John Healy, in a way. When I was just a young player coming up and playing local ball here in St. Louis, he took me aside once and encouraged me to keep playing ball, and he'd visit with me from time to time after that. Without him, I might be back in the iron and zinc mills down on the city waterfront and would never have made it as a ballplayer. I started my life there, and might have finished it there, too, if not for John."

"I think someone in baseball would have found you," John Ward tells Joyce. "It just happened to be me."

"But you only found me because Comiskey tipped you off. And he tipped you off because Healy told him to take a good look at me."

"True enough," Ward concedes. "John said you were a scrappy kid who argued everything, but that you had an eagle eye, tons of power, and a personality that would remind me of Mike Kelly. He also said to look past your gray hair and remember you were still a kid even though you looked older than me."

24

Joyce gives a hearty laugh, slapping Ward on the shoulder. "Comparing me to Kelly might be going a bit far, but it's true I'm working-class through and through, just like he was. Besides, I don't argue *every* call. Just the bad ones."

"And how many of the calls are bad ones?" Hanlon asks.

"Every call we don't get is a bad call." Everyone laughs again.

"Is it true the *Brooklyn Daily Eagle* once called you 'a kicker from Kickersville'?" Hanlon asks Joyce.

"Yeah, but I'm telling you, the paper blew things out of proportion. So did the *St. Louis Post-Dispatch* when it printed the same thing. Just because I've been known to curse out the bad umpires, all of them, doesn't mean I deserved *that* label."

"Or throw your bat at the umpires you don't like?" Hanlon puts in.

"He deserved that. The pitch was a ball, and my eagle eyes told me so, but the ump called me out. I did what anyone would have done in that situation. I didn't even complain when the ump picked up my bat and threw it back at me." Joyce just gives a broad grin while he recalls the story, and more laughs follow from everyone.

"Besides," Joyce goes on, "it's not like you're one to talk, Ned. Your boys over in Baltimore have cursed out their share of umpires over the years. Those boys know every trick in the book, and some that aren't in the book, too."

"Yeah, they do, but I'm in Brooklyn now, Bill," Hanlon answers him. "Some of the boys came with me, but John McGraw is still in Baltimore. You sure I can't talk you out of retirement to come join me in the City of Churches?"

"Nope. Sorry, Ned, but I'm done with major league baseball. I only hit .258 last year, and I led the league in strikeouts. I think my playing days are over."

"But you're only, what, thirty or so? Even if you look fifty."

Another grin from Joyce. "Yeah, some people ask me if I'm as old as Anson. But I'm not even close. After all, Anson listened to George Washington's farewell address back in 1782."

Even though he's laughing along with everyone else, John Ward can't help but say, "I'm pretty sure Washington retired from the presidency in 1796, Bill. The War for Independence was still underway in '82."

"Gee, John, I'm just going by what Anson told me himself. You mean Anson's so old he can't even get his dates right anymore? No wonder he finally retired from baseball."

"Are you jealous he replaced you as Giants' manager last year, perhaps?" Ward counters.

"I don't know, John. Anson lasted, what, twenty-two games as manager? And who replaced him when the Giants fired him? Oh, that's right. I did." Turning back to Hanlon, Joyce says, "I can't believe you'd want me in Brooklyn even if I was going to play, though, Ned."

"Of course, I'd like to have you in Brooklyn. All I have at third base is Doc Casey. You'll probably be a better player than he is even when you *are* fifty."

"You're sure about that, Ned? What was it you said about me back in '96? 'He is utterly unreasonable. He kicks at every ball and every strike, and at every close decision against him.' Did I get the words right?"

"You did, but when I need a third baseman like I do, I'll take it back if you ask me to. What do you say?"

"For the second and last time, no. I'm gonna open a saloon here in St. Louis and run it along with Patsy Tebeau. You boys all know Patsy. He's a good friend."

Finally, the baseball conversation having run its course, thoughts return to John Healy. Again, Joyce speaks.

"I'm gonna miss John. He was a good friend, too. Because I feel like I owe my career to him, I'm glad I could pay him back for all his help."

"How did you do that?" Ward asks.

"I'm the one who got him his job with the St. Louis police force. That's why two policemen were pallbearers in the service today."

"How did you arrange a job with the police?" Hanlon asks. "You don't seem like the type who'd enjoy their company."

"True enough, but Jim Cronin's a friend of mine, too."

"Who's that?" Clarence asks. "I don't remember John talking about him."

"Cronin's an alderman, and he works for Edward Butler, the Irish boss of St. Louis. Healy never knew it, but I persuaded Cronin to give John his position, and to let him keep it until his tuberculosis stole his strength, so he couldn't work anymore. It was the least I could do for him after all he did to help me. John always had an eye for new talent and a kind word for young players."

Then Ward asks, "Perhaps this is not the best time to ask, but what will his family do without him?"

Joyce answers, "I feel sorry for Sally, but I believe John left the family well-situated. Between his career playing ball, his work on the police force, and his part-ownership of the hardware store, I don't believe money will be a problem for the family. John had a good head for business, and he was never a gambler or too much of a drinker."

At this point, Clarence takes his leave of the conversation. He knows John's family will not lack—John made sure of that. His hardware business is quite successful, and before he died, he transferred his share to his wife. Sally will be fine. She is no spendthrift, and being a bit younger than John, she'll have ample chances to remarry if she chooses. Clarence isn't worried about the family.

Instead, he has something else on his mind now that the grief from John Healy's funeral has started receding a bit. Spending time with his old companions and hearing about baseball brings back some memories. One former companion who is not in St. Louis bears heavily on Clarence's mind, however. That companion is Fred Pfeffer.

He still hasn't decided when to leave and pursue the lead on his father that Pfeffer provided, but Clarence knows it must be soon.

He's never been to Athens, Alabama, and has no idea what it's like there, but if his father was in ill health when Lincoln Washington met him, who knows what might happen? Although the thought of meeting his father scares him more than a little, Clarence has so many questions he wants to ask. It appears this is his chance, after nearly seventeen years, to find out why his parents left him.

4

Athens, Alabama

While Clarence's train rolls south toward whatever awaits in Alabama, he has plenty of time to think over what might happen when he arrives in Athens. He must sit in the colored section of the train, of course, after the train reaches Charleston, in the southeast corner of Missouri, and prepares to cross into Kentucky. He remembers the decision of the United States Supreme Court in a case known as *Plessy v Ferguson* in 1896. The court made its ruling while he was riding with the Buffalo Soldiers, but Clarence read about it later. The decision stated that segregation was permissible so long as both colored and white people had equal accommodations.

Looking around at the colored passenger car, it certainly doesn't appear as nice to Clarence as the one he just left. The upholstery of some seats is torn, the carpeting worn and uneven in spots, and his car has but one spittoon, so it smells strongly of tobacco. However, Clarence judges this is not the time to complain. His train left St. Louis in the evening, but he's only dozed lightly and fitfully through the night. Too many questions on his mind. It has been years since he's thought much about his parents. Because Clarence has no idea why they left him, he has always assumed his parents are dead or that they abandoned him. Maybe both.

Now, however, he isn't sure what to think. Pfeffer's letter had been vague, unfortunately, on several points. Did his father even want to see him? Clarence hoped so, but what if he didn't? Did he even care that Clarence was alive? Again, Pfeffer hadn't mentioned what Lincoln told his father. Had Lincoln mentioned Clarence's name or anything about him to William? What if he had, and now William was looking for him and wasn't in Alabama anymore?

Those are just some of the questions Clarence ponders. No matter what comes to mind, however, each question only leads to more uncertainty and more questions. He'll never know the answers until he finds his father, wherever his father might be.

Clarence also thinks back on some of his childhood memories from the years with his parents. He still has some, of course. Before his separation from them, following which he moved to Chicago, they'd lived on their Kentucky farm. Well, it wasn't *their* farm. They'd been sharecroppers, not farm owners, but Clarence still remembers the place, even if he'd been no older than six and some of the memories have become fuzzy.

His favorite time of the year in Kentucky had been the late summer, when he'd wandered through the rows of corn, feeling the green leaves with his fingers, smelling the ears as they grew and ripened. By then, the corn didn't need so much weeding, so he had had a little time to play. Sometimes, boys and girls from the neighboring farms came over, and they'd play endless games of hide-and-seek while dodging through the corn fields and in and out of the dusty, rocky gullies scarring the farm where no corn grew. The games went on until the sun went down, and sometimes into the night, too.

He had other memories of Kentucky, not so happy. Every spring he was old enough to remember, he'd walked behind his father's mule as it plowed row after row of Kentucky soil. Clarence's job had been to plant the corn seeds in the furrows. He remembered walking, on and on, every day, until his little legs ached. It hadn't mattered whether the weather was dry, and he was inhaling dust, or if it rained and he was ankle-deep in the mud. He just walked behind that old mule for days at a time, it seemed, planting seeds until his bare feet grew raw.

A while later, when the stalks of corn first emerged from the earth, he had to weed the rows, so the corn grew properly. Clarence had hated that even more than planting. Weeding time was later in the spring, the weather was warmer, and he had to lean over in the fields all day hoeing the weeds his father told him to watch for. The sun had beat down on him, and even his straw hat hadn't been enough help on the hotter days. So, he'd leaned over the rows, getting thirstier while his young back throbbed, and walked up and down the rows for weeks on end, his little hands blistering while his tiny fingers curled into the shape of the hoe's wooden handle. His father William worked beside him the whole time, bent and stooped for the same reasons. Mostly, they'd worked in silence because they were too tired to speak to each other. Clarence still wonders how his father withstood the monotony of it all, year upon year.

Despite their efforts, the farm never paid. Always, at the end of harvesting season when his father returned home from selling the corn, William's face was downcast. He'd simply slump into his frame wooden rocking chair with no cushions, mutter something about his debts to The Man, and put his head in his hands before slouching off to bed, broken and despondent.

Other memories about summertime come to Clarence's mind. His family's home had been a rude log cabin that leaned to one side and always looked on the verge of falling over. Its lone window was open, no glass, so during spring, summer, and fall, the mosquitos had tormented him. They swarmed, especially in the evenings, until Clarence barely could see through the clouds. His arms, legs, and face had never been free of their small, itchy pink bites.

But the ants had been the worst. Always, the ants swarmed everywhere. Under the house, through the window and walls, into the trees Clarence liked to climb, it didn't matter where he went, the ants were there. True, there were certain spiders he learned to watch for, and venomous snakes like copperheads and cottonmouths down by the creek where he'd go to cool off when he got a break from his work, but he'd always hated the ants the most because he could never get away from them.

The summer heat hadn't helped, either. A handful of trees surrounded his family's cabin, but between June and August, Clarence rarely slept well because it was so warm. His discomfort stemmed partly from the temperature outside and partly from the potbellied stove his mother had used for baking cornbread. The family had to eat year-round, of course, but baking on that stove just made things even hotter during the summer. Clarence had tried sleeping outside sometimes, but then the ants got him, and he couldn't sleep any better there, either.

Winters had been just as bad, but in a different way. On the cold nights, his father would build a fire and tack tarpaper over the open window, but with all the cracks in the walls of the cabin, it wasn't enough. Their chimney leaned to one side, and it had cracks, too, so much of the heat went outside rather than warming the family's two-room shack.

Somehow, Clarence has a tougher time remembering things about his mother, Rose. Neither of his parents had ever talked much, but she had been even quieter than William. Most of Clarence's memories were of her working just as hard as his father, doing things like washing clothes by hand, cooking, and tending a small garden of tomatoes, beans, carrots, and other vegetables right outside the door to their shack. She'd liked to sing while she worked, though, and Clarence believes that's where his love of singing and music comes from. He couldn't remember the names of the songs anymore, however, and their melodies were now mixed up with all the marching songs he'd learned while leading parades.

He was an only child. Once, he'd heard his father tell a neighbor that his mother almost died bringing him into the world and that they'd been too scared to have more children after that. Clarence doesn't know if it was true, or if that was an excuse because his parents had trouble enough just feeding the family with only one child. He guesses it doesn't matter at this point.

The train slows. Looking through the window, Clarence sits up with a start, his eyes wide and his thoughts clear. It's the sign outside his window. Tuscumbia Station. Tuscumbia. One of the men he'd met in the 10th Cavalry, Thomas Delaney, had lived in Tuscumbia.

That isn't what makes Clarence bolt upright, however. It's what Thomas told him about Tuscumbia, about how a white mob lynched his two brothers and a cousin in 1894 just because they'd had a prosperous farm and their poorer white neighbor was jealous of them. Although the thought had lurked in the corners of his mind ever since leaving St. Louis, the Tuscumbia Station sign brings home the reality to Clarence: He is in the South, and his life could be at risk if he doesn't watch himself.

Clarence tries to push down the thought, but it's too late. Thinking about Delaney's brothers brings the visions back. Once again, he's in the Milk River camp in Montana in 1896. The camp is ablaze, the rancher vigilantes riding at will between the buildings. Again, he hears Clemence Ducharme's wife scream while some of the posse rapes her. Clarence's mind replays the murder of Marie Laverdure, her bloody fingers slipping from the rope holding the horse corral shut.

Then, he's inside the cabin with Mary, his leg dripping blood from a bullet wound while the cabin burns down around their heads. Clarence makes his move to burst through the door, to draw the fire of the vigilantes while Mary gets away, only to see her go down when a burning beam falls from the cabin's roof and collides with her head. Clarence kneels by her body, trying to pick her up . . .

"Sir?"

The end of the question dangles in the air. Head jerking up again, Clarence turns to his right and sees the colored porter awaiting his answer, the porter's white-gloved hands folded behind his back. Clarence sweats and breathes hard.

While pulling out a blue cloth handkerchief to dab the sweat from his forehead, Clarence says, "I'm sorry. What did you say?"

"I said we've reached Tuscumbia Station and asked if you'd like to stretch your legs while we load our new passengers, sir. You look like you could use some fresh air if I may say so."

Clarence gives the porter a weak smile and then replies, "Sorry about that. Old memories I'd rather forget, you know?" Although he means to sound cheerful and nonchalant, he hears a quiver in his voice.

The porter only nods, his navy-blue cap with gold trim bobbing up and down. He turns to leave.

"Say, hold on a minute, my friend," Clarence says to the man. From the ease of his walk, it appears the man's been a train porter for some time. When he turns back, Clarence judges he's probably in his later 40s or early 50s. Lines crease his face, and some of his whiskers are gray. He lacks a Southern accent, however.

Clarence asks another thing that's been on his mind. "You ever been to Athens, Alabama?"

"Train goes through there all the time. Never been much farther afield than the Athens Station, though, if that's what you mean."

"That's my stop, but I've never been there before. Just wondering where it's safe for a colored person to go to get the feel of the place, that's all."

"It's not a real friendly town, from what I've heard, sir."

"How's that?"

"Mostly there's the railroad and the local cotton farms. Not much else. From what I hear, about one thousand people live in the town itself, maybe more. That's it. The town's reputation is that its people are a bit suspicious of outsiders. That's why I never leave the station when the train stops."

Clarence sighs, grimaces, and scratches behind his ear. "That's not much help." To himself, though, he thinks that with only one thousand people, if his father is there, it shouldn't be that hard to find him, especially if he walks hunched over like Pfeffer claimed he did.

"Sorry," the porter replies. "If you want information, you might just try the local post office. It's just west from the courthouse in the middle of town, if memory serves. Once, I had to walk there to mail a letter for a passenger. I can't say what reception you'll get, but I'm sure the local postman knows everyone in town. It's either that, or the college for women, and I'd stay away from there if I were you."

Clarence needs no further warnings when it comes to staying away from white women. During the past decade he's managed to get his hands on some of the newspaper articles written by Ida Wells about all the false accusations used to lynch colored men, but even before he'd been able to read, he'd internalized that lesson. It was one of the few things he still remembers learning from his parents.

After another short time, the train is in motion again, and then, before Clarence has the chance to think much more, it grinds to a halt at Athens Station. This is it. Clarence's heart beats strong in his chest; he's sure that if he could eliminate all the noise from the train and passengers, he'd be able to hear it thumping. Fear begins to knot his insides, too, but Clarence isn't sure what scares him more, being in an unfamiliar Southern town, or what will happen if he finds his father. He feels the sweat bead on his forehead again.

Carrying the dark leather suitcase he borrowed from Sally Healy for this trip, Clarence gathers himself and steps down from the train onto the train platform. It's near midday, and only a few people are boarding or getting off. Looking around, it's a pleasant day. The air is warm, near seventy degrees, and a few puffy white clouds drift overhead on the light breeze. Clarence hears the chattering of songbirds and, from the other side of the train tracks, the rapid hammering of a pair of woodpeckers.

Looking up and down the main street of Athens, Clarence notices the tree species of the Deep South's uplands. He sees oaks, with their twisted and gnarled trunks branching in seemingly random patterns, and hickories, with their straighter trunks and greater height, lining the street. Elsewhere, he sees maples, chestnuts, and pines in some of the town's vacant lots.

Lacking a better plan, Clarence strides toward the post office, headed west from the station. On the way, he passes the Limestone County Courthouse. It's an imposing building for a town this size— two stories of red brick, miniature white dome on top, and entrances accessed by stone stairways and covered by colonnaded porches with four white pillars. There's a statue in front, featuring a man in a Civil War uniform. The inscription on it reads, "1861-1865, Confederate Soldiers of Limestone County." Clarence walks on, wishing he dared curl his lip to show his displeasure.

The post office isn't much farther, a couple blocks. Clarence looks at the front door, his guts nervously churning. His suitcase almost slips from his hand when he sees the Confederate flag flying near the door. Not an American flag in sight. Wiping his palms and swallowing hard, Clarence enters.

The postal clerk at the desk looks up once when Clarence enters and then puts his head back down and sifts through some paperwork. Clarence walks to the desk and sets his suitcase silently on the worn, creaking wooden floor. He waits. The man still doesn't look at him. Clarence waits longer.

Finally, he says to the clerk, "Afternoon, sir."

The man continues looking through the paperwork. While Clarence waits, he looks around the post office. The wooden floor carries its share of gouges and stains. Tobacco juice stains, most likely, Clarence thinks. The walls are white, or at least were at one time. Now they're the dirty white of a fencepost that hasn't been whitewashed in a decade or so, paint peeling in places.

After another long pause, the postman lifts one eye to take another look at Clarence, but only for the briefest instant. Another wait. Then, finally, without looking up, "What you want, boy?"

"I'd just like to know a thing or two, sir, like where a man can find lodging in town, and—"

"I ain't here to take your questions, boy!" the clerk interrupts Clarence with a snarl. "I ask you what you want here, at this post office, not what you in town for. Understand?" With the last word, a bit of spittle falls from the clerk's mouth. Without bothering to wipe it away, he looks down at the papers once more.

Clarence checks his next remark before he can say it. The man, his head still down, picks up another piece of paper. Another awkward pause while Clarence stands, trying to decide what to do next. Without looking up at all, the clerk says, "If you's here to mail a letter, then give it to me. If not, be on your way, boy."

"I'm sorry," Clarence mumbles while picking up his suitcase to leave.

The clerk's head jerks back up, and he says, loudly, "You's sorry? That's all you got to say to me, boy?"

Clarence has already half-turned toward the door. Startled by the man's anger, he looks back a moment. Then, he remembers. "I'm sorry. Sir."

"That's right you's sorry. I can tell you ain't from these parts, boy. You Northern nigras come down here causin' trouble, stirrin' up our local nigras, but we gots our eyes on y'all. You watch yourself, boy."

"Thank you, sir," Clarence says quietly while he walks out the door. The train porter had the town pegged about right, it seems.

Back on the street, Confederate flag waving softly on his left, Clarence extracts his handkerchief from his pocket and wipes his forehead. His guts still squirm. Clarence still has no idea where to start searching for his father.

He decides to head east, back toward the train station, figuring that if the post office and county courthouse are on the west side of the railroad tracks, then, probably, the colored section of town will be on the east side of the tracks. At least the local streets aren't muddy.

Before he gets far, however, a blaring horn startles him while he's crossing Jefferson Street. Clarence looks up in time to take a quick jump backward while a motor carriage rolls past. The black-painted vehicle features one leather bench, a folding top, a footrest for the driver and passenger, and a footrail for climbing aboard, but

Clarence doesn't have time to take in any more detail while he jumps out of the way. The white driver scowls and shakes his head slowly, hits his horn one more time for good measure while grumbling something to himself, and drives off.

It's still an adjustment for Clarence, seeing motor carriages in the streets. St. Louis and New York have quite a few, relatively speaking, but he hadn't expected to see one here in Athens. His ears are well-attuned to the sound of horses trotting by towing carriages, but the chugging of gasoline-powered engines remains new to him.

After crossing the tracks, Clarence discovers he is correct about the layout of Athens. The few houses he sees are run-down frame houses, some with glass windows, some without, most with small gardens of various vegetables—tomatoes, carrots, cabbage, and the like—surrounding the buildings. Then, on the edge of hearing, Clarence detects a new sound. Children playing. He walks in that direction.

Soon, he sees the sign: Trinity School. The schoolhouse is a three-story brick building with panel after panel of painted white window frames. There must be dozens of rooms. Ivy crawls up the brick sides of the building, its green leaves just starting to unfurl. Clarence sets down his suitcase and studies the scene for a moment.

This is not the stately ivy-and-brick of the colleges Clarence has seen in New York. Untrimmed hedges line the dirt path to the school's front door. Weeds and ankle-high grass choke the path itself. The ivy droops over some of the windows, obscuring the view from inside, and trees overhang the hedges in places. The schoolyard where the children play has no toys. Rather, it is a flat field where a handful of colored children play games of tag or toss a baseball back and forth.

Something else is wrong. The number of children playing seems woefully small compared to the size of the school. Still, after his rebuff at the post office, Clarence decides this is a good place to sit for a moment and collect his thoughts. Decide what to do next.

Retreating from the school a short distance, he sits down with his back to a chestnut tree and closes his eyes to think.

He probably only dozes off for a few moments, but Clarence comes awake again when he hears the familiar sound of iron horseshoes clopping toward him. Blinking his eyes alert, he turns to see two men wearing the brass insignia of the local police.

"Afternoon, officers," he says, attempting to sound cheery.

The man on the left wears black suspenders over a while flannel shirt and sports gray trousers. The other man wears the same, except his pants are light brown. Both wear identical black slouch hats. Also, both chomp fat cigars between tobacco-stained teeth. They look similar enough that Clarence guesses they're brothers.

"What you say, boy?" the man on the left drawls.

"James, I believe this boy thinks he can speak to us," the other man growls.

"I think you's right, Robert. This boy's gots lots of nerve for a criminal," James says while placing his hand on his right hip. Gently, it pats the butt of his pistol.

Criminal? Clarence repeats to himself. *Did he just say criminal?*

"Now, you listen here, boy," Robert barks again, dropping down from his horse. Clarence now sees his brown leather shoes. They're scuffed and worn a bit but made of high-quality leather. He smells the powerful scent of stale sweat as Robert approaches, extracts his cigar, and holds it in his left hand.

"I'm sorry, officers, I believe there's been a mistake," Clarence tries to say.

Even before Clarence finishes speaking, Robert's hand drops to his hip, and he draws his own weapon, a Colt pistol. "Now, I said that's enough, boy," Robert tells Clarence, his drawl escaping through grinning teeth while he cocks the hammer back. "You ain't from here, so you's a vagrant, and that's against the law."

Clarence looks from Robert back to James for some sign, but James just extracts his cigar from his mouth, blows smoke, and smiles a knowing grin while Robert puts his own cigar back between his teeth.

"Now," Robert gets right into Clarence's face and blows cigar smoke into his eyes, "you's gonna come with us. We gonna have to take you in." He smiles broadly and gives a short laugh, exhaling more smoke through his nostrils in the process.

Clarence can only blink his eyes, partly because the smoke irritates them, and partly because he can't believe what's just happened.

Robert, his cigar nearly spent, takes the stub from his mouth and extinguishes it by grinding it into Clarence's chest before tossing the smoldering stump away. Clarence looks down at his suit jacket, now with a blackened circle marring the right breast.

Next, Robert claps his hand on Clarence's shoulder. "This way, boy."

5

A Bargain Struck

Jefferson Davis Winston considers the man sitting across from him carefully. Winston's hands rest calmly on the cool, impeccably polished mahogany desk, moving only to adjust his tie, which he notices ruefully is slightly askew. He readjusts the tie so it rests perfectly on his modest paunch. He isn't sure he likes this Yankee, Thomas Brown, and all he stands for. Brown's immaculately tailored suit, brilliantly polished gold cufflinks, and diamond-studded tie pin accompany an affable smile, pleasant if somewhat stilted conversation, and all the right courtesies, to be sure. Winston, in contrast, normally meets the day with his sleeves rolled up, top button on his collar undone, and legal library within reach. Today, however, he's done his best to smarten up in anticipation of his visitor. *Which is why,* he muses to himself while taking his third sip of bourbon, *I feel so out of sorts. It's late March in Alabama, it's over eighty degrees, and I'm wearing this infernal suit and tie.* Brown's glass of bourbon, while politely accepted, remains untouched.

Winston knows none of this mild agitation shows on the outside. He has, after all, commanded others all his life, whether on his farm or as a judge, and he masks his emotions under a façade of unruffled calm that even his close friends and neighbors, Southern gentlemen all, envy. He's always believed his composure is a gift bequeathed by his father, almost as valuable as the seventy-four slaves he inherited on his father's death in 1858. *Even if it does show*, Winston thinks, finishing his earlier thought, *it is of little consequence. Brown needs what I have to offer, and we both know it.*

Winston's gaze returns to the document resting in front of him awaiting his signature. The letterhead reads "Southern Pineland Company" in black block letters as plain and unemotional as the demeanor of the man sitting four feet away.

"As you can see," Brown says with a nasal, Boston accent, "the terms are identical to those I sent by post last week for your perusal. Our previous correspondence indicated you were favorably disposed toward signing an agreement."

"Indeed, Mr. Brown. I found your terms surprisingly generous."

"The Southern Pineland Company values your expertise and influence. Its Board of Directors, of which I am a member, sees great potential in the forest resources of northern Florida. Besides the timber we now harvest there, the turpentine resources of the region are considerable as well. With railroads now penetrating the pine forests, we plan to extract the turpentine to bolster our profits."

Brown looks down at the table and gives the briefest of sighs. Not a sigh of disappointment, Winston thinks; more like a sigh over a temporary inconvenience, such as squashing a spider that's wandered too close. Brown bites his lips together a moment before continuing, "We have one problem, however. The remoteness of the Florida pine forests makes them, shall we say, an unpopular destination for workers. Our company has difficulty attracting workers at the wages we offer for the work."

"A regrettable circumstance," Winston replies. "We in the South have much the same problem in our coal mines and lumber camps, I hear. When workers have the freedom to walk away from employment they find unsatisfactory, we face a constant problem with finding new men and training them to do the work properly."

For the first time, Brown touches his bourbon, slowly swirling the brown liquid around in its glass before taking a short sip. "Indeed. When workers have that kind of freedom, it's bad for business. Bad for the development of the country. And bad for the workers, too. If you pay a man more than he needs to survive, he'll simply squander the money by gambling, drinking, or visiting loose women. It's a moral question as much as an economic one. Sometimes, you must make others do what is good for them."

Winston fakes a knowing smile. "I'm pleased to hear that you Yankees have realized what we of the South have known all along. If you'll forgive the expression, the Black Republicans led your party astray after the War Between the States with their calls for Negro suffrage and Negro rights. It raised the hopes of those who never deserved such hopes to begin with. It heartens me to hear that your party has returned to sound principles of business and social relations. Regrettably, you still allow the Negros to vote in your section, but in other respects you've come around to see the historic wisdom of the South when it comes to the labor question."

Winston half-expects Brown to show some unpleasant emotion over his characterization of the recent history of the Republican Party, but he's disappointed when the dour Yankee simply replies, "Yes, those regrettable days are past, never to return, let us hope. To me, and my company, the skin color of our workers is not so important as is making sure we receive efficient, low-cost labor from them. However, since attracting white labor to work in our Florida timber and turpentine camps at acceptable wages has proven difficult, colored labor must fill the void."

Nodding, Winston replies, "They are, as a group, admirably adapted for such a purpose. Not to mention manifestly unfit for more complex purposes requiring thought and reasoning, lacking as they do our great Anglo-Saxon heritage."

"You of the South have never lacked for theories on that question."

"Not mere theories. Facts. A friend of mine, Charles Carroll, has studied the race question for the past fifteen years. Soon, possibly as soon as next year, he plans to publish his research in his new book titled *The Negro: A Beast or In the Image of God*. I am sure it will be a sensation throughout the country."

"Perhaps it will, although my company and I take more interest in the color of the ink on our shareholder reports than the color of the men who create our wealth. Still, given the lack of success of the Negros in fending for themselves as free men, perhaps there may be something of value in Mr. Carroll's work."

"You don't live among Negros daily like we do in the South. They remind me of rabbits in their breeding propensities. Some of them, you can even see their animal nature in their eyes."

Winston says all of this with outward calm and a matter-of-fact tone, but Brown's occasional sideways glances indicate it's about time to wrap up the conversation and leave the sociological shortcomings of the colored race for another auditor. Instead of continuing, then, he sips again from his glass, giving Brown the chance to direct the conversation toward a conclusion.

"In any case, regarding our need for workers, it is the Southern Pineland Company's desire to obtain a workforce that will not trouble us with men leaving the job for better prospects elsewhere. A stable workforce that will perform a fair day's work at reasonable cost and will not stunt the nation's growth. You've promised to help us acquire dependable workers. We've offered you fair compensation for your help. Are you ready to sign our accord?"

"I believe so, although I do worry that, in such a wild place as the Florida forests, these Negros may revert to a less civilized state. But, I'm sure you've taken the proper precautions to control their animal propensities." As soon as he says it, Winston decides this may be stretching the point too far, but he just can't resist.

Brown only nods slowly, his face noncommittal.

Winston considers for a moment more and then flashes a genuine smile as he endorses the contract. "There it is. In return for your payment, Limestone County, Alabama, will supply you with the requested number of Negro convicts to work in your turpentine camp in Florida."

And I, Winston thinks as his hand pens his name in flowing script, *can continue redressing the grievous wrongs inflicted on the honor of the South by the Yankee North these past thirty-five years. Even if it means making use of some Yankees in the process.* But all he says aloud is, "You will receive a fair return for your investment, that I promise. Shall we drink to it?"

Both men take another swallow of bourbon after raising their glasses to their agreement.

With that, Winston leads Brown outside onto the spacious, colonnaded veranda of his house, if house is the right word for a three-story building with more than twenty rooms, six chimneys, and its own bell tower. The stately columns on the lower veranda, newly whitewashed, shine out here and there as the soft shadows of ancient oak shade trees play across their surfaces in a gentle breeze that isn't quite strong enough to make one forget about the modest spring humidity. Winston whistles loudly, and in a few moments, a team of four white horses hitched to a jet-black carriage pulls up, an elderly colored man in the coachman's seat.

As they shake hands and part, Brown says, "Our agreement calls for you to supply the needed convict laborers for shipment three weeks from today. I trust that will be ample time?"

"I am a man of my word. They will be ready. Now, I bid you a comfortable carriage ride to the railroad depot and wish you and the Southern Pineland Company the best in your enterprise. Henry is a fine driver, one of the best of his kind. Whenever you find yourself in need of more convict labor, as you may from time to time, I trust you'll consider my services again?"

Henry lifts his hat to Brown and bows his head as Brown climbs into the carriage.

After taking a seat, Brown looks to Winston and smiles for the first time. As the carriage slides into motion, he says, "You, sir, are right at the top of our list."

If Brown notices the thick scars peeking out from the open neck of Henry's freshly washed and ironed linen shirt, he keeps his thoughts to himself and makes no remark. Instead, he draws a silk handkerchief from an inside breast pocket and dabbles his forehead.

As the Yankee businessman departs, Winston thinks about the justice of the situation. What Brown said about labor being necessary to improve the morals of the lower classes is quite correct. Doubly so, when it comes to Negros. However, what makes Winston's agreement with Brown so perfect is its benefits to Limestone County and the great state of Alabama. Housing inmates in a prison requires money, and money for public services like prisons requires taxes. By hiring prisoners out to a private business like the Southern Pineland Company, Winston saved the taxpayers of the county an expense, and at the same time, helped rid the county of the criminal threat posed by Negros. In fact, the state of Alabama profits from the arrangement. Like Brown had pointed out, so does private business and the development of the country's resources. What could be more perfect?

A short time later, Winston is back on the porch whistling for his own carriage. He needs to head into town and attend to business.

6

Clarence's Trial

Clarence looks around his jail cell. He's been here for three days now, and he isn't alone. Five others share the cramped cell, and next door are another half-dozen prisoners—all colored men in the prime of life. The cell has four beds, bunked on opposite walls, meaning two men slept on the floor last night. Clarence drew a lucky straw and wasn't one of them. Speaking of straw, that's what his so-called mattress consists of—a pile of straw. Still, it was better than shooing away the rats creeping across the floor like the unlucky prisoners had to do all night.

The only other things in the cell are a bucket of scummy water for drinking and another bucket for the prisoners to relieve themselves. The smell coming from that second bucket fills Clarence's nostrils no matter where in the cell he sits and kept him awake much of last night.

Clarence had been the second man interned in the Limestone County jail cell and said little as the cell filled up with new prisoners yesterday. At first, they chatted with each other about why they were in prison, but a few shouts and threats from the guard soon shut down any conversation above a whisper.

Today is different, however. The sheriff, Robert, the same one who'd apprehended Clarence, comes to the cell and takes the prisoners away, one after another, for their trials. Again, Clarence is the second man chosen; it seems the men's trials happen in the order of their bookings yesterday.

On the way upstairs to the courtroom, the sheriff keeps a firm left hand on Clarence's right shoulder.

"Hurry up," Robert growls while he shoves Clarence up the worn, creaking wooden stairs. Not expecting the shove, Clarence stumbles, bracing himself with his palms. His reward is a bruised shin and several splinters in each palm.

Robert hoists Clarence up by the back of his shirt. "I said, hurry up, you dumb brute."

He shoves Clarence from behind again, but Clarence is ready this time and keeps his balance. Just as it usually does, Clarence's stomach knots in fear of what will happen next. The unknown always makes him a bit nervous; with the Buffalo Soldiers, he'd nearly vomited before every engagement. Clarence thinks this is worse, in a way, because he has no idea what to expect. In battle, at least a man knows what everyone expects him to do, and what his opponent means to do.

When the pair reach the doorway to the courtroom itself, the sheriff snarls in Clarence's ear, "Now, nigger boy, you'll just plead guilty if you know what's good for you. You and your Yankee, New York accent, coming down here to stir up trouble. Now, get!"

With that, Robert turns the tarnished brass doorknob and gives Clarence another rough shove into the courtroom before escorting him to the plain wooden desk where sits a man in a dark gray broadcloth suit unclasping a briefcase. Clarence supposes this man must be his lawyer. Why did the sheriff accuse him of being from New York? Clarence never told the man anything about his past, so why would he say that? Must be how southerners see all northerners; a figure of speech of sorts, he thinks.

Then, however, an idea strikes Clarence. Like a ray of light piercing his cloud of fear, he latches onto the words New York. New York! That's where Johnny Ward practices law! He even remembers Ward's address from the letter he received in St. Louis:

96 Broadway. If Clarence can but get a message out to Ward, perhaps he can do something to help. The question is, how?

Clarence sits down in the only chair available at the unpolished, rectangular wooden table. The chair, likewise, is a rough, unpolished wooden frame chair with a low, straight back. The lawyer turns but does not offer to shake hands. "Seth Dean," the man says quietly while leaning in close, almost as if he's trying to avoid attention.

Dean wears a tie over his pressed white shirt, his short hair parted on the left, and pince-nez glasses.

Clarence nods. "Clarence Duval. What am I charged with, Mr. Dean?"

The lawyer, a young man probably not more than five years older than Clarence's age of twenty-two, tilts his head a bit and cocks an eyebrow. "You aren't southern," he says in a thick drawl.

"No. Chicago, Butte, and St. Louis."

"You lived in *Montana*?"

"For a while."

"How'd you get here?"

"Passing through. Looking for family." Clarence hopes that giving his last name might trigger recognition; if his father is here in Athens, perhaps this man would know. But if that is true, Dean doesn't show it. Then, Clarence continues and asks again, "Why am I on trial?"

"The sheriff, Robert Lee Winston, and his younger brother and deputy James arrested you for loitering, vagrancy, and trespassing."

"I'd been in town barely an hour when they collared me. How could I have done all those things?"

"Doesn't matter. See those three men across the aisle from us?"

Clarence looks briefly, from the corner of his eye and without turning his head, then nods.

"They all claim they witnessed you breaking the law. We have no witnesses willing to testify that you didn't. You'll have to plead guilty."

"I've never met any of those men."

Dean looks up from his notes long enough to nod in the direction of the jury box. "You think the twelve white folks on that jury will believe you if you say that?"

"Guess not. What's the penalty?"

"Hard labor to pay off the fine and court costs."

"I've got ten dollars. It was going to pay for my train ticket home. Is that enough?"

"No. It'll get you a shorter sentence, but it won't pay for everything."

Clarence sighs and looks down at the floor. The wood is old. Old and worn, like the floor of the cabin he grew up in. He bites his lower lip a moment, then closes his eyes. They show a bit of wetness when he opens them again. His voice sinking quieter still, he says to Dean, "Will you do one thing after my trial is over?"

"What's that?"

"I need a pen and some paper to write a letter to a friend. Will you send it to him?"

"You can write, too?" Dean says with rising emphasis on the last syllable of the word write. Now both his eyebrows rise.

"For all the good it's done me."

"I suppose. Here." Shaking his head, Dean opens his briefcase and extracts a blank piece of legal paper and a fountain pen. "You can probably write it now; the trial won't start until the judge enters."

While Clarence pens his letter in brisk pen strokes, Dean considers what to make of the young man. A colored man who speaks without a Southern accent, is literate, and speaks formal English is a new experience for him. Athens has a handful of colored merchants, it's true, but they all speak with the rhythms of the South. This man does not.

He notices something deeper, too, but it's hard to pinpoint. When he looks in Clarence's eyes, Clarence looks back rather than lower his gaze. The cringing fear and deference he normally sees from colored men in Alabama isn't there. Dean can see Clarence's hand quiver a bit while he writes at the table, which is understandable, considering the circumstances, but fear does not paralyze this man's mind. These facts alone make Dean more than a little curious who this letter is for.

Writing as quickly as he can with his quivering hand, Clarence dashes off a note to John Ward describing what's happened to him. The penmanship is shaky, for sure, but legible. He signs it with his name and the phrase, "Dress ranks there," so that Ward will know beyond doubt it's from him.

Clarence hands the letter to Seth Dean, who glances at it and places it in his briefcase. Then Clarence looks up and scans the courthouse thoroughly for the first time.

As he does, Clarence notes with some surprise that many colored people have come to the trial. They are all, however, standing in the second-floor balcony, women and men alike trying to fan themselves against the unusual late-March heat. Wiry arms ending in weathered, coarse, calloused hands either wave makeshift paper fans back and forth or rest on threadbare pants legs, patched knees caked with dirt from weeding cotton earlier in the day.

Then Clarence's gaze drifts to the courtroom floor. It's packed with white people. A few wear suits and appear to be businessmen or merchants. Many, however, wear farm overalls and appear, at first, little different from the colored farmers standing above them. Except for a few things. While the people in the balcony simply watch somberly or whisper to each other, those below converse boisterously. Some have brought food. Clarence sees cornbread emerge from baskets, for instance, which young children gnaw hungrily while sitting on the laps of their mothers.

Despite the seeming gaiety, most of the white farmers present a struggling appearance, Clarence notes. Many already sport the sunburned necks and arms of people who work outside daily under the warm sun, and wear clothes no cleaner than those of the colored farmers in the balcony. Meanwhile, their wives sport white, dull gray, or peach-colored dresses, most of which have seen a few too many washings. Many of the children the wives watch over have bedraggled hair, and some wear clothes hardly better than the rags Clarence sported when he was a homeless kid on the Chicago streets. Almost none of the children wear shoes.

There's more, however. Several of the farmers scratch their arms constantly, with white flakes of dead skin falling off in the process. For some of them, the skin on their arms appears cracked and scaly, while others seem to have a rash. Even among those farmers without skin ailments, many have a sallow, yellowing complexion. The smell of sweaty men pervades the stuffy courtroom.

The final difference, and perhaps the most important at present, however, is that many of the white Alabama dirt farmers have shotguns in their laps.

Before Clarence can look any further, the bailiff's voice booms through the courtroom. "All rise. The honorable judge Jefferson Davis Winston presiding."

After the preliminary announcements relevant to the trial, everyone sits back down, and Judge Winston initiates the proceedings. "Prosecutor, you may present your case."

"Yes, suh," the attorney says with a drawl almost as thick as the courtroom air. This man has a large paunch; his belly juts out considerably from his body, so that the suspenders holding up his pants strain when he moves. As he strides forward to address the jury, a trickle of sweat rolls down his cheek, which he stops to blot out with a cloth handkerchief. The man clenches a cigar between his stained teeth, taking it out only when he begins speaking, the words drawling from his lips thicker than sweet tea.

"We will prove that the defendant, a Negro by the name of Clarence Duval, is guilty of the crimes of loiterin', tresspassin', and disturbin' the peace. Specifically, he is in violation of the Vagrancy Act, which stipulates that all Negros must be able to prove lawful employment or else the courts must deem them vagrant. This heah shiftless roustabout was, just a few days prior to today, seen by three witnesses who'll testify as to the truth of this heah situation. All mah witnesses are honorable gentlemen and rank among the many upstandin' citizens of Limestone County. They all will testify that the boy all y'all see in front of you today spent all afternoon on the day in question loiterin' in town and badgering decent citizens in public."

"Please proceed."

One by one, the witnesses take the stand and give their testimony. The first two claim they saw Clarence enter the post office of Athens, Alabama, and each man states that Clarence had, after leaving the post office, "wandered aimlessly" and "been pesterin' good folks" for the better part of half an hour while they went in and out of the post office themselves. Clarence had also, according to Athens tobacconist Tom Turnipseed, "walked on the same sidewalk as white folks, and refused to doff his hat for 'em."

The third witness, Hoss Williams, states he is the field manager for one of Mr. Winston's plantations. Williams claims that, while riding into town to buy a new hoe to replace one that had broken, he watched Clarence enter the schoolyard of the Trinity School and harass the pupils there, and he had then called on sheriff Robert Lee Winston and deputy sheriff James Longstreet Winston to apprehend him. Seth Dean does not cross-examine any of the witnesses.

Finally, it's Clarence's turn to take the stand. He walks to the witness's seat trying, but failing, not to tremble. When he sits down and looks out on the grizzled, hardscrabble white faces staring motionlessly, impassively, monolithically, toward him, his right hand continues shaking, so he puts it behind his back. Clarence has no idea what to do. He hasn't done any of the things the three men accused him of. Being an honest man, who has furthermore just sworn on the Bible to tell the truth, the whole truth, and nothing but the truth, he shrinks back from the thought of lying to the court and pleading guilty. But for a colored person, a Yankee, to challenge the word of a white man—no, make that three white men—is far more dangerous, and potentially fatal. He decides to lie. He survived the Buffalo Soldiers; he can survive this, too.

The prosecuting attorney rises and begins his questioning, his leather shoes echoing softly through the quiet courthouse while he approaches Clarence. "Now, it's well known to all heah that the Negro's place is in the cotton field, under the kind, paternalistic care of his white employers. Ah can mahself verify, though it scarcely requires verification, that this town has always been friendly toward its peaceful Negro population, and that no man need fear from the law so long as he keeps his proper place. Yet, this boy, this outsider, comes into our town and, within a single day, starts causin' trouble, givin' all the Negro people of Athens a poor reputation. Isn't that right, boy?"

Clarence hears the blood pounding in his brain while he contemplates what to say. His life could be on the line; the pressure is too much. His entire reality narrows to the point where all he can see is a confined tunnel between himself and the attorney. Even the all-white jury, only fifteen feet to his right, has lost definition. They, like the rest of the spectators, become a formless blur surrounding the prosecutor's black-suited form.

"Objection," Dean breaks in just before Clarence opens his mouth to speak. "The prosecution is leading the witness. He cannot be made to testify against himself."

"Sustained," replies Judge Winston.

"Very well, I apologize, your honor." Smiling confidently, obnoxiously, even, the prosecutor continues. "Now, boy, where were you yesterday afternoon?"

Clarence looks toward Dean pleadingly, but the defense attorney only nods, as if to say, "you know what you have to do."

Clarence stammers, "I arrived on t-the t-train, went t-to the post office, then visited t-the school."

"Would that be the Trinity School, boy?"

"Yes, sir."

"And you took to pesterin' the children there?"

Clarence sits and thinks. The silence stretches out. His ears start ringing. He feels the back of his shirt soaked with sweat, clinging to him.

"Boy?" the prosecutor says, a note of impatient irritation evident in his question.

"Yes, sir."

"Why?"

"I was new in town. I didn't know where to go, so I decided to look around."

"To cause trouble and stir up the law abidin' Negro people of Athens?"

"I'm sorry, sir. I didn't know the local customs."

"Just like a Negro, always thinkin' of himself, not considerin' what his actions will cost others. Ah'll bet you was fixin' to steal something from Travis's Local Store before checkin' your grip for the next town down the line, now, weren't you, boy?"

"Objection," Dean breaks in. "The defendant's future intentions, whatever they may be, are immaterial to the charges against him."

"Sustained," Winston says, though only with effort does he suppress a faint smile as the laughter dies down in the rest of the courtroom. Turning to the prosecutor, he says, feigning impatience, "Please stay on point."

"Your honor, let me conclude. The prosecution has produced three witnesses of upstandin' character who have testified that this boy, this vagrant, this Yankee, was not only loiterin' near the post office yesterday, but also disturbin' the peace by botherin' decent folks. It is a tribute to the fine character of these folks that they requested the defendant's arrest rather than resorting to, shall we say, a less formal style of justice. With that, your honor, we rest our case."

"The defense may now question the witness."

Rising slowly and adjusting his tie, then his glasses, Dean begins. "Gentlemen of the jury, allow me to say a few words on Clarence Duval's behalf. I offer that although the defendant has admitted his guilt in this situation, you consider certain facts when determining his punishment. Firstly, Clarence Duval is, although an outsider unfamiliar with the customs of the South, a good Negro. Furthermore, please consider his age, a mere twenty-two years. Being born after the War of Northern Aggression, he has always been a free man. Duval has never known the civilizing and paternal hand of slavery and has never experienced slavery's discipline and its tendency to moderate the worst aspects of his race. Therefore, while he is to blame for this crime, the predisposition of the Negro race toward crime and lawlessness is also to blame."

"Ah object, your honor," the prosecutor calls out.

"On what grounds?" Judge Winston inquires.

"Ah believe Mr. Dean has been all too charitable in his characterization of this boy's situation."

"Please explain."

"Your honor, although ah'm tempted to agree with the defense, and with the noted theologian Philip Schaff that, given time to run its course, slavery would have delivered the Sons of Ham from their ancient curse, ah fear that is too generous a description of the situation. Instead, consider that Negros do not appear in the *Holy Bible*. Their history is as blank as that of the monkey or the cow. While perhaps among the more evolved of God's animal creations, they remain animals. It is a fact needing no repetition heah that Negros are not mentioned on the Ark, where Noah and his family escaped The Flood, so they must have been created among the other beasts in the Garden of Eden."

"Although it appears to have little bearing on the matter at hand, your objection is noted," Judge Winston replies. "Now, can the defense finish its closing statement?"

Dean resumes. "I have little more to add, your honor. Given the shortcomings of his kind and his unfamiliarity with our local customs, I ask that the jury judge Clarence Duval lightly for his crimes and offer a lenient sentence in response to his conduct on the afternoon in question."

After the prosecution declines to enter any further argument, the jury departs to discuss the case. In fewer than five minutes, it returns. No one present in the courtroom even stirs when the jury foreman reads the verdict of "guilty" on the counts of vagrancy and disturbing the peace. Now, it remains for Judge Winston to pronounce a sentence.

"Clarence Duval," he begins, "a jury of your peers has found you guilty of the crimes of vagrancy and disturbing the peace. As a result, you will spend the next ninety days incarcerated. Furthermore, as your actions brought on this case, and the financial burden to Limestone County and the state of Alabama that it represents, you will also be responsible for the court fees incurred to try the case or, in lieu of payment, a longer work sentence to compensate the state for today's court costs. Those court fees total fifty dollars. Are you able to pay this sum in cash before your sentence begins?"

Clarence drops his head when he hears the ruling. After a moment, and with the sniffling of someone on the verge of breaking into tears but determined not to, he answers, "No, your honor. I have only ten dollars. It was supposed to be my ticket home."

"Very well. In that case, you must pay back the remaining forty dollars of court costs by your own labor. The court therefore rules that, for the duration of your ninety-day sentence, you will work for the Southern Pineland Company to pay off your debt. Once your ninety days are over, you will continue in its employ until your work has paid all relevant court costs, in this case, forty dollars, at which time you will return to society as a free man. This case is closed."

7

Seth Dean

When he leaves the courthouse later that afternoon, after pretending to represent six poor, mostly illiterate, and deathly frightened colored men, Seth Dean alternates between looking at the verdant green of the courthouse lawn with its beautiful Kentucky bluegrass and the fresh, clear blue of the Alabama spring sky. Normally, he'd enjoy this excellent spring weather and admire the sky as the occasional puffy white cloud drifted overhead, but today, it just doesn't look the same.

Only eighteen more cases like today's over the next three days, he thinks to himself. *At $10 for every case, I'll be living high on the hog soon enough.* This really is his lucky break. All his life, Seth wanted to study law. No way will he end up like his pop, an angry drunk who could barely pay the yearly rent on the 80-acre farm where Seth grew up in the northern Alabama hill country. An angry drunk who'd beaten him weekly until Seth learned to hide down by the creek when he heard his father come home at night. A pitiful man who'd died when Seth was fifteen, he had drunk himself into such a stupor one night that he'd fallen off his horse and snapped his neck. Yes, indeed, this is his break.

A part of him, however, doesn't quite believe it. What would his mother say, if she were still alive rather than eight, no, nine now, months in the grave? "Do unto others." "Love thy neighbor." "Remember those who are in chains, as bound with them." How many times had she repeated the Lord Jesus's commandments to him?

Daily, he thought, *and twice a day when I told her I was going to study law*. Today, he had played a role in sending an innocent man to prison. No, not one innocent man. Six innocent men. He barely put up a defense. Seth just went through the motions, observing the formalities, upholding the pretense of justice. Furthermore, Judge Winston expects him to do the same thing again and again over the next three days. And so on, whenever the situation calls for it.

Instructing any of the accused to plead "not guilty" was pointless, he knew. Defending a colored man in northern Alabama against the word of white witnesses, in front of an all-white jury, when every colored witness who might have taken the stand was too terrified of the lynch mob even to consider the possibility, well, what could he have done? Not to mention that, had he put up a spirited defense on behalf of a colored person, he risked ostracism from the community where he hoped to make his name as an up-and-coming attorney.

Next, Seth's thoughts turn to Emily. He'd begun courting Emily Winston, Judge Winston's daughter, a little more than three months back when they'd met at a New Year's ball in town. The way she looked that evening, with her pure white ballroom gown trailing behind her while they danced, was like the first time he'd ever seen a rose in full bloom. He'd never forget it. Her long, auburn hair, pale skin, high cheekbones, and piercing blue eyes enchanted him. Seth had called on Emily again the next weekend, and the next, and they'd seen each other whenever possible from January onward.

The fact that Emily is Judge Winston's daughter is not a problem, exactly, but a caution. Winston is, without doubt, the most powerful man in Athens. Probably the most powerful man in Limestone County. So long as Seth stays in his good graces, all is well. That is, in part, why he'd made such a pitiful effort today. Judge Winston needs convicts periodically. When he does, his two sons, the sheriff and deputy sheriff of Athens, round up whoever happens to be on the streets or passing through town. Seth makes sure the juries have no reason not to convict and receives a payment from the judge for each person convicted.

Seth doesn't know exactly what happens to the men after their conviction, other than they go to work somewhere to pay off their sentences and court costs. He doesn't know where they go, who they work for, or what becomes of them once they get there, other than the most general details. This batch of convicts will go to the pine forests of Florida, Judge Winston told him, but that is all Seth knows. The only thing he knows for certain is that nine of every ten men he pretends to represent in court is a colored man, and he's never seen any of them in Athens again, even the ones who lived in town and whose faces he recognized before their trial.

Seth also knows, however, that if he is ever to marry Emily like he hopes to someday, he must stay on Jefferson Winston's good side. Not to mention that if he has Winston in his corner, he has no reason to stay in Limestone County forever. He is young, just twenty-eight, and with the Judge's help he might rise considerably in the Alabama bar. Then he can use his influence to make up for any injustice he helps perpetrate now.

Besides Emily, that's the other thought that rarely leaves his mind. Making his way in the world. All the kids who used to tease him, who'd called his father a worthless drunk to Seth's face, he'll show them. Seth Dean will rise higher than any of them, and someday, they'll come to him when they need help. Maybe he'll even end up owning the farms on which they work.

That isn't good enough, what remains of his conscience scolds. *And ma would say so, too, if she could.* While Seth walks slowly up Jefferson Street toward his boarding house on the north edge of town, he keeps his head down the whole way as the argument continues unabated in his thoughts.

Unbidden, something his father told him once, in a rare moment of full sobriety, comes to mind. "Son," he'd said to Seth in a twangy voice rendered pathetic by misery and failure, "do better than your pa's done. Get on in the world. But, whatever you do, don't let The Man get you. I might be as worthless as they come, as worthless as a nigger, even, but I ain't never sold my soul to The Man. I ain't never polished his shoes, or asked for a crumb from his table, and I never will. I'm a lousy, mean, no-account drunk, and I'm poor as dirt, but I'm an honest drunk. When I die, at least they'll say that I was honest. It's all I'll leave to our family, an honest reputation. Don't squander that when you grow up. Don't take from me the only thing I've got."

After that, his father gave Seth one of the few hugs he remembers getting as a child, and Seth saw the tears forming in his father's eyes as he shambled away to hitch up his mule and return to their fields. His father's patched and re-patched overalls were almost indistinguishable in color from the rocky Alabama soil of their rented farm.

Seth had hated the farm as a boy and hated it just as much now. After his father died, his mother moved the family into town in Athens, took in washing and did household work for a couple merchants who were bachelors, and made sure Seth and his sister went to school regularly. He'd never go back to farm life. Never. Besides his dislike for farming itself, Seth believes that Alabama cotton farming might be in trouble. He reads the papers, and he's heard of a new pest that has shown up in south Texas called the boll weevil. It remains in Texas for now but spreads some miles north and east each year. Who knows if it will someday strike Alabama? All Seth knows is that the boll weevil decimates cotton crops wherever it appears, that everything farmers try to use to kill it seems to fail, and that many farmers in Alabama grow cotton. That isn't a future he wants to be part of.

Suddenly, he realizes where he is. The Methodist Church of Athens comes into view on his right. It's the church Seth attends, and among the most opulent buildings in Athens. It looks a bit like the county courthouse. It's almost as large, for that matter. Like the courthouse, it has three floors and a dome on top. The front steps of the red brick church lead to a second-floor porch, shaded by a colonnaded overhang, that gives access to the sanctuary. The porch is wide enough for the church to have three front doors.

Although his mother brought him up a Christian and remained a churchgoer until her death, Seth isn't sure he qualifies as a devoted Methodist. He enjoys singing the hymns; practicing with one's voice has its uses in the legal profession, after all. But because of his legal education, the whole idea of miracles and reading the Bible as literal truth troubles him. Mostly, Seth goes to church there for the prestige. He can sing hymns anywhere, but most of Athens' finest citizens attend this church, so Seth does, too.

Seth considers heading back to his boardinghouse, which means continuing straight on Jefferson for another block, but on the spur of the moment, he decides to call on Emily instead, so he turns right, heading east. He's had a long day and wants to talk with someone besides himself for a while.

Judge Winston lives a bit east of town on his plantation, so Seth needs to hire a carriage to get there. It isn't hard to find one on Jefferson Street, however, and soon, he is on his way.

Knowing that Judge Winston will still be in town for a couple hours yet completing paperwork, Seth hopes that he and Emily can get a little time alone, so he can tell her what's on his mind.

When he knocks at the front door of Winston's vast plantation house, Henry, one of the Judge's faithful colored servants, answers.

"Afternoon, marse Dean," Henry says while removing his hat and placing it over his chest, bowing slightly.

"Hello, Henry, is Emily at home?"

"Yessuh, she here, but she not in de house. She go for a walk down by de creek. She say it too warm inside today."

"Thank you, Henry. I'll go find her."

It doesn't take long. Seth knows Emily's favorite spot and, sure enough, that's where Emily is. She has on a sky-blue dress and a white sun bonnet and carries a parasol with her for shade, although she's set the parasol down now that she's underneath the branches of the creek's black willows. This is one of the few areas in the county where one finds black willows, and Emily likes them. She must have heard Seth coming because she looks over at him right away after he comes into view.

"Seth! I wasn't expecting you to call today."

"I know. I wasn't planning to, either, but just changed my mind on the way home. I need to talk to someone for a while."

"You live in a boardinghouse. You've lots of people to talk to."

"True, but they aren't friends in the way that you are."

"Something's troubling you, Seth. I can tell."

"Is it that obvious?"

Seth sits down on a section of wood that one of Winston's servants sawed to chair height and placed here for Emily. Emily already sits on a similar section of her own.

"Sometimes, you get a bit of a twitch in your left cheek when you're nervous. You should practice not doing that. When you must try cases someday, someone might notice."

Seth puts an arm around her shoulders. "Well, darling Emily, that's part of what I was thinking about on my way home."

She draws back. "You're thinking of leaving Athens? Setting up as an attorney in Tuscaloosa or Birmingham?"

"No," he says with a little laugh. "No, I'm not leaving Athens. Not right now, anyway. Someday, maybe, but not today. Or tomorrow."

Her shoulders sag as Emily exhales audibly. "You scared me there for a moment. Shame on you." She leans back into the hug, the momentary fright gone out of her face.

"I saw Henry when I came to the house. He said you were too warm inside and came down here."

"Don't change the subject like that, Seth Dean. You were going to tell me about something that happened today."

Another small laugh from Seth. "Maybe you should join me in law, Emily. You've got as good an eye for details as I have, it seems."

Emily gives a polite smile. Not the real, light-up-the-room smile that captured Seth's heart the first time he saw it, but still beautiful. She says, "You know my father. He wants me to be a lady, a real Southern belle, but he won't suffer fools. I hear the same lectures from him about attending to details that my brothers do."

Seth puts his head down, gathers up a couple pebbles from the grass, and lobs them into the creek. Their tiny splashes barely audible amongst the twittering of a few goldfinches perched above, he tosses them into the water until he has only one left.

Emily continues. "Are you going to get to the point or not? You said you came here to talk, and now you don't want to. Did something go wrong today?"

"Well, I wouldn't say it went wrong, exactly, but some unusual things came up, and I'm not quite sure what to think."

"About the trials?"

"One of them, yeah."

"Did you have to defend a white man charged with a crime? I know that always makes you uncomfortable when you have to do that."

"No, he was a colored man. All six of them were. But this man was different. He was from the North and spoke perfect English. Better English than most people I know here in Athens. He was just passing through town, said he was looking for family, when your brothers arrested him and brought him in."

"What did he do wrong? And if he was Northern, was he sassy and cheeky?"

"Not at all. He was quiet, calm, and composed. He looked me in the eye when I spoke to him."

"Sounds cheeky."

"But he wasn't, Emily."

"What were the charges?"

"The usual. Vagrancy. Disturbing the peace."

"Then he must have been cheeky to Rob and Jimmy."

"Maybe. But here's the strangest thing. This man could write. He asked me to send a letter for him, and he just sat there in the courtroom and scribbled it out right before the trial began."

"That *is* strange, Seth."

"I thought so, too."

"Who is the letter to?"

"I haven't looked. I was waiting for the trial to begin, so I just filed it away with my other papers. I'm a little curious, though."

"You've got your briefcase with you. Let's give it a look."

Seth stoops down to retrieve his leather briefcase. Setting it in his lap, he releases the brass clasps and sifts through the papers until he finds the letter. Giving it a full look for the first time, his eyes go wide, and he silently mouths the word "wow."

"What is it?" Emily asks, her eyebrows now arching in surprise, too, as she leans in for a look.

"Look at who it's addressed to: Mr. John Ward, 96 Broadway, New York City."

"Who's that?" Emily wonders aloud.

"Who's John Ward? Only one of the most famous ballplayers ever to live."

"He plays baseball?"

"Used to. He played for the New York Club for many years. Providence and Brooklyn, too, but mostly New York. He's retired now, however. I heard once he planned to go into law, so I guess we have something in common."

"Is it a bad thing that this man wanted the letter to go to John Ward?"

"No, I think it's a great thing. I've never told you, Emily, but I dreamed of being a ballplayer, a shortstop like Ward, when I was younger. When I studied law, the one luxury I allowed myself was a subscription to *The Sporting Life*."

"What's that?"

"The premier weekly sporting newspaper in the country. I would have subscribed to *The Sporting News*, too, but I only had enough spare money for one of them. Anyway, John Ward was my hero until he retired. The paper always said how smart he was and what a heady ballplayer he was. I even bought a copy of his book, *Base-Ball: How to Become a Player*. Maybe I should have studied it better."

"Sounds like he'd make a good lawyer, then."

"I think I'll send him a note along with this letter. Just to tell him how much I admired him. Maybe ask for some advice on lawyering. You don't think your father would mind, do you?"

"Why would he?"

"Judge Winston has taught me most of the practical points of how a lawyer should behave. I know the laws, but he's the one who gives me advice on how to act in the courtroom."

"Do you want me to ask him, Seth?"

"No, I'll do it if things come to that. He might find it unmanly if you do it for me."

"You don't think I'm smart enough!"

"Of course, I think you're smart."

"No, you don't. Because I'm a woman you think you need to do things for me."

"I know you're smart. I know you're smart because I can tell you're teasing me right now," Seth says, breaking out his best smile and putting both arms around her shoulders for a hug.

Emily laughs. "I'm teasing, but I'm serious, too. Someday, women will vote in this country, you know."

"Now you're really teasing. That's nonsense, and you know it."

"They already can in a few states out West."

"How do you know?"

"I went to a suffragette lecture last week."

"I can't believe the Judge let you go, Emily."

"I told him I needed a new bonnet, but it took me a long time to decide which one I liked. I think he believed me." She giggles at the recollection.

"You really do have an eye for detail. Maybe you should join me. We can be the first husband and wife legal firm in Limestone County someday."

"Seth! You shouldn't say that! We've only been seeing each other a couple months."

"Sorry. My turn to tease you for a bit."

"But you weren't teasing."

"Yes, I was. Promise."

"You sure you don't want me to ask my father about writing to this John Ward?"

Seth pauses and looks down again. Almost without thinking, he tosses the last of his pebbles into the creek.

"You're still hiding something, I can tell," Emily says, the slightest note of concern slipping into her voice.

Another pause. Finally, Seth turns, looks Emily in the eye, and asks her, "Emily, how much do you know about what your father does?"

"What do you mean?"

"Does he ever talk to you about how he makes money and runs his plantation?"

"Only a little. I know that we live here and that he has tenants and sharecroppers who work for him. He owns thousands of acres in the county. I don't know how many for certain."

"What about his work as judge?"

"When the Negros cause trouble, he calls on Rob and Jimmy to round them up, so they can't cause trouble or threaten women. He keeps us all safe."

"Do you ever stop to think what happens to the people he convicts, Emily?"

"They go to prison, or to work, where they belong. He always warns me about how dangerous the Negros can be, how criminal their race is, and how I should always watch them for hints of trouble."

"That isn't exactly what I mean. Do you ever think about what happens to them when they leave here? Where they go? What happens to them once they get there?"

"I can't say that I've ever given it much thought. But, if they're guilty, don't they deserve whatever they get? I mean, they're criminals, aren't they?"

Seth just stares out across the creek to the cotton field beyond, elbows on his knees. The green stalks of the cotton plants have sprouted, but it'll be some time before the white bolls peek out.

"Although," Emily says thoughtfully, "two days ago, my father had a guest at the house. He introduced me, and then said I should leave them to business. But he said the guest was a director of some Boston company. I think it was the Southern Pineland Company."

"Was something wrong?"

"No, I wouldn't say it that way. It's just that this man struck me as cold. Not just in the Yankee way, either. He just had no expression at all when I met him. He didn't look happy. He didn't look sad. Or friendly. Or pleased. Or anything. His face was like a wall, or a sheet of ice. He didn't strike me as someone I'd want to know more about."

"Did your father mention his name?"

"My father introduced him. His name was Thomas Brown. I sometimes forget names when I meet father's friends and associates the first time, but this man just stood out in a way that made me want to shiver. Do you want me to try to learn more about him?"

Seth pushes up from his knees and stands up. He extracts his pocket watch and gives it a look. "Your father will be home soon. I think I'd better get going. And no, don't worry about Thomas Brown. It sounds like you'd rather forget him, anyway."

"You don't want father to know you visited?"

"Oh, it's not a secret, and Henry knows I'm here anyway, so you can tell him if he asks. Just tell him I wanted to go home and prepare for tomorrow's day in court."

"When will I see you again, Seth?"

"Soon, I hope. Once this current load of cases is over with, for sure."

"Perhaps we can head to town for ice cream. You know how I love ice cream."

"That sounds wonderful. Oh, but leave one thing out if you talk with your father. Don't mention the letter to John Ward. I'll handle it myself."

With that, Seth gives Emily the lightest of kisses on the cheek and then strides off toward the Winston house.

8

Leaving Athens

Clarence sits in his cell for four more days until it is time to depart Athens and begin his sentence. It's miserable. Two nights ago, it was his turn to sleep on the floor, since the cell has six residents but only four beds. Well, the word sleep isn't quite accurate. Better to say he lay on the floor not sleeping while listening for rats and brushing away the cockroaches and ants.

His company, the same five men as on the day of his arrest, are in the cell with him the entire time. Each is a colored man like him, most are about Clarence's age, their "crimes" are the same as his, and their sentences are identical. The only exception is Ezra Tompkins, who is old enough to be the father of any other man in the cell. The Southern Pineland Company has, it seems, contracted for all six of them to go to Florida and work off their sentences under company supervision. What that work entails, no one knows for certain, but no shortage of speculation exists among the cellmates. The day after their trials, that is what everyone wants to talk about.

"I bet we're going to work on the railroad they're building from Pensacola to Tampa," Tom Morton offers. Besides Clarence, Tom is the only prisoner who has some education. He has been to school for eight years, he tells everyone, and is the only other person in the cell who can read and write. Tom is also the youngest, fifteen years old, and might be five-foot-two inches tall, at most.

"How'd you get here wid us po' folks?" Emory Wilson asks Tom. "How'd dey get you?"

"I was on my way through town, just riding my horse, heading south toward my cousin's house. He's older than me, and he works in a warehouse in Birmingham, moving bales of cotton before they're loaded onto the railroad. I stopped in town to send a letter ahead to my aunt and uncle, just to let them know I was doing fine and when I'd be there, but then, just as I was about to leave town, two men, the sheriff and his deputy, stopped me. They said they were arresting me for vagrancy. That was four days ago. I just want to get moving, so I can get my sentence over with and get back on my way. Someday, I'm gonna try and get some more schooling; I hear up north they have good colleges where colored folks can go. Howard, for one. I want to go there some day. Maybe I'll even make it as a lawyer. Then I can come back here and help colored folks who get in a pickle like we are."

"Shut up, boy!" shouts the guard as he looks up from the chunk of wood he's whittling into something that Clarence can't quite make out. Although the guard isn't suffering from the unseasonable heat quite as badly as the prisoners, everyone can see the sweat stains in the armpits of the guard's uniform. "You keep talkin' that nonsense about niggers getting' more schoolin', and I'll take a strap to ya. School only ruins a perfectly good field hand, and that's a fact. College!"

Clarence doesn't recognize this guard. It isn't one of the brothers who brought him in, but this one doesn't appear any kinder, wiser, or more humane than the Winston brothers.

"You listen to him, now, son," the older man, Ezra Tompkins, counsels Tom. "You know that he ain't jus' talkin'. Pipe down, now." Tom and Emory give Ezra an open-mouthed stare; this is the first time Ezra has said anything other than "yes" or "no" in the days that the men have sat in prison.

71

"See?" Ezra says, wincing as he slowly peels off his tan-colored linen shirt. "You don' want to look like me. You's young and got a future. Look."

Ezra's back, which should be a light shade of brown like his bearded face, is instead a crisscross of purple, red, and dark pink scars. Almost every inch of it. The scars form a ghastly kaleidoscope of streaks, indescribably hideous yet riveting in its own macabre way.

"I sassed too much when I's your age," Ezra explains, "and massa whip me all da time. I's like to be dead, excep' den de war came, an ol' massa got killed at Shiloh, or somethin' like dat. Don' be like me and larn de hard way."

"How old are you?" Tom asks.

"Don' know for sho'. I's born in slavery times, 'course, but no one kept count of my age. Don' know whens my birthday. I think I's about twenty when de war begin, so I's about sixty now."

"Last warning for all y'all!" yells the guard. "Now, eat your slop and sit quiet."

Slop is an apt description of the food passed through the bars of the cell, Clarence thinks. A hunk of black bread and a ladle of beans is all each man gets, breakfast, lunch, and dinner. Yet, he eats it hungrily enough because he's always hungry. More than the food, however, Clarence is thankful for a dipper of water. Even though it is late in March, he's still in Alabama. The temperature is warm, his cell is small and crowded, and its one barred window doesn't let in much of a breeze, especially on a day like today when little breeze exists, anyway. The cell's only redeeming feature is that the outside wall faces east and gets the morning, rather than the afternoon, sun.

Clarence spends his time saying little, even without any warnings from the guard. His initial anger at his unfair predicament has given way to resignation to his fate and a determination to get it over with as quickly as possible, but that, in turn, starts fading as fear and trepidation gnaw at him. With so much spare time, Clarence has time to think. Too much time. All the extra time allows the negative thoughts to drive a wedge, slowly but inexorably, into Clarence's determination. What work will he have to do? He's done all sorts of odd jobs in Butte and St. Louis, but he's never worked outside for long and has no experience building anything. What if he can't learn quickly enough? Will that mean a longer sentence? Worse? What about the other prisoners, the ones already there? As Clarence muses on all these things, he scratches his head. A small tuft of hair falls to his lap. That's when he realizes his right hand is shaking again, just like in the courthouse.

Clarence manages to do a little more than just worry during his four days, however. He gives some thought, and perhaps it is long overdue thought, to his future. Assuming he ever gets out of his current predicament, what will he do? He's done what he's always heard a person is supposed to do to get ahead in America. Learn to read? Check. Learn to write? Clarence can do that. Work hard and stay sober? Absolutely. Don't gamble away your earnings? Clarence gave up playing craps long ago. Where had all his good habits ever gotten him? He'd tried to get a job as a clerk or recordkeeper for people like doctors and lawyers in St. Louis, but none ever hired him. That is partly why he gave Williams and Walker a try.

Clarence hates the thought of working in a factory. Besides, after what had happened to him the one time he tried in Chicago, he knows factories are dangerous places. Often, on the streets of Chicago and St. Louis, he's met youngsters missing fingers, sometimes an entire hand, that they'd lost in factory accidents. He's seen other men, men only ten years or so older than he is, walking, stooped at the waist, with a cane from the backbreaking labor. He'd swear that some of the men were closer to sixty than to thirty from the way they walked, if he didn't know better.

For the same reason, Clarence knows he can't work in mining. He still means to keep his promise to Louise Healy and never enter a mine again, which isn't hard because of his fear of being underground. Even though he made that promise years ago when he lived with the Healys in Butte, Clarence will never forget it because it's one of the last things Louise told him before shooting herself. In addition, Clarence knows that miners have a short life expectancy, possibly even shorter than factory workers. Either an accident in the mines kills them quickly or the coal dust clogging up their lungs kills them slowly.

Sometimes, Clarence thinks back on his time in the Army. He hadn't been a very good soldier, unfortunately. He had followed orders as well as the next man, but he'll always remember how nervous he had gotten just at the thought of being in combat. During his time with the Buffalo Soldiers he had never been in a true firefight, but Clarence doubts he would have been very helpful even if he had. His marksmanship was middling on a good day, and those days in the field ushering the Cree and Métis to the Canadian border rank as the most grueling thing he's ever done.

What, then, is he truly any good at? The fact that Clarence has difficulty deciding how to answer is a bad sign, he thinks. His second acting career ended better than his first, it's true, but Clarence doesn't see much future there. He can sing respectably and dance tolerably well, but those roles pay just enough money to avoid starving while the company tours. Clarence knows he doesn't have enough sense of humor to ever be a leading player in an act like Williams and Walker, so he isn't likely to ever make much money in acting because he'll never be a headliner.

What about farming? Clarence likes plants and growing things. Whenever he had the time, he'd helped Sally Healy tend the backyard garden she kept in St. Louis. The idea has potential but also pitfalls. Foremost among them, Clarence owns no land and has little money with which to buy any. Furthermore, without much experience in farming, he doesn't know how to begin.

The same holds true for starting his own business. Clarence learned a little from unloading supplies for the hardware store John Healy co-owned but doesn't know much about the business of running a store. And again, how will he get merchandise and open a store with no money? Will a bank make a loan to a colored man? He also questions how many white customers he can attract because of his color.

For an instant, Clarence wonders if, perhaps, he should have listened to Elizabeth Tucker and stayed with her in Harlem. Although he is in the prime of life, just twenty-two, sometimes Clarence thinks about finding a steady girl and maybe getting married. Then, from nowhere, he remembers Harry Palmer's jokes about moving to Utah with the Mormons and getting six wives. When Clarence and the Spalding Tour passed through Utah back in 1888, Palmer, the Chicago newspaperman, continually cracked jokes about how in Utah a man could marry several women at once. Clarence thinks he recalls reading that Utah finally changed its laws and that polygamy isn't legal there anymore. Still, he chuckles, thinking back on the more carefree times of that trip a decade ago.

Several others in the cell turn and look at him. They've been talking in low voices to avoid aggravating the man on guard. "Sorry," Clarence tells them. "Just an old memory."

Because he rarely says anything, no one pays him much heed, so he returns to his thoughts. The break, however, banishes any further thoughts of Elizabeth Tucker from his mind. She's an attractive young lady; no one can hold that against her. It's what got her the part she had in *The Gold Bug*, Clarence guesses. Elizabeth is one of a handful of women in the company who sang the female parts of the songs while the actors on stage danced. Considering that her voice is a little shaky at times, and she sometimes has trouble remembering the lines she practices, Clarence can't imagine what else convinced Walker and Williams to employ her.

She'd taken a liking to him shortly after he joined the show. Clarence still isn't sure if it was because of true affection or if Elizabeth thought she could manipulate him due to his quiet nature. Maybe some of both. Elizabeth is fun to spend time with, and she has a better sense of humor than Clarence does, but when she spoke to Clarence, he felt like she just expected him to go along with whatever she wanted. Not once did she ask him anything about himself or his life before he joined Walker and Williams. It was for the best, though, in a way. If Elizabeth had ever learned he'd traveled all the way around the world when he was only twelve, her jealousy probably would have stopped her from ever speaking to him again.

The other thing about Elizabeth that Clarence finds most annoying is that she can never stop talking, especially about herself and what a brilliant actress she'll someday be. Once, Clarence tried encouraging her to follow her dreams after a show where she hadn't performed well, but he found that only made her more obnoxiously self-obsessed, so he'd never tried that a second time.

Finally, actresses are bad luck. Clarence knows from talking to John Healy that Johnny Ward's marriage to an actress, Helen Dauvray, had not worked out and that they'd parted ways eventually. No, he decides, if he ever makes it out of Florida, he has no need to write to Elizabeth Tucker or try to see her again.

No nearer an answer about his future than when he began, Clarence eventually drifts into sleep, having nothing else to do besides sit with his back to the cell wall and daydream.

On the fifth day after the trial, it's time to leave for Florida. Deputy sheriff James Winston and his brother Robert, each toting shotguns and smoking cigars, order the convicts to remove their clothes while several other men without uniforms, also armed, watch warily. Most of the prisoners are only too happy to do so because to a man, their shirts and overalls are dirty and exude the foul stench of repeated sweat soakings from spending four days in close confinement in the Alabama heat and humidity.

In exchange for their old clothes, the officers toss each prisoner one shirt and one pair of pants. Both are of the same heavy material, denim, and both feature alternating two-inch black and white horizontal stripes from top to bottom.

"Enjoy your new outfit, nigger!" one of the guards exclaims to Clarence while he puts on his new set of clothes. Clarence doesn't dignify the man with a response, just a quick glance.

What he sees is a familiar look—the same one he had seen from the vigilantes who had attacked his camp on the Milk River in 1895. The hatred is there, yes, but also a beaming grin. The *joy* this man takes in hating is what Clarence just can't understand, and that look of triumphant hatred takes him hours to dismiss from his memory.

"All y'all look better this way. All the niggers should wear ring-arounds!" a second guard jeers.

"What's ring-arounds?" one prisoner asks.

"Your new clothes for the next six months," the man replies.

"That's enough," growls James Winston. "Get 'em ready to move. Train'll be here this afternoon, and we gotta get 'em to the platform on time."

Clarence soon finds that "getting 'em ready to move" means clapping all the prisoners in hand and foot shackles and then chaining the lot together to further hinder possible escape. *Not that we could get away anyway*, he thinks, *with the officers armed and on horseback, and each of us already chained hand and foot, just like in slavery days.*

Shortly after 10 in the morning, the group shuffles off toward the train platform, moving at well under a walking pace. Fortunately, it's only a few blocks from the courthouse to the station. It isn't long, however, before a man falling on top of Clarence from behind knocks him to his knees.

"Aaah!" he cries, a sudden pain shooting up his left leg from his ankle.

"Sorry," Emory Wilson pants while untangling himself from Clarence. "I ain't used to dese chains, dat's all."

The nearest guard cackles and extracts his cigarette from his mouth long enough to say, "Get up, boy! So clumsy and stupid, they can't even walk right. You really ain't much better than an ape, you know that?" Then, the man gives Emory a sharp kick in the side with his booted foot to emphasize his point. "Git up, boy. Walk!"

Emory grimaces and clenches one fist. Clarence sees the anguish burn in Emory's face while he helps him up, although Clarence isn't sure if the anger comes more from the pain of the kick or the humiliation. For a moment, he fears Emory will say something back. "Let it go, Emory, it's not worth it. We'll be okay."

Teeth gritted and muscles tensed, Emory finally remembers his position and composes himself. "I'se sorry, Clarence, my legs still hurt somethin' fierce, tha's all."

With everyone now back up, the group continues its shuffle toward the train station. Then, Clarence remembers. Two days back, Emory complained about the moldy bread the jail served him at one meal. Three guards took him out of his cell and administered a series of kicks and punches in front of all the other prisoners, just to send a message. Emory's beating was so savage Clarence finds it a wonder no bones broke. He doesn't doubt Emory still feels the bruises while he rises and shambles along again.

The nearest guard remembers it, too. "Yeah, you's the uppity nigger, ain't you? If you wasn't already holdin' us up, I'd give it to you again, you ape. Now, walk like a man instead of a monkey, if you can."

"Yes. Suh." Emory grunts through clenched teeth, eyes on the ground.

At first, Clarence fears he's sprained his ankle, but to his relief soon finds the pain bearable and diminishing; he's merely given it a nasty twist. After what seems like hours, they reach the train station. Each man receives two dippers of water on arrival and another before boarding. The day already promises to be another warm one, and it isn't yet noon.

9

The Journey to Florida

After waiting what feels like hours just standing in his chains on the platform, Clarence hears the telltale whistle of a locomotive. Next, he sees the familiar plume of dark smoke visible over the buildings of Athens, and then the train itself rolls into sight, locomotive plowing forward like a hungry beast prepared to devour anything in its path. If Clarence had believed in such things, he might have thought the locomotive's shrill whistle the unearthly shriek of some ancient goddess or righteous angel descending in wrath upon the quiet Alabama town, there to extirpate the population in retribution for its sins. But, alas, no. As soon as it lumbers to a stop, Clarence notes this is no passenger train. Rather, the locomotive pulls cattle cars instead. He sees six of them, each emblazoned with the words "Southern Pineland Company" in black, block letters.

Once the train is still, operatives emerge from the one passenger car at the rear of the train and open the cargo doors for each boxcar. Clarence's feels his insides sink. "Have mercy on us all," he whispers.

The Southern Pineland Company has divided each boxcar into cages, six cages in each car. One by one, the convicts embark and, while armed guards and law officers cover them with their shotguns and rifles, the railroad workers chain the prisoners to the side of a cage, both hands and both feet, confining four prisoners in each cage. Clarence does some quick math. At four prisoners per cage, six cages per boxcar, and six boxcars, that makes one hundred forty-four prisoners if the train is at capacity.

Then, commotion.

One of the prisoners, a man Clarence doesn't know, lunges away from the guards when they release him from his jailhouse chains but before they can load him into the car and shackle him with the other set. The man tries to make a break for it by ducking under the railroad car and rolling out on the other side. None of the guards chase him. In seconds, Clarence learns why. Several gun blasts shatter the still afternoon air, and a man screams and moans in pain. Then, a few seconds later, everyone hears one single shot. The screams and moans end. There must be guards stationed on the other side of the tracks, Clarence realizes.

"Dumb nigger," Clarence hears the guard closest to him say. "Like no one's ever tried that before. We's onta all those kinds a tricks."

From the other side of the train, Clarence hears someone shout, "Where should we put the body?"

"Ah, just leave it," another invisible voice responds. "Let the Negros take care of their own."

Soon, Clarence's turn comes. One guard releases him from his irons while another pushes him toward the boxcar, shotgun pressed in the middle of his back.

"You sees what happens when you boys try to run," the guard grunts at him, his breath a combination of cheap beer and onions coming through his bearded maw. "I can't think of nothin' betta than shootin' criminals, so you jus' test us. Jus' go on an run, if you like."

Clarence doesn't reply.

"Oh, so you's the quiet type, is you? You's too good to speak to me, is you?" The guard jabs Clarence in the back with the point of his gun. Clarence, unready for the blow and unable to see it coming, lurches forward, his chest colliding with the side of the boxcar. It takes most of the wind out of him. He gasps while sucking air back into his lungs.

"Well, your day is comin', you arrogant monkey. Your day's comin'. Sho' is. You'll see. You'll see."

Before Clarence can do anything else, two guards in the boxcar grab him by his arms and hoist him aboard. In moments, he's chained, both hands and both feet, just like everyone else. Tom Morton is on Clarence's left. He doesn't recognize the two other men in the cage with them, but one is tall and very muscular. They both appear terrified and do not speak.

"What do we do if we have to relieve ourselves?" a prisoner chained behind Clarence asks a guard.

The man just gives a twisted smile, grunts, and turns and walks away.

Tom looks at Clarence. From the way his eyes dart about nervously, Clarence can see the fear growing. He remembers that look well from his homeless days in Chicago. "What will we do, Clarence? What'll happen to us?"

"Just hold on, Tommy. When we get there, stay close to me. I don't know what's going to happen, but let's stick together if we can."

"Okay, C-Clarence," Tom says. His mouth works up and down, like he wants to say something else but can't get the words out.

"Don't panic. It won't be easy, but don't go and lose control, Tom. Don't be like the man who just tried to run and got himself shot. That won't help. I've been in some tight spots before. Try not to let your fear get the better of you."

Tom nods. Clarence has lots of sympathy. He remembers well how, on his trip around the world with the ballplayers, he froze in fear more than once. Somehow, his time with the Buffalo Soldiers helped him lose his fear of action, and he doesn't lock up in panic anymore, but, still, he's drilled and had training. Even with training, Clarence remains as frightened as ever on the inside, but he knows how to handle that kind of stress on the outside now. Tom, obviously, hasn't had any training. Instead, he is on the frail side, and before changing into the ring-arounds that all the prisoners wear now, had sported a velvet purple vest over a tailored shirt.

Clarence tries to think of something to calm Tom down. He knows that, on the one hand, Florida is their destination. Florida borders Alabama, so the trip might not be that long. On the other hand, he has no idea what part of Florida they'll work in. If it is somewhere in south Florida, the trip could be very long, indeed. Unable to reassure the young man that their trip will be brief, instead Clarence asks Tom, "You like books, Tom?"

Tom nods, but it doesn't stop his teeth from clattering together. Clarence recognizes that look, too. He'd seen it on a few of the newer Buffalo Soldiers at St. Peter's Mission. A violent shiver wracks Tom's body, despite the fact it's quite warm in the boxcar.

"You ever read *Uncle Tom's Cabin*?" Clarence asks the young man.

Tom nods again, swallows several times as if his mouth is too dry to form the words, and finally says in a croaking voice, "That's how I got my name." He gives the tiniest of smiles. "My parents were very religious, and they admired Uncle Tom's faith."

"Where are your parents now?"

"They died in a railroad accident. My aunt and uncle look after me."

"That's sad, Tom. Where did you live before you came here?"

"Birmingham, but some other cousins live in Evansville, in Indiana. I was coming home from seeing them when the authorities collared me."

"What other books have you read?"

"Oh, you know, the famous ones. Frederick Douglass is my favorite. I've read his autobiography about seven times."

Clarence smiles, both at the fond memory of reading the book himself and to help Tom keep up hope. "It's one of the first books I learned to read, too. The man who taught me to read, Newton MacMillan, gave a copy to me the last time I saw him."

"Is he your favorite, too?"

"One of them. I read a new book just last year, though, by an author whom I'd like to meet some day. His name was William Edward Burghardt DuBois."

"That's a lot of names," Tom says with another weak smile. "His parents must've had a hard time deciding what name they liked."

"Yeah, I suppose they did. Maybe—"

Before Clarence can continue, one of the guards calls out, "All full. All prisoners accounted for."

A man at the side of the railroad car jumps down onto the platform, and together, the two men close the door to the cattle car where Clarence and Tom stand chained. Total darkness descends except for a couple slivers of light filtering through slats in the side of the car. Next, Clarence hears a man outside say, "Secure the doors." A couple clicks follow, as if any of the people inside were about to break their bonds and escape.

A chorus of voices breaks out in the prisoners' car. Everyone begins babbling at once, some excitedly, some in low voices speaking to the man next to him, but the combined effect unnerves Clarence. He knows that keeping his mind clear is the most important thing right now. If he's to ever get out of this pickle, he needs both luck and smarts. He can't lose his composure.

To his relief, Clarence discovers that the darkness of the railroad car does not bother him or bring on a panic attack. He's ridden in railroad cars before—often, in fact—but this seems like being underground more than anything else, and in the past, his fears about going underground caused him to break down and be unable to think.

It isn't long, however, before another problem becomes manifest. The cattle car isn't large, and it has twenty-four people inside it. Quickly, the temperature inside the car rises, and the air gets stuffy, too.

After a time, the noise dies down to a low murmur when the passengers realize that no one has answers, and no one knows how long they'll be here or what's to become of them.

"Clarence," Tom whispers, "my right shoulder hurts."

"How come? Are the shackles too tight?"

"No, I'm too short. The manacle on my right wrist is the same height as everyone else's, but I'm smaller, and it's stretching me so much I can't relax my arm. It's burning my muscles already, and the skin on my wrist is rubbing raw. What can I do?"

"Can you stand on the tips of your toes?"

"I already am. It helps a little, but not enough."

"I don't think I can do anything to help, Tom. I can't reach over there."

"But, what should I do?"

"I don't think there's anything any of us can do. Close your eyes, I guess, and try not to think about it."

"I'll try."

For what seems like a very long time, Clarence's world consists of an inky, stifling blackness. The moans of his fellow prisoners are all he hears while the train rolls monotonously and inexorably toward its destination. Tom alternates between a low moan and quiet sobbing because of his pain. Clarence, before long, starts experiencing the same sensations. He's a few inches taller than Tom, so the pain is not quite as bad, but the fact that he can't put his arms down makes his shoulders very tired, and before long they throb with a dull pain while, at the same time, his muscles start burning. From the sounds of the lamentations he hears the other prisoners aren't doing much better.

"Help me, Lord," becomes a constant refrain of many as the train rolls on. A few prisoners cry out intermittently. Moans and grunts, some quiet and some loud, rise above the noise of the train at uneven intervals.

The other thing bothering Clarence most is the temperature. Sweat flows freely down his back, but also into his eyes, stinging them, and eventually down his legs, too. He uses his biceps to wipe away as much as he can from his face, but things continue getting hotter and more suffocating.

Then, quietly but suddenly, a new sound. The trickle of water, just loud enough to hear over the hum of the tracks. Where is it coming from? Clarence licks his lips, which are getting dry and, he fears, close to cracking. He can certainly use a drink by now, but soon his nose tells him what he should have realized all along. What he heard was a man nearby relieving himself. The train car has no provisions for this, of course, and even if it had, what did it matter with everyone chained hand and foot to the wall of their cage?

"Lord, give me strength to get through this." Clarence hears men mutter some variation of these words to themselves again and again as the time stretches on. At one point, the suffocating heat of the closed boxcar makes him swoon, and he comes near to blacking out. How long have they been on the train? Sunlight continues filtering through the slats in the side of the car, so it must still be light outside, but that's all he knows.

A couple times Clarence asks Tom Morton how he is and encourages Tom to persevere, but as the day inches along, such noble thoughts as compassion for others fade. How can he survive this and keep his sanity? Clarence is almost hyperventilating now. Not because of fear, but because the suffocating air inside the train car makes just breathing a challenge. Clarence's mind begins disregarding all other considerations one by one, narrowing its focus until the question of just breathing and surviving completely overwhelms him, and he can think of nothing else. Even *trying* to think about something else feels like striking a brick wall in his mind. Soon, he completely disregards all other sensory input besides breathing and air temperature.

Clarence doesn't even notice the train stop, he's lost so much awareness of his surroundings. Taking him completely by surprise, the door clangs open, bright sunlight scalds his eyes, and fresh air rushes into the infernal tomb of the railroad car. Now, Clarence can see all the sweat stains soaking his ring-arounds, but he doesn't care. He merely hangs there, gulping in the free air as if breathing too much now will allow him to save some for later. Clarence glances to his left and sees Tom. He'd forgotten all about Tom in his panic. Morton sobs hysterically, like a child. *He practically is a child*, Clarence thinks, *fifteen years old*. Clarence can also see what's happened to Tom's wrist. Because his arms stretch so unnaturally, the manacles chafe his skin so badly that blood runs down Tom's arms. Some has dried in place already, but some is fresh.

Breaking his gaze away from Tom, Clarence belatedly realizes the reason they've stopped. He almost breaks down himself when he sees a new group of convicts boarding other train cars, under guard, just as he'd done. To his surprise, a few of these are white men, but only a few. While some of the guards chain the new convicts in place, others come around and offer a dipper of water to each man in Clarence's car. Each man gets two dippers to drink, and that's all.

When one guard gets near Clarence, he sniffs the air. "Smells like someone couldn't hold it," he says, a goofy smile plastered across his face. "Just look at you boys. Ya stink. Like animals. Can't even control your bodies, like a dog."

Tom whimpers to the man, "Please, sir, can you adjust the height of my chains? It's paining me something awful and I'm bleeding."

The guard kicks Tom in the shin with his booted toe, and Tom screams. The guard says, "Shut up, boy! You's a prisoner, that's what you is. Prisoners don't ask for things. You'll take what you gets. Hear me, boy?"

Tom's too busy shaking in fear and pain to reply. The guard stands there waiting, arms folded over his barrel chest, looking at the poor young man. Suddenly, his face contorts, and without warning he kicks Tom's leg again, roaring out, "I says, you hear me, boy?"

Another scream of pain from Tom. Somehow, he manages to whisper, "Yes, sir."

"That's better." The guard turns and walks away, muttering something to himself. Clarence thinks he hears, "Dumb animals. Nothing but stupid animals."

Clarence can hardly believe what he just saw. The guard's twisted smile. His grunts of delight as he kicked Tom. The lack of hesitation to hurt another person. He's seen these things before, especially during his time with the Buffalo Soldiers in Montana. The worst was the attack by the vigilantes in the Milk River Valley but Clarence saw similar faces amongst the people of Great Falls when the Buffalo Soldiers escorted their prisoners into town. Thinking back farther he remembers the same look from members of the mob in Chinatown during his tour with Al Spalding and the baseball teams. He's never been able to comprehend the mixture of pride, anger, and rage, but also of delight and satisfaction, that he's seen in people's faces at times like these.

Trying to gather his thoughts, Clarence also notes that he can't yet see the sun; it remains high in the sky overhead, so he guesses it must be past midday but not yet evening. It takes some time to get all the new men aboard, but once the guards finish doing so, a whistle blows, and Clarence hears the engine getting up steam again.

The door slowly rolls shut, clanging into place, and the near-complete blackness returns. If Clarence could fall to his knees, he would. This is only the first stop. How many more will there be?

When the train lurches into motion again, Clarence's previous sensations return, but much sooner than the first time. The heat. The stench of sweat. The inability to breathe fresh air. Soon, it all mixes with the smell of other men relieving themselves when they realize the guards won't unchain them and they won't have the chance to get relief during the train ride.

Time passes. How much, Clarence can't say. The atmosphere in the train car is smothering. It must be one hundred degrees inside, maybe more than that. Before he realizes what's happening, Clarence's chin drops forward and bounces off his chest, startling him fully awake. He tries to suck in air, but it's so thick, it barely helps. Panting, he feels like a fish in the bottom of a boat, just gasping with his mouth open. Most of the other passengers have long since gone silent, trying to survive the ordeal while conserving all the energy they can.

Clarence knows he's coated with sweat; by now it's stinging where his arm and leg manacles have rubbed his skin raw. As if his aching shoulders weren't pain enough already.

After another indeterminate stretch of time, Clarence finally notices that the darkness inside the train car has become more complete. It has always been dark, other than the small shafts of sunlight coming through the sides of the car, but now even those begin fading. Or have Clarence's eyes have started losing focus instead? He isn't sure, but he thinks it's the former. That would be good. Maybe if the sun goes down it will cool off inside the boxcar?

If that's true, though, he can't notice the change. More sweat burns and stings his eyes, making them water while he tries to blink out the irritation. As soon as he does so, however, his legs begin wobbling. *I must be getting dehydrated*, Clarence thinks to himself. *My muscles are losing strength and want to give out*. His right leg almost goes, but that just tugs on his right arm, where the manacle digs into his raw skin, forcing him to stand back up with a muffled cry of pain.

He feels something new trickling down his right arm. In the dying light, he puts his nose to his bicep, then sniffs it. Yes, that metallic smell. Some of his own blood.

One cage over from him, Clarence sees the head of another prisoner loll to the side, dangling limply from his body. The man's chained right wrist turns at an unnatural angle, and his arm twists, too, torqueing his shoulder, but instead of crying out, or even moving, the man hangs there silently.

Again, Clarence tries to focus his breathing. Breathe in. Breathe out. It's almost painful sucking in air so dense and putrid he feels ready to vomit.

After rolling on through the deepening darkness for a time, Clarence hears the train stop once more, but the door does not open as he expects. It might be cooler now, but if so, Clarence has trouble sensing it. He hears some clanging sounds and then the engine whistle blows, and he hears the train start up again. Why have they stopped? The pause was far too brief to take on more prisoners.

As the whistle fades, Clarence realizes that his car isn't moving. With a sound that's deafening because it's so unexpected, the door opens, finally. Eyes bulging, mouth agape, Clarence sucks in fresh air. In the process, he can see outside the car. They're in a forest. Mostly pine trees, it looks like, although it's tough to be sure in such darkness.

A few lanterns give off light in the area outside the train car, but that's all. The one directly in Clarence's sight flickers, not because it's running low on fuel, but because flying insects swarm it.

Guards board the car and release the shackles holding the men's arms in the air. Not their feet, however. Those manacles remain in place. Clarence gasps in relief when his arms drop to his side for the first time in half a day. He never thought he'd know pain as bad as he'd felt while sitting on the fence rail at Fort Assiniboine, but this is close. Momentarily, he thinks about the irony. In Montana, he'd been wrongly accused of deserting the Buffalo Soldiers and forced to sit on a fence rail all day as punishment. Here, it isn't much different. Another wrongful arrest followed by excruciating pain.

Next, a guard brings around a dipper of water to the prisoners. When he gets to the hanging man one cell over from Clarence, the guard says to a man waiting outside, "Looks like this one didn't make it."

"I think that makes three who died on the way if you combine all the train cars," the other man replies.

"What do we do with the body?"

"Unchain him and drop him on the ground out here."

The guard inside the train car complies, unlocking the man's feet and arms, dragging him to the edge of the boxcar by his shoulders

89

and then lugging him over the side, where the dead man lands on his face with a soft thud in the dirt and sparse grass below.

The guard outside unholsters a pistol and shoots the dead prisoner in the middle of his back. The report from the gunshot is so loud in the still forest air that Clarence recoils.

The man on the ground bounces from the impact and then doesn't move at all, but now blood spurts from the open wound in his back.

"Yep, that one's dead, all right," the outside guard says while he kicks the corpse in the shoulder with a little laugh of satisfaction. "Henry, it's time!" he yells over his shoulder.

Another man appears with a burlap sack. He extracts chunks of bread from it, tossing each prisoner a half a loaf. "There's your dinner, boys. Enjoy it because tomorrow you all are gonna go get to work. Sweet dreams, boys."

"Where do we sleep?" one of the prisoners calls out in a hoarse, exhausted voice.

"Right where you is," the nearest guard replies. Next he says, as if just remembering something important, "Oh yeah, and here's your bucket if you need to go. Just pass it around." He tosses a metal bucket into the boxcar.

"Henry, is Travis ready with the dog yet?" the guard outside says to the man who'd brought the bread.

"There he is, he comin' right now," Henry replies.

Clarence looks over to see what's about to happen. A man approaches with a huge German shepherd dog on a chain leash. All the other guards back away when Travis approaches. The man chains the dog to the nearest tree. From there, it has just enough chain to cover the entire doorway to the boxcar. When it sees the prisoners, the animal bears its teeth, snarls, and barks ferociously.

Travis, the man who controls the dog, gazes into the car at all the bewildered, exhausted, demoralized, and terrorized prisoners. Smiling, he removes the blood-soaked shirt from the dead man lying on the ground, lets the dog have a sniff, and then puts it back on the dead body. Looking at the dog, he says, "Get 'em!"

In two bounds, the dog reaches the body, buries its teeth in the dead man's arm, and slashes and tears at it so violently that blood and human tissue sprays this way and that. It can't be more than a minute before the dog rips the dead man's ulna bone from his arm and brings it to Travis, fleshy hand and fingers still attached.

"Nice souvenir, ain't it?" one guard says to Travis.

"'Night, boys," Travis calls as he and the other guards walk away.

10

Clarence's Letter

One Monday morning in early April, John Ward arrives at his New York City law office. He feels great; the weather has been unusually warm for New York in April and he's played several rounds of golf over the weekend. He loves golf almost as much as he loves baseball, and, he must admit, these days it's a whole lot easier on his body.

"Good morning, Mr. Ward," his secretary calls out as he walks into his office.

"And good morning to you, Mr. Lewis," Ward replies. "Anything interesting for me to look at before I begin my casework this morning? I've got a busy day in front of me, so it'd better be good."

"Well, maybe," William Tecumseh Lewis tells Ward. "I see a letter here from Alabama. I wasn't aware you had any clients in Alabama, but the return address is the law office of someone named Seth Dean. Did you go to law school with him, perhaps?"

"I don't recall anyone by that name in my classes at Columbia. Well, let me see it. It's worth a look for curiosity's sake if nothing else."

Ward opens the envelope with care and unfolds the note, which comes typed on cream-colored stationary. At the top is the address of Seth Dean, a lawyer in Athens, Alabama. *Still doesn't ring a bell*, Ward thinks to himself. He reads down the page.

Mr. John Ward,

Allow me to introduce myself. My name is Seth Dean, and it is a pleasure to write this note to you. You see, when I was a young boy you were among my heroes. When I was going to school, I read all about you in *The Sporting Life* and *The Sporting News*. Even though I knew I'd never achieve my dream of becoming a crack shortstop like you, I lived through your exploits and always cheered for the Giants while you were a member of the club.

Although I didn't realize you had a law degree while in law school myself, it's a pleasure to know we now are in the same profession and have something in common at last. Although the odds seem against it, it would be my honor to make your acquaintance in person someday. As a relatively young man just entering my career at law, perhaps in time I can enter such eminent circles as you now travel in.

At this point, Ward puts down the letter. Lewis looks up from his typewriting and raises an eyebrow. "Anything interesting, Mr. Ward?"

"No, not particularly. Just fan mail. It can wait."

"Fan mail? About your baseball career?"

"Indeed."

"How long has it been since you've received a letter from an admirer of your baseball talents?"

"Some time, Mr. Lewis, although I can't say how long for certain."

"Well, at least you know that people remember you. It's more than anyone will ever say about me, I suppose. I've certainly not lived up to my name, at any rate."

Ward gives Lewis half a smile. "Now, that's not quite true. You're an excellent secretary. I'm lucky to have you in my employ. You're at least a two-star general of secretaries, maybe three."

"You'd never convince my father of that. I think he's still sore at me for not joining the Army and becoming an officer."

"After a decade? He's still upset with you?"

"I don't know for sure, but I think he is. He fought in the Civil War, you know. Marched with Sherman all the way to Vicksburg back in '63. He lost a leg during the siege when a cannonball hit nearby, but he still idolizes the man. He hoped I'd follow in Sherman's footsteps and become a military man, but here I am, a secretary instead. My father barely thinks I'm a man at all, just sitting at a desk sifting papers all day."

"I'm sorry to hear that," Ward replies. "I suppose it's hard for him to understand that we've not been at war much since the Civil War ended. We trounced the Spanish last year, it's true, but that was over so fast one hadn't much time to make a name for oneself as a soldier."

"He wrote me telling me I should enlist, offer my services to my country in its time of need, but I never did. John, my father just doesn't understand that a day is coming when we won't need war to settle disputes anymore. Someday, reason and diplomacy will solve our problems instead, and war will be a thing of the past."

"Although I find your pacifist beliefs admirable, I'm not sure I share them. The British are, along with ourselves, the most civilized people on earth, and even they remain embroiled in a colonial war in South Africa as we speak, just as we do in the Philippines."

"Well, my beliefs help your law practice at least, don't they?" Lewis says with a wry smile. "You don't have to worry about your secretary coming home with one arm and having to train a new one, do you?"

Ward laughs. "You could learn to type with one hand. For a while, a man named Hugh Daily pitched in major league baseball, and he only had one hand."

"Well, maybe I wouldn't make the worst soldier ever to strap on boots, but I'd rather keep both my arms, given the choice. Say, if there were a Brush Plan for secretaries, what grade would you classify me in?"

"If we had a major league of secretaries, you'd make the cut. In fact, I'd classify you in Class B, at minimum."

"Only Class B? I thought my deportment and habits were better than that," Lewis says back with a smile of his own.

Ward laughs a bit but looks down at the floor when he does so and closes his eyes. Next, he sighs and looks up at Lewis with one eye.

"Sorry, Mr. Ward, maybe that went a little too far?"

"No, it's my fault. I shouldn't tease you about your beliefs and your pacifism. It was only fair play for you to remind me of the failure of the Brotherhood of Professional Baseball Players. Although I don't regret what we did back in '90, trying to start our own major league when the National League tried to enslave the players with the Brush Plan and control our salaries, it sure didn't turn out the way I thought it would."

"I still think you might have pulled through, had your backers shown a little more faith."

"You may be right, but they didn't. We failed. That's all I can say about the matter. Well, in any event, I'd best see to my cases for the day. I'll let you know when I'm ready to dictate something to you for a client."

"Yes, sir, Mr. Ward. Should I keep the windows open? It's a very pleasant April day once again."

"Sure, keep them open. I'd really like to get out for more golf today, but my workload may prevent it."

With that, Ward picks up the letter from Seth Dean and hands it to Lewis to file it away. Fan mail is nice, Ward thinks to himself, but the hope of saving time for golfing in the afternoon is even nicer, so no need to read the rest right now.

11

Extracting Turpentine

The pounding noise begins registering somewhere in Clarence's mind. Somehow, he knows it means something important, but it's distant, like when he nearly drowned in the Marias River and the light on the surface of the water remained out of reach even as he strained and tried swimming to it. Except this time, his mind moves toward the light, rather than away. It keeps getting brighter.

His eyes finally open. It remains dark outside, but the men around him begin sitting up. One of the guards bangs on the side of Clarence's uncoupled railroad car with an ax handle. It's a different guard from the men Clarence saw last night.

"Up 'n at 'em, boys! It's four in the mornin', time to get movin'. The turpentine ain't gonna extract itself. You gots five minutes before we leave, so pass that bucket around and be ready to go."

Freed from their shackles but still under guard, the prisoners take turns limping to the bucket to urinate, and then the march through the forest begins on achingly empty stomachs.

The guards divide the twenty-three remaining men in Clarence's boxcar into groups of four and chain all four men together by their right leg. The guards mount up. One, who seems to be the leader and whom the other guards call "Captain Thomas," says, "Come and grab your tools, boys. This way."

Clarence sees that the body of the dead man remains where the guards dumped him last night. A horde of flies swarm the poor man's corpse. So many crawl along the shredded skin of the dead man's right arm that Clarence struggles to even see any skin. The giant German shepherd eyes them warily and growls low as they drop down from the boxcar and follow Captain Thomas.

He leads them to a shed where two more men stand guard. These two men distribute the work supplies to the prisoners. Some men get axes while others get metal pans to carry. Two men end up transporting huge metal drums that look like they hold about fifty gallons of water. Clarence carries two axes, while Tom Morton, still next to him, receives one of the metal pans.

The group shambles off into the forest, six groups of four men chained together, along with four guards on horseback toting loaded shotguns, all the men carrying work tools.

The men trudge through the forest, stopping for only one two-minute break on the way to their worksite. During the break, in the fragile light of the approaching dawn, Clarence introduces himself to the other two men chained together with Tom and him.

"Clarence," he says, extending his hand to the nearest man.

The man, who appears to be about the same age as Clarence, is the very large and muscular man Clarence saw the previous night. He looks at Clarence and, without saying a word, shakes. The man has a crushing grip, but his eyes dart about, and although his jaw muscles move like he wants to say something, he puts his head down.

"He can't hear you," the fourth man of Clarence's group says. "He's deaf and mute."

This man puts out his hand for Clarence to shake. He looks like the giant man but seems a few years older and is of normal stature. "I'm Elijah Maxwell. That's my younger brother, Matthew. He can't talk. Never could. Least ways, not more than baby sounds. Can't hear, neither. We have a system of hand signals, so I can tell him what to do."

No sooner does Elijah say this than Matthew manipulates his fingers and hands in front of Elijah.

"What's he telling you?" Clarence asks.

"He appreciates your courtesy," Elijah says with a smile. "He's pleased to meet you."

"He's as strong as a country horse," Clarence says, flexing his hand a bit in hopes the blood will flow again.

"Yeah, Matthew is as strong as an ox. He's as hard a worker as they come and can work all day if you just keep him fed right. I'm not surprised that Winston dragged us off our farm to get us to work down here. Matthew's the strongest man in Athens, and everyone knows it."

"You two are sharecroppers?"

"Tenants."

"What's the difference?"

"A sharecropper grows the crops but turns them over to the landowner in exchange for payment. A tenant rents the farm. We make a cash payment every year, but whatever crops we produce, we sell ourselves."

"Who's your landlord?" Clarence asks Elijah.

"We rent a farm right next to the Johnstone plantation and pay Sam Johnstone our rent. He's the second biggest landowner in Limestone County, right after Judge Winston. Or so I hear."

"Were you always a farmer?"

"No. I was going to school at the Alabama State Agricultural and Mechanical College for Negroes for a while. I wanted to be a teacher. But then my father died. So, I went back to help Mom and Matthew on the farm."

"You said that Johnstone is the second largest landowner in the county after Winston, right, Elijah? They work together to set you up?"

"Well, that's what I'm not sure of, but I don't think so. They aren't friends, for sure. Had a couple lawsuits against each other over some land titles a few years back. That's what people say around Athens, anyway. No, I reckon that Winston's son arrested me to get back at Johnstone somehow, take away two of his best tenants. Don't make much difference to me right now, though. Matthew and I are still here, not back on the farm, and I don't imagine this is going to go well. If we ever do get out of this Florida forest, maybe I can find out the truth. Look sharp, now."

Elijah nods in the direction of one of the approaching guards. The man wears a pith hat that nearly covers his eyes. A beard falls nearly halfway down the man's chest, and from the bulge in his cheek, it appears to Clarence that chewing tobacco is a favorite pastime. From horseback the man spits a stream of tobacco juice in the chained quartet's direction.

"Time's up, boys. Get a movin', now."

When the guard rides closer, Clarence can see that, besides his shotgun, the guard also has a black leather strap that looks like it weights several pounds. Clarence swallows hard while struggling to his feet. "Yes, sir," he remembers to say.

Tom Morton hasn't said a word the entire trip. He merely sits on the ground, his face somewhat flushed with color. He rises mutely on command. Tom stands there and nods that he's ready to go on, but Clarence sees that his legs wobble and nearly buckle when he tries to get up.

When the group resumes hobbling toward its worksite, the brightening sky showing dawn isn't far off, Clarence takes in his surroundings. They are deep in a longleaf pine forest somewhere in Florida. The ground they're trudging over is rather flat and supports stands of tall grasses, although Clarence isn't sure what kind of grass, and the soil is somewhat rocky and a little sandy in places. The forest has no paths to speak of; the men just trot along behind the guard whose horse leads the way. It's cool, but only for the moment. Humidity is in the air, and when the sun does come up, it's going to be rough. A few birds chirp from their perches, but no other sound besides that of grunting men breaks the stillness.

They stop at a stream, and the prisoners have a chance to take a drink. Clarence also splashes a bit of water on his ankles where the chains have rubbed his skin nearly raw already. He notices Tom Morton blankly staring off in the distance.

"You all right, Tom? Try to drink more water," he says to the young man.

As if returning to the moment from somewhere far away, Tom turns to Clarence and looks at him, still with a blank stare. Slowly, his eyes refocus.

"Tom, you hear me? Drink some water."

Tom blinks a few times. "Right, okay, good idea, Clarence," he says softly.

Clarence is about to ask Tom what's distracting him when the nearest guard shouts out, "That's enough. Move along."

The prisoners reach their work area just as the sun ascends above the eastern horizon. One guard dismounts, and while the others cover the prisoners with their guns, he takes an ax from one of the convicts.

"This is how to harvest turpentine. Watch closely, you dogs, because I'll only show you once. You chop away the bark like this."

He takes a couple hacks from the right side, striking the tree at a downward angle and then turns to the left side and does the same. Chunks of bark fly and chips of wood arc through the air before coming to rest in the long grass. When he's finished, everyone can see how he's cut the bark from the pine tree. To Clarence, the shape of the cut looks like the letter "V," or, better yet, the chevrons on the uniforms of the officers when he served in the Buffalo Soldiers. Slowly, a substance begins oozing from the wounded tree.

After a few more hacks that deepen and lengthen the cut, the guard with the ax stops and addresses the group again: "That's how you start. Once you've cleared away a healthy section of bark, then you make a horizontal cut like so."

More chopping, the ax blade digging straight into the tree this time. After a few minutes, the guard stops and grabs a pan from one of the men.

"When your cut is deep enough, you insert this pan into the cut. This catches the turpentine when it drips down the trunk of the tree. Once you've finished your cuts on one tree, move on and chop another. See?"

Most of the men nod quietly. Clarence simply watches.

"After a while, you come back and check on the first tree. When the pan's full, you bring it back to the metal barrels y'all brought with you and dump it in. By the end of the day, we'll have a wagon out here that you roll the barrels onto, and we take 'em back to camp that way. Now, get goin'."

The men spread out to work. At first, it's hard for Clarence to get the technique correct with his ax, and because he's not that tall, he has trouble reaching as high on the trees as he should with his cuts. At one point, a guard, the one with the long beard and leather whip, rides by.

"That the best you can do, boy? Didn't you larn to do it right?"

"Sorry, sir, I'm trying my best to learn."

"You betta learn faster, boy. You see this?" He holds up the heavy leather strap.

"Yes, sir."

"This is for anyone who don't work fast enough. Got it?"

"Yes, sir."

"Only time I'm gonna warn you. Now, get to work."

By midday, when they stop to eat their meal, Clarence's arms feel ready to fall off from swinging the ax all morning. The meal isn't very helpful. The men get another half a loaf of dark bread and a ladle of beans on a tin plate, and one apple.

By now, the sun's been up for hours, and the temperature is well on its way past eighty degrees. Like yesterday, Clarence can see the sweat stains on the armpits, chest, and waistband of his prison uniform, and he's quite aware of how strong his body odor is. At the same time, the flies swarm all day. They sting Clarence again and again on his neck and forearms. Brushing them away is pointless. After a while, he stops trying.

Tom continues struggling with the pace of the work. Matthew sees it, too, and a few times he takes the ax from Tom and lets him sit down to catch his breath while Matthew does extra work. Tom thanks him from his hands and knees.

The warm temperature means the risk of dehydration, Clarence realizes quickly, but it also brings another problem. The mosquitos. They, along with the large black flies that sting, torment the men without end. By the time the midday meal is over, Clarence looks at his arms and sees red bite marks. More of them than he can count.

Try as he might, Clarence simply can't keep up the pace of the work all day. Elijah does better, and Matthew better still because they're used to hard farm labor. Even at that, the two brothers sweat profusely, stop occasionally, and breathe hard the entire time. Tom Morton is the worst off. By mid-afternoon, he moves from one tree to the next slowly and listlessly, taking tiny steps. Several times, he stumbles and falls. After each fall, he rises slowly and unsteadily, even with help from the others, to get back to his feet and continue. Clarence hasn't heard him speak a coherent word in hours. None of the prisoners say much; they realize conserving energy is more important than talking.

At last, the sun drops toward the horizon, and as dusk sets in, Clarence hears one guard blow a whistle. The men gather round, hobbling and limping as they do so.

"You boys worked like shit today. Look at this. Only a barrel and a half of turpentine. Now, I'se gonna give you boys a break this time because this is your first day on the job. Tomorrah, if you don't fill both barrels, we gonna keep workin' 'til theys both full, even if it takes 'til midnight. Now, in two minutes, we get movin' back to camp. You dogs grab the tools."

Clarence swoons to the ground. He's awake and alert, but his arms ache so badly he has trouble pushing himself back up to a sitting position. The muscles of his forearms spasm continually, and he has difficulty flexing his fingers because they've curled into the shape of the ax handle. Clarence also sees enormous blisters on both palms. Tom Morton lies face down next to him, breathing shallowly, little puffs of dust blowing away from his lips each time he exhales.

"Tom, can you walk? We've got to get our tools and head back now," Clarence tells him. Tom opens his eyes but doesn't answer.

"We got 'em," Clarence hears Elijah Maxwell say as he stands near Clarence and Tom. "He's not doing well, is he?" Elijah asks, pointing at Tom.

Rising to his knees, Clarence shakes his head.

"Here, help me get him up," Elijah says to Clarence. "Matthew and I will help carry him back to camp if you carry the tools. Can you handle them all?"

"I think so, but it's been a while since I've done physical work like this. About three years."

"You made it, though. This boy, Tom, he don't look too good. We've gotta help him."

Matthew lifts Tom to his feet and drapes one of Tom's arms over his shoulder. Elijah grabs the other arm and does the same. They nod to Clarence.

"Move out!" one of the guards shouts. The men limp and stumble back toward their camp. Clarence, when he can manage to lift his head for a moment, notices a few of the other men look almost as exhausted as Tom Morton. They drag their feet through the long grass. A few men fall forward as they try to walk. They crawl for a bit before rising to stumble onward until their legs give out once more.

As the men plod through the deepening darkness and finally return to their train car prison for the night, the obvious thought finally breaks through the haze of numbing pain in Clarence's mind: *This is only my first day.*

12

The Governor

"I say, John, old boy, your skill on the links is almost on par with your skill on the diamond," the burly man with the mustache, close-cropped hair, and pince-nez glasses says to John Ward.

"Maybe, but you're a better golfer than you let on, my friend," Ward replies.

"Perhaps, but remember, you aren't to tell anyone that I play the game. A reform administration that proclaims its desire to take on and tame New York's robber barons and Tammany's grafting bosses must be careful about having the public see me playing an elitist sport such as golf," the man replies, a grin spanning his face as he sips brandy in Ward's Broadway law office. A polished oak desk separates them.

"Don't worry, Governor Roosevelt, you know your secret's safe with me. I can bluff and keep a secret with anyone. Well, maybe anyone except Spalding," Ward says with a little laugh before clinking his own glass with Theodore Roosevelt's in a light toast.

"Yes, that was some plan you hatched back in '89. You almost pulled it off, too. Whether baseball is better off because your plan failed, I'll leave to others to decide."

"Always the politician, governor, always the politician."

"I've always liked baseball, the manliness of the sport and its clearly defined rules. The gumption it takes to play successfully is something we should cultivate in all young boys."

"I still remember you saying as much in your speech at Delmonico's after we got back from the Spalding World Tour in the spring of '89."

"That was quite an evening, John, I'll not deny. The atmosphere at Delmonico's that night was quite a change from my days ranching in the Dakotas. It helped reinforce for me that public service was my true calling. That evening was also, as I recall, the first time we met."

"Indeed. It's a pity we didn't meet sooner considering how many years I played ball in New York, but, as you said, ranching in the Dakotas occupied your life for part of that time."

"It was a good life out there in the West, even if things were a bit primitive. It helped reinforce for me the importance of initiative and physical activity. And, it helped me deal with my grief, too, away from the pressure of New York City. When I came back, I was a new man. And, I hope, a better one."

"To the old times," Ward says as the glasses gently clink again.

"You ever miss playing ball, John? The camaraderie, the strenuous competition?"

"A little, but a ballplayer's career only lasts so long. Everyone must bow out sometime. My career lasted longer than most. Seventeen years."

"It's hard to believe you've been out of the game for, what, five years now?"

"Yeah, this year will be my fifth season since I last took the field."

"You know, John, it won't be long before people begin to forget all you accomplished on the ball field. It's a sobering thought, isn't it?"

"For sure. Although, come to think of it, I got a piece of fan mail about three weeks ago. Some lawyer from Athens, Alabama, of all places. I didn't take it too seriously at the time because things were so busy that week, but maybe I should go back and read the whole thing. It never hurts to get a little confirmation that what you did mattered to someone else, does it, Governor?"

"Never. I suppose that's part of what drives me, too. The fear that one day, the world will forget my name and all that I've tried to do. I'm frightened of the thought that the name Theodore Roosevelt will get lost in a history book that no one will ever read."

"I rather doubt that, my friend. You've written books and received a nomination for a Medal of Honor, and now you're the governor of the most populous state in the nation. Those are just the most notable things, too. I don't believe anonymity will be your fate."

"You may be right, but still, I hope the best is yet to come for me. I think you are right, too, that it doesn't hurt to have someone tell you that you meant something to them. Go back and read the letter you mentioned. You are old enough and wise enough that a little praise won't go to your head. At least, I hope not," Roosevelt says with another grin as he stands to leave.

"Thank you, as always, for the company today, Governor. You can bet that what little influence I still possess I will deploy on your behalf during the next campaign."

"Don't sell yourself short, Johnny. A good friend and an honest man like yourself is worth more than a vote. A man in public life must have solid friends who command the confidence of the people if he's to go very far. You can never have too many of them, and I'm pleased to call you a friend."

With that, the two men shake hands, Roosevelt dons his hat, and departs. Ward finishes his last sip of brandy and walks to his files to fish out the letter from the Alabama lawyer. While sifting through his papers to find it, he thinks back on that majestic evening in April of 1889 when he first met Theodore Roosevelt. The tremendous pomp and patriotism, the great speeches and nine courses of rich food, all of it. For a time, he'd tried to organize a yearly reunion of all the members of the Spalding Tour to relive the old times together. He'd succeeded in holding one, but only some of the men came, and afterward he lost enthusiasm for the idea. Some of the other men had lost enthusiasm, too, considering the hard feelings generated among several of them by the aftermath of the Brotherhood's experiment of organizing its own major league.

Now, Ward wonders when he'll ever see any of the old crew again. Five of the ballplayers, Jim Fogarty, Ned Williamson, Ed Crane, Marty Sullivan, and now John Healy, he'd never see again. A sixth tourist, one of the organizers he barely knew, was dead, too, so that made six people with whom he'd traveled the world who hadn't lived even ten years after their return. It was a sobering thought, considering that all five ballplayers were superb athletes in the prime of their career during the tour. Fogarty had a sprinter's speed. He stole ninety-nine bases in 1889 and one hundred-two in 1887. Yet, by 1891, he was dead. Williamson and Crane had been the champion distance throwers on the tour. Both dead, like Fogarty.

Ah, there it is, the letter from Seth Dean. Ward reads the opening paragraphs again and smiles. Soon, however, his smile fades, his cheeks flush, his eyes grew wide, and his jaw drops slowly.

This attorney wrote about how he'd defended Clarence Duval against charges of vagrancy and disturbing the peace in Athens, Alabama, but believed the young man innocent and the charges fabricated. Dean couldn't believe that Clarence knew who Ward was, but Dean reported that Clarence had asked Dean to send a letter to Ward after the trial and that he'd enclosed Clarence's letter in the envelope. Dean also mentioned that the judge sentenced Clarence to the turpentine forests of Florida to work off his sentence and court costs, and that Florida is probably where he is now.

Frantically, Ward grabs the envelope and looks at the date of its postmark. Nearly four weeks ago! He curses himself for waiting so long to read Dean's letter. Clarence is in trouble, and his response is already three weeks tardy.

With trembling fingers, he extracts Clarence's letter. While the writing is unsteady and looks hurried, he has no trouble reading it.

Mr. John Ward,

Mr. Ward, I've run into trouble in Athens, Alabama. The local sheriff has accused me of crimes of which I am innocent. I was only in Athens for a few hours before my arrest and did nothing wrong. My lawyer informs me I must plead guilty, however, because the jury will ignore my testimony.

If it is within your power, can you please find a way to help me? I'm told by Mr. Dean that the court will send me to a work camp somewhere to pay off my court costs. I pin my hopes on you that you might use your legal knowledge and connections to investigate the situation, help me prove my innocence, and get me out of here.

As always, your friend,

Clarence Duval

P.S. – Dress ranks there!

Ward smiles at Clarence's reference to his days leading the parades on the Spalding Tour, but only for an instant. By the next moment, he's already decided he must do something to help Clarence, both because Clarence helped him long ago, and to honor the memory of their mutual friend John Healy.

Striding toward the door of his office, Ward opens it and bursts out. Then, realizing he's forgotten his hat in his haste, he darts back inside to grab it from the hat rack.

"In a hurry, Mr. Ward?" Mr. Lewis, his secretary, calls to him.

"I need to catch up with Governor Roosevelt. A friend stuck in Florida needs our help."

"Isn't Mr. Roosevelt the governor of New York? What can he do in Florida?"

"The governor has many connections. I'm sure he'll be able to think of something."

13

May in Florida

"Aaah!" Clarence bolts awake with a start, squirming furiously, his chains clinking. His skin burns and crawls!

Instantly, he realizes that ants are swarming over him and biting away at him already. Frantically, he swats his arms and shakes his body to get them off as best he can in his restrained condition.

"Aaah!" More bites. Clarence tears off his shirt and pulls down his pants to get the rest of the ants, swatting them away with his stinking, stiff, salt-crusted, sweat-stained work shirt.

Throughout the prisoners' train car, other men do the same. The enormous German shepherd strains at its chain, trying to leap at the men, barking furiously at all the commotion and frothing at the mouth. It runs back and forth across the entrance and howls at the men. Within a couple minutes, Clarence hears the shouts of guards and sees bobbing lantern lights as some of his jailors run in his direction from their barracks.

In a minute or so, they arrive and begin counting heads.

"Still twenty-two men," Captain Thomas confirms.

"So, there's no escape? What the hell caused all the commotion, then, you bastards?" another guard yells out at no one in particular.

"Ants, suh," one the prisoners replies. "They's big, and they swarms us while we's sleepin', and they bite."

"Leave 'em be," Captain Thomas grunts to the other guards. "You boys gots plenty to do tomorrah, so git your rest."

Clarence wonders if the irony of that statement has any impact on Captain Thomas. Most days, when Clarence wakes to work in the morning, he does so with great effort. Generally, the men go to sleep around ten o'clock at night and wake by about four in the morning. Because they work so hard and don't have enough time to sleep and rest, they're always tired and can't work very well.

In the past when Clarence has found himself in high-stress situations like this, he has had nightmares. Vivid, lifelike dreams revisiting horrors from his past always seem to haunt his rest. For the past month, however, he's been unable to even have nightmares because he's too exhausted to dream. As soon as he closes his eyes, he's asleep instantly, and it feels like his eyes only stay closed a moment before he must get up again and go into the forest and work.

Clarence has no idea what time it is when the ants attack, but no one sleeps much the rest of that night because the ants continue disrupting their rest. As a result, when the guards return a few hours later, ready to march everyone back into the forest to extract more turpentine, all the prisoners are even more exhausted than usual.

Like he always does, Clarence worries about Tom Morton. Tom was never very big to begin with; when he and Clarence came to the camp a month ago, he probably had about one hundred pounds on his five-foot-two frame. Now, however, Clarence guesses he must be around ninety. The shoulders on his ring-arounds sag, he uses a length of rope tied at the waist to keep his pants from falling while he works, and his skin looks drawn and ashen.

After relieving himself in the one bucket all the men must share, Clarence gives himself a look over and realizes he isn't doing much better. His fingers won't quite uncurl from the shape of holding an ax handle. Sometimes he tries to straighten them out, but they go right back to curling. Today, his hands have faint bloodstains from the blisters that broke yesterday while he worked, and they pain him fiercely. His ring-arounds already are wearing thin at the elbows and have a tear in the back from snagging on a tree three days ago.

The smell is worse than the state of his clothes, however. The men get to bathe in a small creek near the work camp once each week. While they bathe, everyone does his best to clean his clothes, too, but without soap, it only helps a little. For the other six days, they work in the sweltering heat getting sweaty and dirty, their ring-arounds becoming sweat-stained and foul, and the men work in their own reeking stench until Sunday arrives and they can clean themselves again.

Normally, Clarence, Tom, and Elijah say nothing on their way to their work site in the pines, choosing to conserve their energy instead, but today, Elijah feels like talking.

"Where've you been the last two days?" he says to Tom quietly, hoping to avoid too much attention from the nearest guard.

"The guards sent me to work at the big turpentine still instead of going into the forest with you all."

"Is that the big building on the other side of the tool shed?"

"Yeah."

"What did you do there, Tom?"

"I fed the furnace that heats the still."

"From the big pile of firewood on the edge of camp?"

"Yes. While I did that, other men rolled the barrels we collect in the forest to the edge of the still and dumped in the contents. The still is twelve or thirteen feet tall, and it's really hot."

"I've always wondered what happened to the barrels after we fill 'em up."

"That's where they go, Elijah. After someone dumps out the contents, another person cleans them with boiling water. All the jobs are dangerous because everything is boiling hot. There's also some salt residue left after heating the stuff. It'll burn your skin if you don't handle it right."

"Why does everything have to be so hot and dangerous?"

"I think because you have to boil the turpentine to separate it from the pitch and dirt we also collect when we tap the trees."

"That makes sense, I guess," Elijah says with a shrug.

"If it gets on you, then you're really in trouble because it's boiling hot and still sticky. I saw one guy from another train car get careless, and it got on him. He screamed while his arms blistered and burned, Elijah. The guards just laughed at him and called him stupid and clumsy."

"Well, I'm glad you got to skip working with us the last two days. You just do what you have to, so you can keep up your strength."

"Elijah, we both know that's why I got that job in the first place. It's because I'm weak. I don't work as fast as you, Matthew, or Clarence, so I'm a liability out here in the woods."

"Doesn't matter. You're with us. So long as we're out here, you're our little brother, and we're watching out for you."

Tom gives a wan smile and shakes Elijah's hand in gratitude.

After that, Elijah falls back a step and looks over at Clarence. He shakes his head slowly and sighs, blowing some air between his lips. Clarence looks at Tom again and then nods back to Elijah in understanding. They both know Tom won't make it unless they can do more to help him.

Two days ago, the first day Tom stayed in camp to work at the still, Clarence and Elijah talked about what they could do to help Tom. They know he isn't healthy and can't keep up the pace of the work much longer, so they agreed to help him by doing extra work whenever possible. Matthew had signed his agreement to Elijah, as well. He started crying while he did it. When Clarence asked Elijah why, Matthew signed that the previous night he'd woken up by chance. Tom had taken his rope belt, tied it into a noose around his neck, and was looking for a place to tie the other end. Matthew had grabbed the rope from him and given Tom a huge hug while Tom cried into his shoulder.

The memory over, Clarence looks at his friends. All have the scruffy beards of men who haven't shaved in several weeks, except for Tom, who is too young to have a full beard. The first week, one guard passed around a razor blade for anyone who wanted to try shaving without a mirror, but one prisoner tried cutting his own throat and almost bled to death, so the guards took that away.

Elijah is, or was, a healthy man. He stands four or five inches taller than Clarence, about five-foot ten, and has a strong frame. Clarence guesses Elijah is a couple years older than he, probably in his late twenties. Matthew is about Clarence's age and he's huge. He stands about six-foot, three-inches, and Clarence isn't sure how much he weighs, but certainly well over two hundred pounds. Matthew's muscles are big enough that they stretch the arms of his ring-arounds, and his pants bulge as well because they are too small for him. At least, that was true when the men arrived in Florida. Looking at Matthew now, Clarence notes that's not the case anymore.

Even for two men in the prime of life, just a month in the Florida forests is taking a brutal toll. Clarence shuffles over to Elijah.

"How's your ankle, Elijah?"

"Still hurts. I twisted it two days ago, but it's not getting better very fast. Don't think it's sprained, but I injured it pretty good. I'll live, but we don't have much time to rest and heal, you know?"

"Right. What about Matthew?"

"His left shoulder is bad. The guards made him push one of those full barrels by himself the other day, and I think he strained something. How're your hands?"

"In pain. I still can't uncurl my fingers, and I have all these blisters that make them hurt worse."

"You're losing weight, too, Clarence. Doesn't show as much as with Tom, but you're thinner than you were."

"I know it. We're all losing weight. No way to avoid it with the puny amount of food we get. How are Matthew's spirits?"

"Low, but no lower than yours or mine. He's resilient, but he can only take so much."

At this point, one of the guards rides in close and grunts at Clarence and Elijah. They stop talking and resume shambling along.

While Clarence walks silently, he thinks about waking up in the night. Twenty-two men left, Captain Thomas had said. Yes, he thinks, that's right. Another man died to go with the man who asphyxiated on the ride here. About two weeks after arrival he tried to escape into the forest after getting free of his shackles somehow, but the guards used dogs to trail him and run him down on horseback. That left twenty-two of the twenty-four who'd boarded the train with Clarence in Athens. How many have died in the other railroad cars, Clarence has no idea.

He also has no idea what happens to the bodies of the dead men. The corpse that the dog attacked and dismembered the first night just lay on the ground for five days, its decaying smell nauseating everyone, until the guards finally dragged it off somewhere unknown. Clarence supposes the guards left it in everyone's view that long as a warning. By the third day, however, the biting black flies swarmed the body so furiously that even the vicious dog stayed away.

Finally, the prisoners arrive at their worksite and begin hacking away at the pine trees to make them bleed turpentine. The grove where they work today stands next to an area of the forest where most of the longleaf pines are dead. Because most of the dead trees have cut marks, Clarence guesses this must be an area where the Southern Pineland Company cut timber and extracted turpentine in years past.

Clarence hopes that two days away from the forest will help Tom Morton keep up better, but if they do, the boost doesn't last long. By mid-morning, he's struggling again. Then, a little while before the men break for their meal, ominous, dark clouds roll in from the east. Before long, they open, and a deluge comes down.

Normally, the men appreciate some rain. Occasionally, thunderstorms roll through during the afternoon, drenching the prisoners for a while. Clarence doesn't mind the storms; he gets soaked, but the temperature drops for a while, and the wet clothes cool him further while they dry. The humidity goes up even higher afterward, it's true, but it's a trade Clarence finds acceptable.

Today is different, however. Instead of a brief thunderstorm, nature produces a steady, pounding rain that does not relent. By early afternoon, the men work in ankle-deep muck, slogging about in slow motion while their mud-coated boots get heavier and heavier. Predictably, Tom is in the most trouble. Exhausted, he falls face down in the quagmire and just lies there for a while, dropping a pan of turpentine in the process. It spills when it hits the ground.

Unfortunately, one of the guards is near and notices that Tom isn't moving. It's the one with the long beard, shotgun, and leather strap. He rides over and dismounts.

The guard walks over to Tom, the squishy sound of mud sucking around the guard's worn, brown leather boots. He prods Tom with the barrel of his gun. "You dead, boy?"

With trembling effort, Tom lifts his head. Slimy brown muck covers his face, so he can only see from one eye. "No, sir," he manages in a whisper.

"Then git up and work, boy!" A spit of tobacco juice splatters near Tom's head.

"Yes, sir," Tom whispers again.

Tom pushes his torso out of the mud and gets to his knees. He tries to rise the rest of the way but falls back to one knee, legs shaking.

"I said, git, boy!" The guard kicks Tom's shoulder with some force. Clarence sees Tom wince in pain and blink his eyes a few times.

"Yes, sir," Tom murmurs again, barely even a whisper this time.

Then the guard notices the pan of turpentine spilled on the ground. It lies, face down, in the tall grass near Tom.

"You drop that, too, boy?"

His face blanching as he looks over at the spilled pan, Tom looks back at the ground. "Yes, sir."

"Stand up, boy!"

By this time, one of the other guards rides over to check out the situation, attracted by the first guard's shouting.

The bearded guard says to the new arrival, "Watch these dogs. I got to administer some punishment." He pulls the leather strap from his belt. It's about three feet long and three or four inches wide. "Hold out your hands, boy."

Tom, now standing but wobbling a few feet away, does so. With quick reflexes, the guard whips the strap through the air. Clarence hears it whistle as it strikes Tom's palms.

Tom screams. Welts rise on his hands, and Clarence sees the crimson red of blood spots appear immediately. Without warning, the guard swings the strap again, in a backhand motion, and it strikes Tom's hands for the second time. He goes down with another scream of pain, writhing in the long grass.

"Git up, boy, we got three more to go. This'll teach you to drop the goods."

Clarence notices that little red spots appear in the mud when Tom lifts his hands from the clinging muck. Finally, he's seen enough and speaks up.

"It's my fault, sir. I bumped Tom on accident. If you must whip someone, I deserve it, not him."

"That so, boy?" the bearded guard drawls, turning to Clarence now.

"Yes sir, it's so," Clarence lies.

Another spit of tobacco juice. "Take your shirt off then, boy, and put your hands on that tree."

Biting his lips hard, Clarence does so and prepares for the pain. Since he's now facing away from the guard, however, the only warning he has is the whistling of the leather strap while it cuts the air. It isn't enough time to brace himself for the impact.

Smack! The echo of the leather striking his bare back pierces the moisture-sodden air. Now it's Clarence's turn to scream, even as the rain continues coming down and blurring his vision.

The shock of the initial blow is like nothing Clarence has ever felt. He'd fallen off his horse while training with the Buffalo Soldiers, but when that happened, he knew he was about to fall and could prepare for the impact. When the vigilante at the Milk River shot him, it hurt incredibly, but that was only a one-time event, and the bullet didn't hit him squarely. This time, the shock of the impact takes all the breath out of his lungs. After his scream ends, he makes an animal-sounding gasp while he tries to suck some air back in. It doesn't work well enough.

While these memories cascade through Clarence's mind, suddenly the whistling sound comes again. Smack! The shock returns, and again Clarence struggles to breathe while the wave of pain reverberates from his fingers to his toes. His left arm begins shaking.

"Three!" the bearded guard shouts as soon as he swings again. Through the stinging and the pain arcing through his body, somehow, Clarence gets the feeling of moisture on his bare back. He doesn't know if it's the rain or blood. Probably both.

After five, the whipping guard pauses for a moment. Clarence squeezes his eyes closed, but tears flow out from between his eyelids anyway. Maybe his torment is over. He falls to both knees.

"Stay there, boy!" the guard commands.

The other guard says, "I think he needs a stiffer punishment. I don't think this one's been tough enough to larn him."

"You're right," the bearded guard responds. "It's like whippin' a big animal. You gotta do something special just so the pain will register, and they'll learn their lesson."

While he says this, the guard with the whip bends down and slides the entire leather strap through the mud and dirt. Lifting his right arm back up, he brushes off the big globs of mud, leaving sticky dirt and grainy sand coating the leather. He draws his arm back and swings again, throwing his weight into the swing.

The pain explodes through Clarence's whole body, and he tries to scream. All that comes out is a loud wheeze because all his breath catches in his throat. Not only is the strap heavier, but also, the dirt and sand embed themselves into his bleeding cuts. Whenever he moves, even to breathe, they abrade the lacerations and keep his back aflame.

Thwack! "Seven!" the bearded guard shouts.

Clarence drops to a knee. He wants to reach back and try to rub some of the sand and dirt off his back. He begins to try, right arm quivering uncontrollably.

"Arms up!" the guard with the shotgun shouts.

As soon as Clarence complies, he's hit again. Eight.

From the corner of his watering eyes, Clarence notices Tom Morton watching, mouth agape, bleeding hands covering his face, smudges of blood on his cheeks and mud-coated shirt. Clarence sets his mouth, even though he can barely breathe.

After the tenth swing, Clarence falls, face down, into the slime and grass. Every muscle he has screams. Even his legs spasm while he lies there.

"That all? Just ten?" the mounted guard with the rifle asks his fellow.

"Yeah, for now. That's the first time for this boy, so I'll go easy on him. Y'all get workin' again," he growls to everyone watching the whipping. Then, to Clarence, he shouts, "And you got two minutes to get up and go back to work, or else you gets another ten."

That evening, when Clarence staggers back to his train car for the night, he knows there'll be no sleep. Every step, the pain lances through his body again, every inch of his back screaming. Most of the blood from the cuts has clotted, but walking tends to open the cuts again, causing fresh blood to trickle down his back, and the salt in his blood only makes the pain worse as it contacts fresh cuts and raw skin. He leans on Elijah Maxwell while he drags himself forward. Now and again, Elijah tries to help by brushing off some of the dirt and dried blood, but every time he does, Clarence must suppress a yell.

"You want me to stop, Clarence?"

"No, keep going. It'll help in the long run."

"You sure? Your face contorts every time I clean something away."

"I know. Every time you touch me, it's like a fire burning me, or getting scalded by hot water. But it's not good to have the dirt just stay there. Keep going. I'll take it."

Lying chained in the train car that night, face down so his back won't rub the floor of the car, Clarence decides that his letter to John Ward was in vain. No help will come get him out of Florida. He's certain that he'll have to get away on his own. Staying here will kill him, so he needs to plan a way out.

14

Visiting Judge Winston

Eric Hoffman steps from the Louisville & Nashville train onto the platform of the Athens station in mid-May. He's prepared for the worst in terms of the weather, wearing a light linen shirt in anticipation of balmy heat, but this morning Athens offers overcast skies and modest humidity. *Probably the only thing I'll find comfortable on this entire trip*, he thinks to himself while carrying his single suitcase from the platform. He has an address for the hotel where he'll stay, and the hotel isn't hard to find, considering it's on the opposite corner of the intersection from the train depot, at the corner of Monroe and Washington streets. Hoffman ambles in that direction, his leather suitcase in his left hand, leather briefcase in his right.

In his heart, this isn't an assignment Hoffman wants. He feels like an outsider whenever venturing below the Ohio River, like a traveler to another time in another country. His family owns a prosperous farm in western New York state and is well-established there. They're well-established enough, in fact, that they sent him to Harvard's law school when he showed great promise as a youngster. An uncle is involved in state politics in New York, too, and those facts help explain why he is here, in Limestone County, investigating a recent spate of arrests.

As he walks, Hoffman analyzes his situation one final time. He knows why the Justice Department gave him this job. While at

Harvard, in 1878, he'd met a young man named Theodore Roosevelt and sparred with him in the boxing ring a few times. They'd struck up a friendship, and the bond strengthened after the death of both of their first wives.

About a week ago, Roosevelt had telegraphed Hoffman regarding a suspicion of unusual activity in Alabama. Roosevelt believed that local authorities in Athens may have subjected people to wrongful arrests and had asked him to take the case if the Justice Department saw fit to investigate. Roosevelt specifically requested that Hoffman look into the fate of a young colored man named Clarence Duval but to keep his eyes open for greater irregularities as well.

Well, Roosevelt is governor of New York, and the Justice Department did not turn down Roosevelt's request, especially given that Roosevelt is a rising star in the Republican Party, and the current president of the United States, William McKinley, is also a Republican. So, out of friendship for Roosevelt, Hoffman accepted the assignment. His uncle had urged him to take the case, too, when Hoffman mentioned the possibility to him. Both Hoffman's uncle and Roosevelt are known as Progressive Republicans, a group proclaiming an interest in reform and making politics more responsive to the people.

Hoffman tends in this direction as well in his political loyalties, so he volunteered, but reluctantly and with misgivings. He is a Republican; Democrats rule the South. He is a Progressive; to him, the South is anything but. Hoffman believes in the United States and its representative government; the South started a civil war within his lifetime to secede from that government. He believes in the Fourteenth Amendment and that all Americans deserve equal rights; the South has Jim Crow laws and public segregation. Likewise, the Fifteenth Amendment gives all male citizens the right to vote, but the South uses poll taxes, literacy tests, grandfather clauses, white primaries, and violent intimidation to make sure that not all men exercise that right. Finally, and at the most basic level, Hoffman believes colored people deserve the right to exist in the United States as free people; given some of the pamphlets and books published by Southerners over the past two decades, he knows many Southerners don't even accord colored people the status of humans, let alone the right to live free in the United States.

Hoffman shivers, even though it isn't cold. No, this is not a plum. His salary from the U.S. government isn't opulent, by any means, and he'll earn every penny on this trip, and then some, unless he's quite mistaken. Yet, one part of him does relish the opportunity. Partly, so he can put his beliefs about equality into action, but also because if he makes a success of this investigation, his reputation will climb a notch higher in the Justice Department. It isn't that Hoffman is a man with ambitious images of grandeur; better to say he likes a challenge, takes pride in doing his job competently, and has enough talent to succeed most of the time.

Preoccupied by these thoughts, Hoffman barely notices anything about his hotel, the Commercial Hotel, except that it is more like a large house than a typical Washington, D.C., hotel. White pillars support a roof over the front veranda two stories high, each room has large windows that the occupants can open to let in the breeze, and a shingled roof covers the wooden frame house built on a brick foundation. A one-story building connects to the hotel in the back, probably the kitchen, from the smell of things. About a dozen wooden steps take him from the walkway to the front door. Hoffman also notices the hotel has an entire city block nearly to itself. Only a pair of residences to the north dot the grassy lot spanning out north and east behind the hotel.

Before entering, Hoffman takes a moment to put on his suit vest and a tie. When he goes inside, a man wearing a white shirt, gray suspenders, and a black bow tie sits behind the desk just inside the door. He wears a clerk's hat. "Afternoon, suh," he drawls.

"Good afternoon," Hoffman replies, removing his black derby hat and setting it on the counter.

"You from up North somewheres?" the man says, now sitting up straight and taking an interest in someone who speaks without any Southern accent.

Hoffman nods. "Sort of. Washington. I trust you have rooms available?"

"Yessuh, we do. How long you thinkin' of stayin'?"

"I'm not sure, but I'd guess at least a few days."

"You here on bidness, suh?"

"Of a kind, yes." Hoffman makes sure to finger his silver cufflinks conspicuously and then pulls a watch on a gold chain from his vest pocket. After checking it, he continues. "I think I'll be able to get something done today, but if it's all the same to you, can we just arrange payment when my stay is over? Or, I can pay you each day. It's of no consequence to me."

"We usually take payment each day if our guest don't know how long they plans to stay."

"That will be fine. Tell me, my friend," Hoffman adjusts his silver tie pin while addressing the man and smooths the fabric of his pinstriped vest a bit, "I'm to conduct business with Jefferson Winston and Sam Johnstone while I'm in Athens. I've never met either. What can you tell me about them?"

"You's here to meet the Judge and Sam Johnstone both?"

"Yes. You act like that's unusual. They are the two most important men in Athens, are they not?"

"Yessuh, they is. But they don't get along so well. Least ways, that's the word I hears. What bidness is you in, anyway?"

"Cotton. I'm hoping to strike a deal with at least one man for supplying my mill. Maybe both, if things break right."

"Oh. Well, that makes sense, I guess."

"I hope it will make some cents as well," Hoffman puns with a wry smile while he pulls a shiny new silver quarter from his pocket, just in case the clerk needs a hint to get his joke.

The hotel clerk chuckles. "Tha's a good one. 'Specially for a Yankee. Everyone says y'all Yankees don't have a sense of humor, but you's funny."

"Some of us do more than count coins and look at inventories all day, it's true."

"Well, now, I can say Judge Winston, everyone says he's the smartest man in Athens. All business. If you was like most Yankees," the clerk says with a wink and an easy smile, "you'd like him. He's stern, but courteous. Least ways, that's what people say. I've never met him myself."

"I take it, then, that Mr. Johnstone is a different kind of man?"

"Why, yessuh, he's a gentleman through and through, he is. Always has a kind word for a friend and a comfy chair for a guest. That's Sam Johnstone. You'll not find a more Christian soul in Limestone County."

"Thank you, good sir. You do know how to make a stranger feel welcome here in Athens."

"Thank you, suh, we tries our best."

Hoffman nods, smiles again, and picks his hat up off the counter. "Like I said, I would like to begin today."

"Oh, yessuh, let me show you to your room, then," the clerk says. "Would you like the first floor or the second?"

"First floor suits me just fine. Thank you, my friend. Is this your local newspaper?" Hoffman says while picking up an eight-page sheet lying on the desk counter.

"Yessuh. It's the *Alabama Courier*. It's a fine paper."

"May I have one?"

"Goes with bein' a guest, suh."

"Much obliged," Hoffman says while he tips his hat to the clerk.

After the clerk walks him to his room and then leaves, Hoffman shrugs while unpacking his clothes. He hadn't lied, exactly, when he claimed he was in Athens on business, except for the cotton part, but he needs all the information he can get before meeting Jefferson Winston later today. It appears the judge might be a tough nut to

125

crack. Johnstone could be too, for all he knows. A polite and gregarious exterior sometimes masks a calculating mind.

Hoffman decides to shave before meeting Winston. Looking in the washroom mirror, he doesn't need it too badly but decides to play his role to the hilt just in case, so he pulls out his razor and begins scraping away. *Damn*, he says to himself after nicking a spot under his chin and drawing a bit of blood, *now I'll have to wait a moment while the bleeding stops*.

With nothing better to do to kill a few minutes, Hoffman opens the local paper and looks through it while waiting for his chin to stop bleeding. Tearing off a corner of the back page to staunch the blood, he holds the scrap of paper to his chin with his left hand while turning pages with his right. Hoffman glances over the usual reports of local news, much of it about the state of the cotton market in Alabama, plus a few articles on national news that are several days old. Ever since his wife died, Hoffman likes to read the obituaries, so he looks for those. He isn't morbid; rather, he likes the obituaries because it makes him feel good to read the stories of deceased people who, like his wife, had lived full and energetic lives.

This issue doesn't contain many obituaries, but one name catches Hoffman's eye instantly. William Duval. The entry is short. It simply reads that William Duval, a sweeper in a sawmill, died during an accident at the mill the preceding week, his wife had predeceased him, and he had one child. *Might be a coincidence*, Hoffman thinks to himself, but he decides to file the information away in his mind, just in case. If William Duval had one known child that makes it possible, maybe even probable, he was the father of the Clarence Duval Hoffman is supposed to look for.

Finally, he feels ready and leaves the hotel, walking the two blocks to the Limestone County Courthouse even as the pleasant early afternoon weather makes part of him wish the trip was a little longer. The local trees, mostly oaks and hickories, line his way along Washington Street, while some town lots also sport maples and chestnuts.

After Hoffman reaches the courthouse, it isn't long before a secretary ushers him into Winston's chambers. After shaking hands, the two men sit down to discuss Hoffman's purpose for traveling to Athens.

"I trust you received the telegram stating the reasons I'm here," Hoffman begins. "The Justice Department received word that there may have been questionable arrests in Limestone County about two months ago. We've made no official accusations, of course. I'm merely here to investigate whether the information we received has any validity to it."

"I can assure you that your investigation will turn up nothing because the accusations are baseless, but, nonetheless, you can expect the full cooperation of Limestone County and the city of Athens." Judge Winston shows no perturbation, no hint of nervousness or worry, Hoffman notes. He simply looks at Hoffman across a polished desk with his hands folded calmly on the table.

"Thank you for that. I'm sure everything is fine. Personally, I think the Justice Department has more important things to do than interfere with local affairs in the individual states. This seems more of a state matter to me. But, as I'm sure you know, when a superior asks you to examine something, one has little choice in the matter. I hope to conclude my investigation as quickly as I can."

Winston gives the faintest smile. "Just as I said before, I'll provide whatever resources you need to carry out your investigation."

"To begin with, I'd just like to have a look at the arrest records for the month of March."

"Certainly. I'll have my clerk bring out the books. You're welcome to sit in our records office and study them as long as you'd like."

A few minutes later, looking through the county records, Hoffman sees what he expected to see. The people who'd appeared in court in March were, almost to a man, colored. Their crimes were the predictable ones as well: loitering, vagrancy, petty theft, and the

127

like. For each man, the sentence was time at hard labor to pay court costs and whatever fine their crime dictated. In every case, the court authorized leasing the prisoners to the Southern Pineland Company and putting them to work in lieu of monetary payment of their fines and costs.

After reviewing the books, Hoffman returns to Judge Winston's office. "I just have a few questions, Judge Winston, and then I'll be on my way for this afternoon. The records all look clear enough. Do you have any speculation as to why your county experienced a sudden wave of criminal activity on the part of its colored population in March?"

"The Negros around Athens are an unpredictable lot. Because so many are shiftless roustabouts, we get a number of them in town early in the year, poking around, looking for work. When one accounts for their dissolute habits and fondness for alcohol, sometimes these boys get into trouble, and we have to bring them in to protect the law-abiding citizens of the town."

"I see," Hoffman says, scribbling notes on a legal pad. "And, I trust, things have been peaceful since March? I saw very few incidents in the records after that point."

"Indeed. Negros in Alabama can learn from example. Some of them, at least. After they saw us round up so many of their kind because of unlawful behavior, the local Negros calmed down and returned to their normal, satisfied condition."

"I'm sure the citizens of Athens are relieved that you've restored order to the town."

"That's what the courts are for."

"I also notice, Judge Winston, that your court leased each convicted man to the Southern Pineland Company. Can you explain how the leasing of convicts works, just to make sure I understand things correctly?"

"Certainly. The system is a nearly perfect one. Because the arrested men tend to be shiftless and oftentimes unemployed, we remove a threat to the community's safety while, at the same time, helping the convicts learn a trade under the watchful eye of a company. In our case, we've chosen to contract with the Southern Pineland Company. In most cases, the convicts cannot pay the court costs for their trial. So, to work off the debt they've incurred, we lease them. The company pays the county, or when employing state prisoners, the state of Alabama, a sum of money for the right to lease the convicts. The county uses this money to carry on the functions of government. The convict lease system lessens the burden on taxpayers thereby and removes the necessity for local communities or the state of Alabama to maintain prisons as well. So, you can see, the system benefits all involved. The local population remains safe, the leasing of convicts funds the functions of government, and the convicted men learn a trade, thereby improving their station in life."

"I see. And does the county, or the state of Alabama as the case may be, exercise any oversight on the prisoners during their time working off their fines and costs?"

"It does not. The companies are private business."

"Indeed. That makes sense to me. Thank you for that fine explanation, Judge Winston. I think that will be all for today. I'll inform you if I have any further need to examine court records or documents."

"You're welcome, Mr. Hoffman. Like I said previously, Limestone County will cooperate with your investigation as best it can, so you may be on your way promptly."

The two men shake hands and Hoffman exits Winston's office.

From his window, Jefferson Davis Winston watches Eric Hoffman cross the street, retracing his steps toward the Commercial Hotel. Winston runs his hand over his chin a few times and sighs. Something doesn't feel quite right. Hoffman appears sincere and hadn't pressed him hard on why his court convicted so many men within a few days back in March, it's true. Perhaps he means what he says about wanting to conclude his investigation and be on his way. But, perhaps not. Something about Hoffman's manner strikes Winston wrong. Almost like Hoffman had tried too hard to act like he isn't very interested in the investigation. Winston sighs again, cupping his chin in his hand.

He'd telegraphed Thomas Brown immediately after getting the Justice Department's initial telegram, of course. Brown replied that Winston should report back after ascertaining the motives of the investigation. So, Winston thinks to himself, he'd better get more information on what, exactly, those motives are. He stands up and walks down the hall to where his sons, the sheriff and deputy sheriff, sit playing checkers in Robert's office.

James looks up first. "How'd the meeting go, Father? Do you think that man has any inkling about what happened?"

"I'm not sure yet."

"You couldn't tell?"

"Mr. Hoffman looked uninterested in his assignment and gave me to understand he was just here going through the motions, but I'm not so sure."

"Well, you're usually right about reading people," Robert puts in. "If you're suspicious, there's probably something suspicious afoot."

"That's what I'm thinking, too," Winston replies. "Robert, why don't you keep an eye on Eric Hoffman. You know the clerk over at the Commercial Hotel, don't you?"

"Only a little. His name is John Putnam. We went to school together as youngsters, but our paths haven't crossed too often since then. Not too much happening over at the Commercial Hotel. You know the owner, Sid Powell, is a teetotaler, so we don't collect any money from him for us to look the other way while he distills and distributes alcohol like we do from other hotels in town."

"But you know John, and he knows you."

"Of course."

"Go talk to him and ask him to send a bellboy over here every time Hoffman leaves the hotel. I want to know when he leaves, where he goes, and who he talks to. You and Jimmy both watch this lawyer, Hoffman, too. Get some local kids to help you if you need to avoid suspicion. Tell them you'll buy them ice cream for their help."

"Sure, Father. John'll listen to me."

"If he doesn't, Robert, you know how to lean on him."

"Absolutely."

"Good. Now, get going. We need to know what Eric Hoffman really plans to do in Athens."

15

Sam Johnstone

Eric Hoffman gazes into the washroom mirror, straightening his tie. He checks his pockets again, making sure he has enough money to hire a carriage to take him to the Johnstone plantation. While he does so, he thinks about yesterday's conversation with Jefferson Winston. The judge had been formal, but cooperative, exactly the way he expected a judge to behave, but Hoffman doubts that everything in Athens is what it seems. The judge's explanation of why so many arrests had happened all at once is weak, certainly, and the fact that no one exercises any supervision over the treatment of the convicts after their lease troubles him badly.

Hoffman also knows that Judge Winston's two sons are both law enforcement officers and had made most of the arrests. They may be qualified officers of the law, or they may not, but that certainly smacks of nepotism and makes him more suspicious.

After stepping into the street and hiring an omnibus to transport him to Johnstone's plantation, Hoffman thinks further about the prior day. He didn't think he'd given away too much during his conversation with Winston. He wanted to come across as a man who just wanted to get things over with and hoped he'd done so, to put the judge more at ease, but who knew how Winston had viewed him?

In any case, after about half an hour, he arrives at Johnstone's house. Yesterday's weather had been very pleasant, but today promises to be much warmer and more like the Alabama he'd planned for, so Hoffman is glad his arrangements call for meeting Johnstone early in the morning.

Johnstone's house is every bit what Hoffman anticipated. It looks like a plantation house built before the Civil War: two stories, about twenty rooms, several chimneys, a wide front porch, and enormous oak trees everywhere providing shade.

Stepping onto the porch, the door opens even before Hoffman can knock. "Come in, Mr. Hoffman, please come in, sir," a white-haired man with a thin white goatee says. "I've been waiting for your arrival all morning. I'm Sam Johnstone. Please, come in. Can I have my maid get you some coffee? Or, perhaps something a bit stronger?"

"No thank you, Mr. Johnstone. I appreciate your offer, but I'm fine for now. It seems a bit early for anything stronger than coffee, at any rate."

"You can call me Sam, Mr. Hoffman. All my neighbors do. Unlike some Southerners, I don't stand on the formalities and glories of the past."

Hoffman can't help but smile. "Department policy is to use formal titles, but I suppose calling a man by his preferred name won't hurt anything."

"As you wish, but feel free to call me Sam. Let's head to my study to conduct our interview, shall we?"

"Absolutely. Please, lead the way."

Johnstone leads the way through the foyer of his home, and Hoffman notes a few things about his host while following him down a hallway to the study. Although he looks over seventy, Sam Johnstone shows no signs of frailty. He walks erect and with purpose in his stride, like he'd been an officer in the Army in his younger days. His black suit shows sharp creases and appears freshly pressed. When he shook Hoffman's hand, his grip had still been firm.

After sitting down in a plush armchair, Hoffman opens his briefcase and brings out his legal pad to take notes. He decides to float a couple test questions to try to get a better feel for the man and see if the outward courtesy is genuine. "Mr. Johnstone, I mean, Sam, you mentioned a minute ago you weren't interested in the glories of the past. Can I ask what you mean by that?"

"It's a reference to my service in the war."

"You fought in the Civil War?" Perhaps, Hoffman thinks, he's not as old as he looks. Or, he really was an officer.

"No, not the War of Secession. Bah. Worst thing to ever happen to this country. Worst thing to ever happen to the South, at any rate. I've never lived in the North, so I suppose I can't say if it was the worst thing for the Yankees. No, I meant I served in the Mexican War back in '47 and '48."

"You fought in Mexico?"

"Yes, sir, all the way to Mexico City and the Halls of Montezuma."

"You may be the first veteran of that war I've met. Well, the first in many years, anyway."

"It's true, I'm getting up there in age, but that can't be helped, I suppose. It's better than the alternative, at any rate," Johnstone says with a cheerful laugh. "It's 1899 now, so I may just live to see a second century. You sure you don't want something to drink? I've got some Tennessee bourbon if you'd like. It's excellent stuff. Nothing but the finest."

"No, sir, although that's quite generous of you."

"Don't mind if I do," Johnstone says in a relaxed tone. "I've been enjoying good bourbon all my life, no need to hold back now." Partly filling a glass, he returns and sits down opposite Hoffman, raising his glass after doing so.

"Yes, it's true I fought in Mexico. Interesting times, those days were. Army life had it's good and bad side back then."

Hoping that Johnstone will let fall some clues, Hoffman decides to encourage him to keep going about his war years. "What were the good points, if I may ask?"

"Well, the people you fight alongside and lead into action, some of them stay your friends for life. I served under Ethan Allen Hitchcock while in Mexico. You know that name, Mr. Hoffman?"

"I remember Ethan Allen, the Revolutionary War hero, from my books in school, and I know that the current Secretary of the Interior is also named Ethan Allen Hitchcock."

"Same family. The one I fought with was the grandson of the Revolutionary War leader, and, let me say, one of the best men I've ever met. The man you mentioned who works with you in Washington is the nephew of the man I served with. I don't know him, but if he's anything like his uncle, you've found a good man to run Interior. The Hitchcock family may not be too creative with its names, but it's produced some fine men."

"I've never met the one in Interior, either. I just know he used to be an ambassador, although I forget where. Russia, I think."

"Fighting with brave and honorable men like Hitchcock was what made military life bearable for me. The food certainly didn't help. And the whiskey, bah! Cheap, horrible stuff."

Hoffman smiles and laughs. Tenting his fingers in front of his face, he asks, "Anything else you didn't like, besides bad food and bad whiskey?"

"Sure, lots of things. That war was nonsense, for one. Just like Hitchcock said, we didn't have a particle of right to be there. It was all Polk's scheming. But, at the time, I was young and gullible, so I joined up when some friends of mine did. Thought I was a great patriot in those days. Wasn't until I learned what army life is like that I realized how stupid I was. Luckily, my father had money and got me a commission as an officer. Otherwise, it would have been even worse."

"How so?"

"You ever seen men get shot right next to you, Mr. Hoffman? Seen their shoulder explode when a bullet shatters every bone they've got? Or seen army surgeons sawing off the legs of wounded men? That's what the battlefield is like. In Mexico, the enlisted men also had to deal with scorpions, rattlesnakes, and every camp disease you can think of. At least officers like me got regular pay and didn't have to sleep underneath tents that rotted and fell apart right before your eyes."

Hoffman just shakes his head while giving a short whistle.

Johnstone gives a kindly laugh. "Well, don't feel bad that you haven't seen those things with your own eyes. It's not an experience I'd choose to relive if I could go back and do it over again, and I don't wish it on anyone else. I suppose army life taught me a few other things, though, like organization and discipline. Didn't have much of either when I signed up, but they've served me well for five decades now, so I guess I got something out of my time and trouble."

"I notice, Sam, you don't ask people to call you by your rank. Most Southerners do, if they have military experience."

"That's what I meant about not standing on past glories. No need for that."

"I'm also surprised you didn't fight in the Civil War. Surely, someone of your experience must have been tempted."

"Not in the slightest."

"No?"

"Mr. Hoffman, all the slaves in the world weren't worth one single young man getting shot and dying. That's what fighting in Mexico showed me. My father owned some slaves, to be sure. About forty, in fact. But I set them all free after he died and I inherited the family plantation. That would have been in 1857. When that fool Taney and his Supreme Court handed down its Dred Scott decision, and then all that Lecompton trouble started up, I said to myself, these people are leading the country into ruin. Besides that, it seemed to me like holding another man against his will wasn't the Christian thing to do. So, I set the family slaves free. Luckily, I was an only child because my mother died in childbirth, so no one else in the family could contest my decision. Otherwise," Johnstone chuckles lightly while thinking back more than four decades, "who knows what might have happened? Those people were worth an awful lot of money. I hate to think of people that way, as being just money, but at the time, they were."

"That was a noble gesture."

"Perhaps. It seemed like the right thing to do, and I've never regretted it. I told all those slave families that I planned to set them free and that they could go anywhere, but I also told them that if they wanted, they could rent land from me to get up some money and then go where they pleased. Most stayed on for a while. A few of those families still rent land from me today. So, I guess you can say I did make some money off the deal in the long run."

"Now I think I understand why you didn't want to fight in the Civil War," Hoffman says.

"You got it. One war was enough for me, and I wasn't exactly in the good graces of my neighbors when the next one came along, if you understand me, so they left me alone, and I sat it out. I always thought the War of Secession was a mistake anyway, like I told you before. I never supported Secession, but down here in Alabama, that put me in the minority."

"You mentioned that some of those families still rent land from you, even today?"

"They do, and that's part of why I'm glad you're here. You see, I have a friend or two working at the courthouse, and when they found out someone from the Justice Department was on his way to Athens to investigate some wrongful arrests, I made sure you'd get to speak with me. Some of my tenants, a pair of brothers named Maxwell, to be exact, were part of one group arrested in March. I doubt they did anything."

"What makes you think so? I looked at the court records yesterday afternoon, but there were enough arrests that I can't remember particular names."

"Well, these brothers never bothered anyone, for one thing. The older one, Elijah, was studying in college to be a teacher until his father died and he came back to the farm to help his mother. Elijah's brother, Matthew, is a deaf-mute. He can't talk or hear anything. Matthew's also one of the gentlest souls I know. He doesn't even like to kill the rats when he catches them in the barn, according to Elijah. I can't imagine how those two young men could get in trouble and get themselves arrested, so I suspect something's afoot."

"I noticed that the sheriff and deputy sheriff are sons of Judge Winston."

"They are, and that isn't good. I don't know what their scheme is, but it sure was suspicious to me when they rounded up all those young colored boys all at once."

"How's your relationship with the judge?"

"Poor. I think everyone in town knows it, so you probably knew the answer before you asked the question."

Hoffman smiles in acknowledgment.

Johnstone continues. "A couple times over the last few decades, we've ended up opposing each other in court over land boundaries. Back in the eighties, he won the cases because the old judge still disliked me for betraying the South and not fighting in the War of Secession. After he retired, Winston became the judge himself, and you can guess what my chances were in court after that happened."

"Right. So, can I summarize things by stating that you suspect foul play but have no proof of it at this moment?"

"That about says it, yes. But here, let me give you the name of someone else you need to speak with. Seth Dean. He's the lawyer who defended the accused in court. I'll bet he knows a thing or two if you can only get it out of him."

"I'll be sure to do that. Thank you for your time, Sam. Maybe when all this is over, I'll take you up on your offer of a glass of Tennessee bourbon." *If they don't run me out of town before that*, Hoffman thinks to himself.

"You're welcome back here anytime, Mr. Hoffman."

"If you think of anything else, I'm staying at the Commercial Hotel."

With that, Hoffman closes his briefcase, dons his derby hat, and makes for the front door. Maybe, just maybe, he's found an ally to help him get to the bottom of things in Athens.

While Hoffman walks down his porch steps to the circular driveway where his carriage waits to take him back to town, Sam Johnstone watches him through a white-curtained window. "This lawyer may have his uses," he says quietly while stroking his goatee. As Hoffman rides away, he walks toward the rear parlor of his home. Alannah, his colored maid, waits there.

"Your husband, the omnibus driver, he knows what to do, right?" Sam says to her.

"Yessir. If the lawyer asks him where to find Seth Dean, he knows what to tell him. And, he knows to suggest it if the lawyer don't ask. Thank you for your help, Sam."

Johnstone nods. "We'll both gain something if my plans work out, Alannah. This lawyer's just a pawn right now, but with a little luck, we can turn him into a knight or a rook. If we can do that, we'll have a better chance of trapping the king."

"Is it time to talk to my brother, do you think, Sam?"

"Yes, I think our chance is finally here. Tell Ben to pay Mr. Hoffman a visit this evening."

16

Hell in Florida

Clarence wakes to the sound of men vomiting. He isn't sure what day of the month it is, having no way to keep accurate count, but he thinks it's sometime late in May. He forces his eyes to open, rather than allowing the blackness to take him back to sleep. As they slowly focus, he sees Matthew retching over the side of the train car. The German shepherd is only a few feet away, snarling and barking demonically, snapping at but just missing Matthew's face, but Matthew just lies on his stomach, throwing up while his body shakes uncontrollably.

When Clarence has the chance to awaken further and form a better awareness of his surroundings, he sees Matthew isn't the only one. A pair of prisoners whose names he doesn't know do the same. When he'd gone to sleep last night, he'd noticed Matthew quivering, breathing hard, and rubbing his head as if he had a headache. Now, whatever's wrong with him, he's added vomiting to the list of symptoms.

Clarence wonders why several prisoners have apparently gotten the same illness all at once. The treatment of the prisoners has been uniformly harsh; there's been no change there. The only thing that's different about the past couple weeks is that after the day of hard rain when he'd taken the whipping to cover for Tom Morton, the rain kept up for most of the next two days. Some of the local creeks flooded their banks and, for a while, part of the camp was ankle-deep in water. The clouds of mosquitoes, while always troublesome, got even thicker for a few days afterward. Clarence looks at his arms, but has no way to tell how many of the red bites are new ones compared to the number of old ones.

Elijah Maxwell is awake, too. Clarence asks him, speaking up a bit so Elijah can hear him over the dog's deafening yowling, "Has Matthew told you what he thinks is wrong with him?"

"Last night he signed that he had a fever, a headache, and trouble breathing. It looks like things are worse now."

"I don't know what those symptoms mean, Elijah, but a couple other men have them, too."

"I'm not sure what the cause is, either. Do you have a guess?"

"Not for sure. Either it's because we're worn down from too little food and the harsh work, or maybe it comes from all the mosquitoes that swarmed us after the camp flooded about two weeks ago."

"You might be right about that. I don't have any idea. How are we going to get out of here, Clarence?"

"I've tried to think of ways, but I'm always exhausted or working. There's barely time to think of anything else because all we do is work, eat, and try to sleep so we have the strength to work."

"How is your back?"

"It still hurts a fair amount, but most of the cuts are closed, and the scabs have fallen away by now. You did the right thing by helping wipe the dirt away, even if it made me cry like a little kid."

"I can't imagine how that felt, Clarence. How did you make it through work the next day? You had to go out and work a regular day, as if nothing had happened to you."

"I don't know. I was half out of my mind that entire day. The pain was so great I literally couldn't see anything that wasn't right in front of my face."

"I remember. When I tried to talk to you a couple times, you just mumbled back to me. You're lucky you didn't cut off a hand with your ax or something like that."

"Do you think one of our axes could cut us out of these chains to get away?"

"Maybe, Clarence, but the dogs would chase us down. The guards are on horseback. The one guy who tried that got killed, remember?"

"We'll have to escape at night, then."

"What about the monster dog right in front of us?"

"I'm working on that part."

"Well, keep working, but here come the guards. Let's keep this between us, right?"

Clarence nods.

A couple hours later the men are back in the pine forest, cutting away the bark of the trees and gathering turpentine like always. Matthew struggles. Although everyone sweats constantly under the sweltering heat of late May, today it simply pours off Matthew. He continues shaking while he tries to work, too. Several times, he drops his ax and must go to one knee to get it. Each time, he takes a bit longer to stand back up. A guard notices and rides over.

"What's the matter, boy? You get to work. You's the strongest one here, and you's actin' like you's as weak as that boy over there."

The guard points at Tom, who now weighs, in Clarence's best guess, eighty-five pounds, at most. His ring-arounds are so baggy that his hands don't even stick out of the sleeves anymore. He must roll the sleeves up, so they don't get in his way while he works.

Meanwhile, Elijah tries to explain to the guard. "I'm sorry, sir, but my brother is deaf and mute. He can't hear you. I'll tell him what you said." Elijah begins signing to his brother.

"He can't understand me? He needs to larn, then."

"Matthew was born that way, sir, not being able to hear or talk. But something new is wrong with him. He and some of the other men were vomiting earlier this morning. He's got a sickness of some kind. See how his arms are shaking for no reason? That's why he dropped his ax."

"I don't care what he's got. He's gonna work, or he's gonna get the strap—"

Just then, before the guard can continue his threat, there's a commotion from another group of workers nearby.

Clarence looks over and sees Ezra Tompkins, the old man whom he was jailed with back in Athens, lying on the ground, holding his foot and screaming in fear and pain. The guard rides over to check out what happened. Clarence can hear the conversation because Ezra shouts due to his panic.

"Snake, suh, snake bit me. I gone and stepped too close, and it bit me. Look at the marks, suh!"

The guard doesn't bother getting down from his horse. "It's just a little bite. Barely swelling. You's fine. Stop whining and get working."

"But, suh, it's a rattlesnake. They's poisonous. Look, there it is!" Ezra points to something in the grass that Clarence can't see from his distance but that he supposes must be the snake.

The guard levels his rifle and fires. Even at a distance, Clarence can see snake body parts arcing through the air.

"There, you's safe now. Go back to work."

"But, the poison, suh!"

"What, old man? You think we gots snake medicine at our camp? We don't got none. You's gonna work, or I'se gonna get the whip."

Clarence watches Ezra swoon and hit the dirt. He pushes up to his hands and knees but shakes his head back and forth. He crawls over to his ax and braces against it to lift himself to his feet. Ezra makes it up, but he stumbles over and leans against the nearest pine for balance.

The guard, meanwhile, lights a cigarette and puffs it while watching Ezra struggle.

Ezra is another of the men who gets to work at the still boiling out the turpentine some days, Clarence remembers. Probably for the same reason Tom does—he's not as strong and healthy as the other men because of his age. Before Clarence can give much more thought to the matter, however, the smoking guard looks over his way, and he hustles back to work.

The day turns out as long and hellish as the others. The flies buzz, swarm, and bite mercilessly. The mosquitoes do the same, the only difference being their bites don't sting. Looking at his arms, Clarence sees as much of his skin covered in pink bite marks as he does his real skin color. It hurts the worst when the black flies bite somewhere that's already an open sore, like on his ankles where Clarence's skin is always raw from chafing at the chains each night.

As each day goes along, his perspiration starts soaking his shirt, and today is no different. That means that the longer Clarence works, the heavier and more clinging his shirt gets, and the harder it is to work. He'd take it off, but he prefers sweaty, clinging clothes to even more mosquito and fly bites.

Then, late in the afternoon, it happens. Another cry. Clarence looks over and sees Ezra Tompkins on the ground again. He's not getting up. Instead, he lies there, spasming uncontrollably and grasping at his throat like he can't breathe.

The twitches and jerks continue for several minutes, but gradually, they slow in intensity. After a few more minutes, they stop altogether. Emory Wilson, another man who was a prisoner with Clarence back in Athens, stands by Ezra's side. He drops to a knee and puts his finger on Ezra's wrist, checking for a pulse.

"He's dead," Emory says. It isn't that loud, but because everyone who can see Ezra just stands there silently, Clarence hears him clearly. Emory runs his right hand over Ezra's face, closing his eyes. A guard rides up. The bearded one with the strap.

"Move him out the way, then get back to work," the man growls.

"We gots to bury him. It's only decent," Emory replies. Clarence sees a glint of the sunlight reflecting off tears.

"Worry about that later. Now that he dead, you got to do his share today."

Emory just stands for a moment.

"Oh, that's right," the guard drawls while fingering the barrel of his gun. "You's the uppity one. I's only gonna say it once."

In slow motion, Emory drags Ezra's body to the side, picks up his ax, and shuffles to the tree where he's working.

Clarence is a bit surprised Emory is still alive. He does have a temper, and it seems like the guards whip him nearly once each week. Again, however, Clarence must return to chopping bark instead of watching how the scene plays out. From a few glances he steals during the rest of the day, however, he knows Emory keeps stewing on things.

When the light is so dim Clarence can't see what he's cutting anymore, another bleak work day ends, and the prisoners trudge back to their train car, heads down, feet dragging. Emory pulls Ezra's body along with him. When they've nearly reached the camp, Emory collapses to the ground from the strain. He doesn't get up right away.

"Stand up, boy; you's almost there," one guard says.

Emory, face down in the sandy dirt, holds up one index finger, signaling he needs a moment.

"I'm tired a waitin' for you monkeys. I said, get up! I wants to sleep tonight, too."

Emory tries, but falls over again after a few steps.

"Leave that body behind. We take care of him tomorrah," another guard instructs Emory.

"It ain't right. We got to bury him decent. It ain't right," Emory answers bleakly.

"I do believe this boy's out of line again," the first guard says.

"We'll take care of him tomorrah, too," the second man replies.

"Should I get ol' Tim and have him ready with the strap?"

"Nah, this boy's run his mouth too often. I think it's time for the sweat box."

"Yeah, the sweat box. I think you's right."

When Clarence collapses into his rectangle of train car where he sleeps, he drifts off trying to imagine what the sweat box is. In moments, however, the darkness takes him. The last thing he remembers is that Ezra's death is the third among the twenty-four men with whom he left Athens. Three deaths in less than two months.

17

Interviewing Seth Dean

"Good morning, Mr. Dean, might I speak with you a moment, sir?"

"Depends. I'm not sure we've met? Mr. . . . ."

"Eric Hoffman. Justice Department, United States government."

The man, who wears a black derby hat and a black vest over a white pinstriped shirt, extends his hand. Seth shakes it, although without as much firmness as he meant to.

"What can I do for you, Mr. Hoffman?"

"I'm here investigating a report my department received that certain arrests that took place in Athens in March might have been in error. You were the defense attorney for many of the accused, were you not?"

"I was."

"In fact, I believe you were the one whose letter prompted us to open an investigation in the first place."

"It's true I wrote a little note to John Ward after the trials, but since I never got a reply from him, I decided to look into things a bit on my own."

"Indeed. Might we sit down somewhere to discuss your findings?"

"Well, seeing that this is the house where I board, I guess we'll have to head upstairs to my room. Follow me."

Clopping up the well-worn but sturdy stairs, Dean leads Hoffman to his room and, extracting his key from his pocket, turns it to open the lock. "It's modest, but it suits a bachelor. I'm looking into buying a place of my own soon."

"Oh, no need to apologize, Mr. Dean, I've seen much worse."

Seth notes that Hoffman said he'd seen worse, not that he'd lived in worse. As Hoffman enters and takes a seat at the room's one table, a small square of plain wood measuring three feet on a side, he opens a briefcase and extracts pen and paper to record notes of their conversation.

"So, Mr. Dean, you say you've looked into the matter more fully on your own?"

"That's correct, sir."

"Care to mention if you discovered anything noteworthy?"

"I've learned a few things, yes. The most important for your investigation is that I could find no evidence of anything untoward or underhanded on the prosecution's part."

Hoffman pauses and looks up from his legal pad, eyebrows raised. He stares at Seth for just a moment. "You found nothing suspicious?"

"No, sir, nothing suspicious."

"What did you find, then?"

"It's true that Athens saw a large increase in criminal activity a bit less than two months ago. That's what got me thinking and worrying that something might be wrong. But I checked the arrest records—I was the lawyer for most of the accused, after all—and everything checked out as normal. The charges were legitimate," Seth states.

"When I looked at the records at the courthouse, they showed that every defendant entered a 'guilty' plea."

"Yes, they did."

"That doesn't strike you as odd?"

"I advised them to, of course, Mr. Hoffman."

"Why?"

"In every case, the prosecution had witnesses who testified that my clients had broken the law. There were no witnesses willing to testify that they hadn't. As a fellow lawyer, I'm sure you know how difficult it is to obtain acquittals when you have little evidence and few witnesses to work with and the prosecution has a great deal of both."

"Indeed, that's true. I do find it strange, however, that you represented twenty-one men within one week and couldn't find any witnesses to defend any of them."

"Have you ever been a trial lawyer in a Southern courtroom, Mr. Hoffman?"

"No."

"Let me tell you one or two things about how justice works in Alabama."

Setting down his pen for just a moment, Hoffman says, "The same as it works in any other state, I'd hope, although I'm sure you're about to tell me that isn't the case."

"In theory, yes, trials work the same everywhere, but a few aspects of justice in northern Alabama are, shall we say, peculiar to the region."

"Go on."

"The jury, most crucially. You probably know that we Southerners do not allow Negros to serve on juries. While that's a good thing as a general principle because rarely are Negros fit for such duty, it does make the jury skeptical of accepting testimony from Negros."

"And why are juries always segregated?" Hoffman inquires.

"Well, sir, finding Negros qualified to sit in the jury box is not easy to do, given all the shortcomings of their kind, both socially and in terms of education."

"I see. What else?"

"When you combine that with the additional fact that white juries tend to give more weight to testimony from whites than to testimony from Negros, you'll see how difficult, indeed, impossible, it becomes to persuade a jury that a colored man is innocent. That's why I advised all of them to enter a guilty plea, in the hope that acknowledging their guilt would result in a lighter sentence."

Pen back in hand, Hoffman just nods while he continues writing. Next, he asks, "Including a young man named Clarence Duval?"

"Yes, his case was the same as the rest."

"It didn't strike you as odd when the sheriff and deputy sheriff arrested him mere hours after his arrival in Athens?"

"Why should it? If he broke the law, which the court fairly determined that he did, it doesn't matter how long he'd been in Athens."

"It's just that you mentioned your original concerns in a note you included in his letter to John Ward."

"It was just the frustration of the moment." Dean lets out a long sigh. "That's why I sent that note saying I thought there may be something going on here. It was frustration, as much as anything else, over losing every case even before it began, and knowing I'd lost the case before it began, that caused my momentary weakness in writing those lines. I wish I could take them back. It would have saved everyone a lot of time and trouble, including you. The ways of the South frustrate me as a lawyer at times, even though as a citizen I understand why they are so necessary. But that does not mean the trials of the men were illegal or improper. The courts followed all due process of law."

"Is that all you'd like to tell me, Mr. Dean?"

"That, and I was a great fan of Johnny Ward when he played shortstop. That's the other reason I wanted to send a note to him when I saw Clarence Duval write a letter addressed to John Ward. Just reliving some old sporting memories and having a legitimate reason to contact an old hero who I admired was the other reason I wrote to him. I'm sure you understand and have a few heroes of your own, don't you, Mr. Hoffman?"

A pleasant smile. "Yes, I suppose I do. Anything else?"

"No. That's all I have to say about the matter. That's all I know."

"I'll add your statement to my notes. Can I reach you here if I have any further questions?"

"Yes, certainly. Or at my office in town. I've no plans to leave Athens by tomorrow," Dean says with a curt laugh.

"It remains to be seen if I do," Hoffman says, his own laugh a little fuller. "Should you decide there's anything else I should know that would be helpful, I'm at the Commercial Hotel."

Hoffman shakes Seth's hand, descends the stairway, and goes on his way.

Once Eric Hoffman leaves, Seth lets out a sigh of relief. Hopefully, that will be the last he sees of the Justice Department. He gives another long sigh and closes his eyes, so he can stand and think for a minute.

After what is closer to fifteen minutes, Seth decides to call on Emily Winston. She is always so optimistic; she'll know what to say to help him feel better. Naively optimistic, perhaps, but even naïve optimism might help right now. Besides that, he trusts her. They've grown closer over the past two months. Not intimate yet, but they have had many serious conversations.

Seth walks a few blocks into town and hails a carriage to take him out to Judge Winston's plantation. The ride gives him more time for reflection.

Nothing serious will ever happen between Emily and him without Judge Winston's permission, of course. In no case will Winston ever allow his daughter to marry the first ne'er-do-well lawyer to fancy her. Seth knows he must have Judge Winston's confidence and trust just as much as he'll need Emily's for a marriage ever to take place.

Is that what he wants, a marriage? He isn't sure yet, but Seth finds his thoughts drifting that direction more often lately. He's yet to discover anything about Emily that makes him think twice about it or doubt her. As far as Seth knows, she's always been honest with him. Emily defers to her father, of course. Any woman in her shoes would, and that is only natural so long as she lives under his roof.

Yet, she has a bit of an independent streak that sometimes shows in their private conversations. He'll have to test that today.

Ugh, another pothole in the road. These carriages never give the smoothest ride. Someday, Seth thinks, he'll buy a motorcar. Maybe someday soon. At least that way he'll only have himself to blame for hitting all the bumps in the road.

Well, not too soon. Automobiles are expensive; he'd done well in March, but other months of the year, it's tougher for a small-town lawyer to find enough clients to really prosper. It sure would help him professionally if he married Emily Winston. With her father's prestige behind him, getting clients would be much easier. In fact, they would come to him.

Still, that isn't a good enough reason for marriage. If they were still alive, his own parents, his mother especially, wouldn't approve of marrying someone just to get ahead in life. If he and Emily are to be happy together, they have to be in love. Are they, though? Seth isn't sure. He'd been thunderstruck when he first saw Emily, and he still enjoys her company and wants to spend time with her, but is that the same thing as love? Maybe he just needs more time to know for sure.

In any case, however bumpy the ride, it's over. Paying the driver, he walks toward the front door of Judge Winston's house and knocks for admittance.

Judge Winston himself opens the door. "Seth, come in, son. We need to talk."

Dean's eyebrows rise, and while his jaw doesn't quite drop, this isn't how he expected things to go. His heart rate jumps immediately.

Trying to recover his composure, he says, "Yes, sir. I didn't expect you'd be at home this afternoon."

"A matter of some importance has come to my attention, and you may have some part in it."

"I assume you mean the lawyer, Mr. Hoffman, from Washington?"

"Quite so. Sit down, Seth. Can I get you a drink?" the judge says while motioning Seth to one of his plush, high-backed armchairs with the beautifully woven flower motifs on its upholstery.

Seth judges it wise to decline. "Not today, Judge Winston, but thank you."

"Were you coming to call on Emily?"

"Yes, sir."

"You know, Seth, she's become rather fond of you. She talked about you after the two of you first met at that New Year's ball, and she very much enjoys seeing you." While speaking, Winston pours himself a partial glass of bourbon and sits down opposite Seth, placing the glass on a sparkling clean and polished wooden table. Unlike the table in Seth's apartment, this one is large, rectangular, and sits a dozen people comfortably.

Winston continues after sitting down. "This lawyer is a problem, as you know, although how great a problem remains to be seen. What did you talk about today?"

"He asked me about trying to defend all the convicts and why I advised all of them to plead guilty."

"What did you tell him?"

"The truth, mostly. That no colored man stands a chance in front of an all-white jury, especially when white witnesses testify against him. I told him that that aspect of Southern justice frustrates me, but I had no choice but to tell the accused to plead guilty and hope for a lenient sentence."

"Did he ask you about the letter you sent to John Ward in New York?"

"Of course." Seth had always guessed that the town postman reported information to Judge Winston. Now, he's sure of it. That the judge revealed the fact to him so casually is, of course, a threat, a demonstration of power.

Luckily, Seth suspected this question was coming and has an answer ready. "The letter I sent to Ward was fan mail. I always thought he was the king of shortstops out on the diamond, and when that man, Clarence Duval, requested I send his letter to Ward, I sent my own note telling Ward how I followed his career as a young man. That's all it said."

"Do you know who authorized the Justice Department to open this investigation, Seth?"

"No, sir, the lawyer didn't mention that in our conversation. He took me by surprise a bit, I'm afraid, since I had no warning he was here in Athens until he arrived at my boarding house."

"One of our state's senators, Edmund Pettus, wired me from Washington that Theodore Roosevelt himself asked the Justice Department to investigate this situation. You know who that is, I take it?"

"I know the name, yes. Isn't he the governor of New York state?"

"He is, yes, but he's more than that. Much more. Pettus also mentioned that some rumors around Washington say he'll be nominated as vice president on the next Republican presidential ticket."

"What does that mean for us?" Seth asks, the words almost catching in his throat.

"That Roosevelt's a very powerful man who commands more resources than we do. If he wants something investigated, he can make it happen, and I can't call in enough political favors to just send this lawyer on his way. We must stonewall the lawyer and admit nothing."

"That's what I did today. I revealed nothing about our deal, or any of the men you hold on your outlying farms against their will."

"Then you did one thing right, at least. Why did you ever send Clarence Duval's letter to John Ward in the first place? You should have destroyed it."

"How could I have known they were friends? Duval's colored and clearly never played ball with Ward because Duval's so young. He came on a train inbound from Missouri, not New York. Nothing indicated I had anything to fear." Even before Seth finishes, he knows it isn't good enough for Winston.

"Yet, here we are, with a lawyer from the Justice Department in town asking questions. I know you did it out of compassion, or, should I say, weakness. Accepting money to send Negros to prison takes getting used to, I suppose, and your conscience slipped in and overruled your practical side."

Seth looks down at the polished walnut arms of his chair, saying nothing.

"Remember what we're about, Seth. It's taken a lifetime of effort, but I'm doing my part to reverse the wrongs inflicted upon the South and its pure, Anglo-Saxon civilization by the North for all these years. You know, just as I do, that Negros are good for nothing but working and breeding. They lack all pretensions to modern, civilized life. Getting as many of them into the convict labor system as we can is for the benefit of both races."

Seth looks up, nods.

Winston continues. "Not to mention, there's money in it. For both of us. I know how you grew up. I know how much you hate farm life, the poverty you come from, and everyone around you looking down on you. There's great potential in you, Seth, and I foresee a fine career ahead of you in law but only if you learn to eliminate sentimentality. It has no place in our world. We deal only in practicality and calculating the odds."

"Yes, sir. You're correct, of course, Judge Winston."

"We may have more trouble to come, we may not. It depends on how persistent Eric Hoffman is and how badly he wants the truth. If he asks you anything further, you'll tell him nothing, understood?"

"Yes, sir."

"Very well. If you like, you can go see Emily now."

"Really?"

"Of course. Why not? That's what you came for. She's always happy to see you, and I like seeing my daughter happy. We may have difficult days ahead, but that's no reason to abandon all pleasure. Like I said, this trouble may all blow over. We must be ready in case it doesn't, and we will be, but in the meantime, enjoy each other's company."

18

Emily Joins the Game

Emily Winston slowly walks away from the back door to her father's house. The dull murmur of voices from the back of the house catches her attention again. All evening after dinner, she and Seth sat on the back porch, sipping tea and talking, until the sun went down, and Seth declared he needed to go. The evening was delightful, except for her brothers playing poker with their friends inside the house. *They are always so loud during their poker games*, Emily thinks to herself, *especially if they've had something to drink, and tonight they've had more booze than usual, if the noise level is any indication.*

Emily walks to the door of the back room where they play, intending to ask if they'll quiet down a bit, so she can rest. No wonder it's so noisy. They've left the door ajar. Again. Stupid pigs. Especially Thomas. Emily can't stand him. She's known Thomas for years, unfortunately, and he repulses her. Not only because she knows Thomas sees her as a prize to win, but also because no matter how many times she ignores him or shows her distaste, he won't leave her alone. He keeps trying to court her, but he's so *bad* at it. Between the off-color jokes, his horrible taste in clothes, and the vile drunkards he spends his free time with, Emily decided long ago she'd have nothing to do with him. He's obnoxious, too. Like at the New Year's Ball where she'd met Seth. When she and Seth left to go home afterward, he "just happened" to be outside, partly drunk, and he'd bumped into Seth intentionally and asked to escort her home.

Because Thomas and Emily's brothers have been friends since childhood, however, he keeps turning up at her father's house, tormenting her with his poor jokes, unshaven looks, and constant need to spit tobacco. Even now, Emily hears his whiny voice as she approaches the door, stopping for a moment to listen to what idiot thing he'll say tonight.

"Damnit, Robert, why's your sister so uptight? You know I treat her like royalty, and that wench just gives me the cold shoulder every time."

"Careful, Thomas," Robert replies. "You know she fancies that no-account lawyer. Cain't see why, but she does."

"Why don't she 'preciate a man of good Southern stock like myself? I's a born and bred Alabamian. That oughta count for somethin'." Thomas belches.

"Everyone in town's an Alabamian, even that lawyer," Emily hears John Clark say. Of all her brothers' friends, he is the closest to respectable and drinks the least. His restraint around alcohol probably accounts for why Emily often hears her brothers mention how well he does in the poker games.

"Aw, shit, that lawyer barely counts. He's a hill country cracker when you peel off the fancy outside. I'd whup him any day of the week," Thomas whines.

"As bad as I'm whupping you at poker?" James jests at Thomas.

"Damn straight," Thomas replies with a shrill, whiny laugh. "Pour me a bit more, would ya, Sam?"

Emily hears a chair scrape the hardwood floor. Probably Sam getting up to get the whiskey. Sam is Thomas's brother, and he's even dumber than Thomas is. At least he is halfway polite and only bothers her occasionally. She almost feels bad that he usually loses at poker because he isn't very smart. Almost.

After hearing Sam sit down again, Emily puts her hand on the door knob to go in and ask them to be quieter, bracing herself for the smell of too much alcohol, cigar smoke, and a lewd stare from Thomas. First, however, she hears her brother Robert speak again.

"Now, Thomas, you just be patient. My pops has plans for Seth Dean. You might get your chance someday if you just play your cards right."

Emily freezes, barely breathing.

"Like this? Two pair, jacks over nines," Thomas yells out, not even noticing Robert's pun.

"Damn, you got me again," Sam says. "Pair of kings."

"Hell yeah!" The clink of coins scraping across the table follows. Then, "Wait, what was you sayin' 'bout that lawyer, Robert?"

"He's in a bit of trouble with my dad. If he don't shape up, he's gonna ship out, if you know what I mean."

"Well, hallelujah, it's 'bout time the Judge did the right thing there. What he do?"

"You didn't know 'bout that Justice Department lawyer in town askin' questions?"

"Why should I? Hell, he didn't come to my farm to ask me no questions while I's hoeing corn today," Thomas says loudly, drawing a laugh from Sam.

"Seth Dean's the reason he's here. Wrote some letter to an old ballplayer named John Ward."

"Never heard of him. Whose ante is it?"

"Well, this John Ward is now a lawyer, and the Justice Department's here lookin' into things, and Seth's the reason why."

"Why don't the Judge just shoot him, then, Robert?"

"We're hopin' the Yankee lawyer goes away on his own. But if he don't, well, that's too bad for Seth, if you know what I'm sayin'."

"Is it something to do with all those Negros you and James arrested back in March?" John Clark asks.

"Yep. Seth was in on that, too, just like we were. Arrestin' niggers pays, I'll tell you. Pays mighty well. These Northern companies want workers, so we give 'em workers. We gets them colored boys off the streets, too. Everyone wins. Then there's those peons out on our land in the countryside. I don't know how much Seth knows 'bout that, even, but they's out there, workin' for nothin'."

"That's sure a good thing you got goin'," Sam says. "Someday, me and Thomas oughta do somethin' like that."

"That's why I's after Emily, stupid," Thomas puts in. "That's how we get a good thing for ourselves. Now, I just gotta get the strumpet to notice I's the man for her."

"Watch it there, Tommy, that's my sister you's speakin' about," Robert growls.

"Well, you know what I mean, right, Robert? She's a fine woman, but she oughta know a good man when she sees one."

Emily avoids retching when she hears all this, as much as she'd like to. She does, however, feel a teardrop tickle her as it slides down her cheek after they mention Seth. Her stomach, once burning in anger over how crude and ignorant Thomas is, now churns in fear. She can feel it, a ball, right in her guts. She wipes away the tear and resolves it will be the only one.

"Now, tell me how you done that again, with the, whaddya call them, peons?" Sam says.

"Done what?" James asks him.

"Get those people to work for nothin'."

"Easy. Me and Robert arrest them and make them sign a work contract for a year."

"But, some of those people have been out there for more'n a year, right?"

"Yeah. Either they make a mistake, and we penalize them with more work time, or we tell them they's still in debt and must work longer to pay off the debt."

"That sho' is smart," Sam's voice trails off.

"Now, don't go changin' the subject. I wanna know 'bout Emily. When's this lawyer gonna be outta the picture?" Thomas butts back in. "I'm in the prime of my manhood already, and if we's gonna get to breedin' some children, now's the time."

"Don't know, Thomas," Robert says. "Depends on what this Yankee lawyer from Washington does. I told you that. Now, let's play another hand of poker and stop talkin' 'bout somethin' that ain't happened yet, can we?"

Tiptoeing away from the door, once she knows she's out of hearing, Emily runs upstairs to her bedroom. Looking in her full-length mirror with the carved wooden scrollwork around the glass, she wipes away the tear stain from her face but refuses to cry again. Next, Emily sits on her bed with her head in her hands for a long while, processing all she just heard and thinking about what to do next. Her mind made up, she rises, finds her favorite walking shoes, puts a silk bonnet on her head, and walks downstairs again, heading for the front door.

One of the family's servants, Susan Anderson, meets her on her way to the door. "Evenin', Miss Emily. Is you goin' out for a walk?"

"Yes, Susan. I'm not tired yet, and I think a walk would do me good this evening."

"What should I tell the Judge if he comes home and you's not back yet?"

"Just tell him the truth. I wanted to clear my mind and went for a walk."

Eric Hoffman sits reviewing his notes from his second day in Athens. The gas lamp on his table provides decent light, but it isn't as good as the electric lighting he's become used to in Washington. Just one more way the South is behind the North. Still, the light source isn't as problematic as his investigation so far.

Thinking through everything, he doesn't have much to work with yet. The court records are, as Seth Dean pointed out, all legitimate. The accused might not have gotten a fair trial in the moral sense, but they had in a legal one. Not much to work with there. He has Sam Johnstone's suspicions, but for the moment that's all they are—suspicions.

Seth Dean surprised him. Hoffman is nearly certain Dean lied, or at least tried his best to cover up something, but he can't pinpoint what. His story of wishing he hadn't written John Ward is flimsy, for sure, but plausible, and so long as the court records show no irregularities, it doesn't really matter.

Running his hands through his hair for the hundredth time that evening and then rubbing his eyes, Hoffman decides he'd best get some rest and think about his next move in the morning. Sometimes, a good sleep is just the thing to revive his energy and generate useful ideas.

Just as he stands up to prepare for bed, Hoffman hears a knock at his door. He glances at his pocket watch. It's late—nearly nine at night. Cautiously and quietly, he strides to the door. While he deliberates on whether to open it, he hears a deep voice whisper through the wooden barrier, "Mr. Hoffman? Are you there?" A short pause, then, "Sam Johnstone told me to find you."

Hoffman decides to open the door. In front of him, in the murky yellow light given off by the hallway's lone gas lamp, stand two colored men. The first is short but stout and bows to Hoffman, doffing his flattened cloth hat in the process. "Ben Walker, sir. This is a friend's father, Dale."

Ben steps aside and motions to the man standing behind him. Dale is one of the most bedraggled men Hoffman has seen in years. Dale is also short but thin, very thin. He wears torn overalls and a tattered linen shirt so threadbare that it has nearly disintegrated off his body. Dale wears no shoes. He holds his straw hat in his hands, fingering the brim while looking down at the floor. Water soaks his overalls to about mid-thigh. A few droplets plop to the wooden floor of the hallway while he waits for Hoffman's response.

"Can I help you?" Hoffman says, not knowing how else to respond.

"Sam sent us to show you something that might help your investigation," Ben tells him.

"And what do you have to tell me?"

"Not tell, sir, show you. Will you come with us? It's a bit of a walk, I'm afraid."

"This can't wait until morning when it's light out?"

"No, sir, not if you want to see the evidence without the Judge knowing."

"Judge Winston?"

Ben nods.

"What're the chances of me getting killed on this trip?"

"You're probably safe. Dale here, he's already thrown the guard dogs off the scent, so we can sneak 'round the back way."

Hoffman looks at Dale again. The older man meets his eyes for an instant and then lowers his head again without speaking. He simply nods his head twice.

Hoffman gives a huge sigh, saying nothing for several moments.

"Sir, will you go with us?" Ben asks in a pathetic, almost pleading voice. At the same time, he glances along the hallway as if worried about someone finding him there.

Hoffman nods and sighs. "Might as well."

19

The Lion's Den

Sam Johnstone strides to the door at the sound of the knocker. He'd almost gone to bed—it's nearly nine at night, according to the grandfather clock he passes on his way to the door—but decides he might as well see who is there. On his way, just in case, he picks up the Colt he always keeps ready for unwanted visitors.

"Who's there?" he calls in a loud, but not hostile, voice.

"Emily Winston. Can I speak with you, Mr. Johnstone?"

Johnstone nearly drops the gun in his hand. Jefferson Winston's daughter? At his own home? At night? Quickly, he recovers his wits and slides his Colt into a drawer of a side table near the door. Next, Sam opens the door with a smile and a bow.

"Miss Winston, this is a surprise. What can I do for you this evening?"

"I know you're surprised to see me, Mr. Johnstone. It's been a good while since we've spoken much. May I come in for a moment?"

"Absolutely. Pardon me, Miss Emily, for not suggesting it first. You took me a bit by surprise, I'm afraid, showing up alone at this hour, but still, that's no reason to forget my courtesy. Would you like some coffee, or perhaps some tea?"

"No, Mr. Johnstone, that won't be needed."

"Here, let me help you sit down, Miss Emily. And please, you know you can always call me Sam. Just because your father and I have our differences, it's no call to insist on unnecessary formalities between the two of us."

After seeing Emily situated, Johnstone sits down opposite her in an armchair with a high back. Leaning back, elbows on the armrests, and tenting his fingers in front of his nose, he says, "Now, what can I do for you this evening? Are you here to deliver a message from your father?"

Emily takes off her silk bonnet and then sits with her hands folded politely in her lap. At Johnstone's question, she shakes her head.

"Your brothers?"

"No, Mr. Johnstone, I'm here on my own account. I doubt my family needs me to deliver messages on their behalf."

"Forgive me, Miss Emily. Like I said, the surprise of your visit has me a bit addled."

"I understand. I shocked myself a bit when I decided to come here tonight, but here I am."

"I would ask how the Judge is doing, but you're much too smart a young woman to be fooled by false courtesy. You know that he and I are not on friendly terms, so I sense you must have some unusual circumstances behind your visit."

Emily nods slowly but calmly, her gaze steady while she looks Johnstone in the eye. Although she sits up straight, her shoulders are relaxed. "Yes, I know that the two of you have had your battles in the past. That's part of why I'm here. You're among the few men in the county with the courage to stand up to my father."

"I don't know if I'd call it courage. I've yet to win, so perhaps stubbornness is the better word."

Emily gives the briefest of smiles. "Use whatever word you please. I'll go with courage."

"Courage it is, then, although I think the word applies equally to you, entering the lion's den on your own, as it were. I always thought you had a bit of an independent streak, and I admire that in people."

"I've entered the lion's den because I need to meet a lion."

"Well, since you've come to see me, an old lion will have to suffice. Why do you need to meet a lion?"

Emily gives a kind, yet nervous, smile. "Mr. Johnstone, I'm here to ask for your help."

"You want *my* help?"

"Yes."

"Your father's the most powerful man in Limestone County. What can I possibly do for you that he can't?"

"I need your help because my father is the problem."

Jefferson Winston sits in an uncomfortable wooden chair underneath the gas light in the Athens telegraph office and reads over the latest communication from Thomas Brown. The Yankee businessman requested Winston do exactly what Winston planned to do anyway. Stonewall the lawyer. Destroy evidence, if necessary. Brown stated he would see to any issues regarding the treatment of the convicts in Florida. Winston doesn't know what that means with certainty, although he has a pretty good guess. In fact, he doesn't want to know with certainty. The less he knows about that, the better.

"Thank you, Albert, for making sure I received this message tonight," Winston says to the sleepy telegraph operator. The man is easily one hundred pounds overweight, his gut jutting out so that his suspenders strain when he moves.

Albert Dunlap yawns before answering, "You're welcome, Judge Winston. You know it's my pleasure to help out a man who's done so much for Athens."

Winston turns to leave, handing Albert a dollar bill in the process. "For staying open late to help me," Winston says, nodding to the money. "You do fine work here, Albert. Maybe, with luck, you'll be over working at the courthouse someday."

"I'd like that very much, Judge Winston. Why, that's very kind of you to consider me when the time comes. If you're done, I'll lock up the office now."

Winston nods and exits the small building, its wooden door with the unadorned glass window creaking slightly as he does so. Normally, the telegraph office is not open at ten at night, but when he told Dunlap he expected a communication, of course Dunlap agreed to wait until Winston concluded his business.

On his way home, Winston thinks about how best to carry out Brown's instructions, especially about destroying whatever evidence he needs to. The records at the courthouse are solid. No need to worry about that. His sons, James and Robert, won't buckle. The weak link in the chain is certainly Seth Dean. If Dean keeps his mouth shut about the plans and deals made to round up Negros and sentence them to prison labor with the Southern Pineland Company, Winston believes they'll be in the clear. He just needs certainty the weakest link will hold. That, or he will eliminate the weak link before it breaks.

As he nears home, he realizes there might also be a third option to send Eric Hoffman back to Washington empty-handed. If it works, Dean's strength under pressure will be irrelevant. Winston decides to try that route first. In fact, he'll initiate the plan tomorrow.

After he walks up the steps to his own front door and goes inside, Winston is surprised to see his daughter, Emily, still up, sitting in his library reading under the electric light.

"You're up a little late, darling."

"Yes, father, I was just reading your book."

"My book? You've never shown interest in that book until tonight."

"I know, and I feel bad about that. I just wanted to read about how the War of Northern Aggression affected Athens, and how it ruined Southern civilization."

"And why, pray tell, are you worrying yourself with that at this hour?"

"I was just curious what it must have been like back then. How much better life must have been when all the Negros were under control, and how the war and the carpetbaggers with their bayonet rule changed everything for the worst."

"It's good to see you showing some interest in our Southern history, but it couldn't wait until daylight?"

"I suppose, but you always say I should be mindful of details, and these are details I never thought about much before."

"That's my girl," Winston says, kissing his daughter lightly on the forehead. "If your brothers did a little more reading like you and played less poker, I'd feel much better about the family's future."

"They're young, daddy. They need some fun sometimes."

"They're older than you are."

"They'll learn. I hope," Emily says with a little giggle.

"I'll see you tomorrow."

"Goodnight, daddy."

Sam Johnstone remains seated in his armchair long after Emily Winston's departure. Much of the time, he sits with his eyes closed, but he isn't sleepy. In fact, Johnstone doubts he'll sleep much at all this night. Excitement runs through him, pulsing in his veins. He can hardly believe his fortune. Hands shaking a bit, he walks to get another drink from his liquor cabinet.

Can it finally be true? Is this the opportunity he's waited nearly two decades for? Johnstone thinks about all the nights he's lain awake in bed, cursing silently at how the South's backwardness held everyone stuck in place and how he was unable to alter it one bit. All the frustration of losing his court battles with Jefferson Winston. The scowls and frowns he sees so often from the people of Athens when he goes to town. If the things Emily told him are true, he might finally get the upper hand and a little redemption.

For years, Johnstone has suspected that Winston uses peonage on his farms, of course, and he's already told the lawyer, Hoffman, about his suspicions regarding the roundup of young colored men in March. He's never had any proof of how the whole scheme works, however, until now. Oh, he could get plenty of colored sharecroppers to testify about how things are in Athens, but no white jury cares about that. The daughter of the most powerful man in Limestone County, however, is another matter entirely.

When the Justice Department lawyer showed up, Johnstone thought he'd captured a pawn who, with nurturing and some help, he could trade for a knight or a rook. Emily Winston is still a pawn, too, but she has the potential to become a queen.

Eric Hoffman trudges along the muddy creek bed, the thick, cloying clods of mud making the going slow and slippery. He's given up caring how often he's fallen. The thought also occurs to him that, if he needs to avoid suspicion, he might just have to throw this pair of pants away. He doubts the Justice Department will compensate him for that.

Ben and Dale plod alongside him. They slip nearly as often but march on without comment or complaint. The smell of damp earth and willows fills Eric's nostrils.

"We're here," Ben Walker says in a whisper just loud enough that Eric can hear him over the murmur of the water in the creek bed. "Dale crossed the creek on the other side of these fields, so the dogs and overseer will be over there looking for him, if they haven't given up already."

Eric looks out over a clearing that the moon illuminates dimly. He can see a cabin on the other side. It's run-down, to say the least, badly leaning to one side. He can see one window, although it lacks glass, and no smoke issues from the chimney. No lights come from inside, and all is quiet.

"How come Dale never talks?" Eric whispers to Ben Walker.

"He's afraid of white folks."

Eric looks over for some acknowledgment from Dale in the dappled moonlight beneath the tree sheltering them, but Dale just looks down at the ground again and won't say anything.

"And how come Dale had to run away from dogs and overseers just to meet you and find me tonight?" *Why didn't I think to ask that before agreeing to go on this little expedition?* Eric asks himself at the same time.

"Because he had to distract the overseer of this farm, so we could sneak over here and take a look."

"But, why?"

"These people are peons."

"Peons."

"You know what that is up in Washington, right?"

"Of course, I know what peonage is. But, it's not legal."

"Who cares about legal? This is Alabama," Ben tells Eric.

"How many others are there?"

Dale whispers something in Ben's ear, who then turns back to Eric and says, "Five peons work the fields here. Winston has more farms like this, though, scattered around the county. Winston owns them all."

"How does he get people to stay and farm for nothing?"

"He convicts them in court and signs them to work contracts to pay off their court costs."

"Sounds familiar," Eric says, shaking his head.

"Yeah, same thing that happened in March, except these people never left Limestone County. When their sentences are almost up, Winston, or his overseers, tells them they ran up too much debt at the local store, and they need to stay longer to pay off their debt."

"Let me guess. Winston owns the store, too, doesn't he?"

"Sure enough, he does."

"But you're not a peon. Is Dale?"

"No, I rent a farm from Sam Johnstone. That's why he told me to find you and show you this."

"Where does Dale come in?"

"His son was my best friend."

"You say that in the past tense. What happened to him?" Eric looks back and forth from Ben to Dale.

In the pale moonlight Eric sees Ben hesitate for a moment. He rubs his eyes with his fists and tries to look Eric in the eye. In a faltering whisper, Ben says, "He got shot and killed by one of Winston's overseers for supposedly trespassing on this farm. Just stumbled over here one day, and the man shot him in cold blood because he didn't want no one to know what happens here. Then, they dropped his body in Piney Creek over yonder. Dale and I heard the gunshot, sneaked over here to investigate, and followed behind when Winston's overseer dumped the body."

Eric looks over at Dale again. For the first time, Dale has his head up and looks him in the eye. The moonlight reflects off the tears.

Ben Walker continues. "After they went away, we fished the body out of the water and gave it a proper burial. It's in the graveyard of the Athens Methodist Episcopal Church now."

Finally, Dale musters his courage and speaks. "Please, suh, help them. An' help me. We got no one else," Then he looks down at the ground once more and silence descends.

Breaking the stillness of the night, across the clearing, the three men hear a dog growl and see a lantern light appear. The light approaches the unlit, run-down shack on the other edge of the clearing. Rather than the wielder of the light knocking, however, he kicks in the door to the shack and takes the light inside. A moment later, a voice screams. The light reappears when its owner drags a young man outside the shack and tosses him to the ground. The angry man sets down his lantern, pulls something small from his belt, and brings it to his lips. He kicks the frightened young man cowering on the ground while the dog continues growling at the unfortunate peon.

Because the night is quiet, and the man is loud, Eric, Ben, and Dale can hear him clearly. "You ain't planted and hoed enough cotton this week!"

"I'se sorry, suh! I tries to do bettah."

"Yeah, you tries. You tries, all right. I'm only gonna say this once, you coon. You don't shape up, you's gonna end up like that boy we put in the river last month. I know you knows about that.

171

Hell, it was on this here property that I had to shoot the dumb nigger for tresspassin'. You don't produce more cotton, you end up like him."

Another kick follows to illustrate the point.

"Yes, suh! I work harder, suh," comes the pathetic, cowering reply.

"Yeah, that's what all of you dumb coons say. This is your only warning! If you're lucky, this'll only cost you an extra couple months of work for neglectin' your duties. Now, get back in your shack and sleep. If I don't see you right early tomorrow, well, you know what that means."

The poor peon simply crawls back inside his shack without any reply. The overseer picks up his lantern, puts his flask to his lips once more and then stalks off, muttering obscenities to himself.

"All right, I think we can go now," Eric says. Not only has he seen peonage for himself, he's heard the overseer confess to murder. Now he understands Dale's fear much better.

He reaches out to shake Dale's hand and says, "Dale, it's okay," but Dale has already begun walking into the darkness to get back to his home.

Once back in his room at the Commercial Hotel, Eric writes some notes. Peonage. He had no clue it still existed. It's 1899, after all, almost a new century, but in some ways visiting northern Alabama is like going back in time five or six centuries. If what Sam Johnstone and Ben Walker have told him is correct, Jefferson Winston is the local baron running his own fiefdom. He owns the courts, the land, and, it seems, even some of the people, just like a medieval duke lording it over his serfs on some English estate. Hell, even Russia, the most despotic nation in Europe, finally ended serfdom about four decades back, and here he's just seen serfdom in Alabama.

Peonage and debt slavery in America.

Suddenly, Eric has a jolt of recognition. This is big news. Huge. If he breaks this case open and exposes conditions in Limestone County to the nation, his name will be all over the Northern papers. Maybe the Southern ones, too, although he doubts they'd present the story in the same light. But, if he plays this right, who knows how fast his star will rise in the Justice Department, especially with someone like Theodore Roosevelt in his corner. This is the type of case that makes careers, the case that comes along once in a lifetime, if a man is lucky.

Eric plans to send two telegrams in the morning. One to his superiors in the Justice Department, informing them of his suspicions, and the other to John Ward. Eric met Ward briefly before heading south to learn more about the man whose letter started the case in motion, Clarence Duval. Besides describing Clarence Duval, however, Ward had also told him of another interested party in Duval's case, a Pennsylvanian who knew both Ward and Duval and had volunteered his help, should it become necessary. Hoffman believes the time has come.

20

Cutting Firewood

The day after the death of Ezra Tompkins, Clarence limps back to his cell on the railroad car. Hands blistered, skin burning from the biting flies, stomach growling in hunger like always, he reaches the clearing where the railroad car awaits. Soaked in sweat and smelling like a man who hasn't bathed in several days, he drops to one knee when he looks at Emory Wilson.

At the edge of the clearing Emory hangs from a wooden crucifix, arms held in place by leather belts. His head droops forward onto his chest, and his eyes have swollen shut.

But the worst thing is the blood and the swelling of the rest of his body. Emory's skin, blistered everywhere, puffs out like someone just punched and bruised every inch of his body. And he's covered in bloodstains. Emory's clothes, arms, legs, face, everything, is stained crimson. It drips from his cheeks, from the ends of his fingers, from his toes, everywhere. Open sores cover his swollen limbs.

A guard stands next to Emory's body, the guard's arm around a box about the size of a coffin but made from tin. Although it has hinges for the lid, the only other opening is a small circle right about where someone's nose would be if they lay down inside.

Once everyone has returned from their day's work, the guard says, "See this, boys? You see this? This is what happens when you don't follow orders the first time. You gets the sweatbox for five hours."

He punches Emory's leg. Emory's lips move, but no sound comes out louder than an incoherent whisper.

"That's right. This nigger here complained, and he got what was comin' to him. Five hours in the box. If he does it again, it'll be ten. He's still alive right now, but I bet he wishes he weren't."

Another punch lands on Emory. His head lifts almost imperceptibly before dropping back down. A couple fingers twitch.

"Sleep well, you dogs."

While other guards lock down all the prisoners, the one who spoke unties the leather belts holding Emory in place. He slumps to the ground and lies there. Two guards drag him to his cell in the train car while the German shepherd yowls maniacally. It only stops barking to lick the bloodstained ground where Emory fell.

As soon as he's locked in his place, the blackness of sleep overcomes the shock and takes Clarence instantly.

Just like two days ago, the following morning Clarence awakes to the sound of men vomiting. Matthew is one of them again. Clarence looks over at Elijah, who just shrugs.

"He was better yesterday, but this looks just as bad as two days ago," Elijah says to Clarence.

The dog bays uncontrollably while the men suffer. Clarence tries to find Emory Wilson. Emory's not so much moving as lying on his side twitching. His blood is dry now, caked to his body and clothes. A low moan comes from his mouth.

Clarence also looks at Tom Morton. Tom scratches his head, and some of his hair falls out. Next, Tom crawls on his hands and knees to the bucket where the men relieve themselves, so he can take care of business.

Before long, the guards arrive to take the men into the pine forest. One of them looks around, scowling while he bites his lower lip. He spits a stream of tobacco juice and says, "Damn, the uppity buck can't work today. He was supposed to chop wood for the furnace that heats the turpentine." The man looks around, jaw working over his chaw. "You, there!" he says pointing at Clarence. "You'll have to take his place. This way."

Clarence finds himself led in the opposite direction of where he usually goes. This section of forest is right near the camp, or at least it used to be. The clearing created by felling trees now stretches several hundred feet from their camp's edge.

About a dozen men, one or two from each train car brought into the forest, make up the woodcutting crew, and Clarence doesn't know any of the men he's with today. No one talks, either. The guards pair them off and give each pair of men a crosscut saw. The prisoners trudge numbly to a nearby tree and, two men to a tree, begin sawing away until the tree falls over. A handful of armed guards on horseback watch the woodcutters.

A few trees are down already when Clarence arrives, their branches lopped off and their trunks mostly sawed into sections. He supposes this must be where the work finished yesterday evening. He's not assigned to work on one of those trees, however. Instead, a guard with a cigarette in his mouth grunts and motions with his shotgun to a nearby standing tree.

At first, Clarence wonders how the men know which trees to cut and which to leave because a few trees remain in the area that no one's cut down, but he soon finds out. When he and his partner for the day reach their assigned tree, Clarence sees that yesterday one of the guards pounded a metal spike a few inches into the tree, indicating it was next. Once the men start sawing, the guard comes by and removes the spike, placing it through a loop in his belt. Clarence guesses there must be an ideal thickness of tree for use in the turpentine furnaces, and that's how the guards mark which trees fit the profile.

It takes a good while, but eventually he and his partner succeed in getting a tree on the ground using their crosscut saw. The man doesn't say a word to Clarence the entire time, barely even looking up other than to make sure they're working in tandem with the saw. When the tree finally topples, crashing to the forest floor, he gives a grunt of satisfaction and gives Clarence a brief nod of the head. Clarence nods back, but that's all. He enjoys smelling the pleasant scent of fresh-cut pine, but quickly the pleasure fades because he must continue working.

Next, it's time to cut off the branches with an ax, so the lengths of the trunk will fit inside the furnace. This takes far more time than Clarence ever considered it might, and within an hour, he's sweating just as badly as he ever did while extracting the turpentine. He's skilled at handling an ax by now, but Clarence's hands still curl into the shape of a "C" even when he puts the ax down for a moment to wipe his brow. He tries to uncurl his right index finger, but it curls up again the moment he lets go with his left hand.

Eventually, the wood piles up in a central woodpile, and a horse and wagon appear to haul it back to the furnace where other prisoners boil the turpentine. Late in the afternoon, which has been mercilessly hot, Clarence and his partner haul another heavy section of pine trunk to the pile. Just as they let go, their section landing atop some others with a dull thunking sound while chips of bark scatter from the collision, Clarence stands up tall to wipe the perspiration from his face. Then, he walks back to grab another section of trunk.

Another pair of men do the same to the tree they've felled a few feet away, hauling the sections to the central woodpile one by one. Clarence notices the guards have their back turned to where he's standing. At that moment, one man from the other pair says to his partner, in a loud whisper, "Now! Do it now!"

"You sure?" his partner whispers back.

"Yes, damnit, now!"

Clarence sees the first man put his left foot on a section of log and then nod to his partner. The partner raises his ax and swings it down with force, connecting with the first man's foot just below his ankle. Blood sprays. Clarence hears bone crack. The injured man lets out a scream of continual obscenities and falls over in pain, where he continues screaming from the ground. Blood spurts in whatever direction his left leg flails while the man wails and writhes. Clarence even sees the rest of the man's severed foot, flesh, bone, ligaments, everything, land a few feet away. The toes of the severed foot continue twitching.

In mere moments, guards arrive to investigate. "What happened?" the first calls out commandingly.

"Ain't it obvious?" his partner answers. "This dumb coon is so bad and lazy with the ax, he cut his own foot off."

"Well, he cain't work like that," the first guard says. "I'll drag him back to camp and see if the doc can get him patched up. What a clumsy fool."

The guard dismounts and pulls out a rope from his saddle bag, which he tries to loop around the injured man's chest. When the guard approaches and hauls the wounded man up, he falls into the guard's arms. Caught off balance, the guard falls into the wood pile, landing on his right side. In the process, Clarence sees something shiny and metal fall from his belt.

Cursing furiously, the guard flings the injured man to the ground and then stands up and clubs him on the shoulder with his shotgun. "Get off me, you clumsy nigger!" he shouts as the man continues yelling, crying out for help. "Now look what you's done. I gots bloodstains on mah clothes 'cause of you!"

Still furious, he loops his rope under the armpits of the wounded convict and cinches the knot, hard. Finally, the guard mounts his horse and drags the wailing prisoner back to the camp, who continues screaming and bawling all the while. A trail of shiny red blood marks their path.

"Take a break for food!" one of the remaining guards shouts from horseback. Each man gets a biscuit today to go with a couple of potatoes.

Clarence ends up sitting in the dirt only one man away from the prisoner who severed his partner's foot. The man between them whispers, just loud enough that Clarence can hear, "What happened? Did he really cut off his own foot?"

"No, he told me to do that to him," the second man whispers back.

"He *wanted* you to cut his foot off? Has he lost his mind?"

"Maybe so. But he's hopin' that with no foot they won't make him work no more."

"He had you cut off his own foot rather than work? What's he gonna do when we gets out of here?"

"Who says we ever gonna get out of here?" the second man points out plaintively. "Men is dyin' left 'n right around this camp. Guess he figured on puttin' an end to his misery sooner rather than later. Maybe he the smart one."

"You think he'll live?"

"We'll find out tonight, I suppose."

"You think his plan'll work?"

"Don' know 'bout that, either."

"Shut up, there, no talking. You knows the rules," a guard comes over and growls in between mouthfuls of biscuit. He prods one of the prisoners with the butt of his gun for emphasis.

It doesn't take long to chew the bit of food the prisoners get, but while he does, Clarence considers what the man who injured his partner said. Maybe they aren't going to get out of here. Perhaps the sentence to work off their fines is only a ruse to keep them working until conditions kill them. That would be almost like the miners in Butte who Thomas Healy used to work with.

He knows he can't think that way, however. He's trusted to his luck before, and, in the end, his luck has never failed him. Clarence thinks back on his past. He's been homeless, fallen into a mineshaft, fallen from a hot air balloon, been bitten by a King Cobra, escaped burning alive on Mount Vesuvius, gotten involved in a murder plot, was shot in the leg, nearly drowned once, killed a man larger than he in single combat, and escaped enlistment in the U.S. Army. He can hold on and survive the pine forests of Florida.

Once the brief break to eat ends, Clarence's first move is to walk straight to the woodpile. It's still there! He bends over and, in the name of moving the injured man's ax out of his way, makes sure the guards aren't looking and picks up and hides the metal spike that fell from the guard's belt. It takes him three tries to pick it up because his fingers still won't uncurl, but, eventually, he gets it.

The day continues, dreadfully hot. Clarence decides he prefers extracting turpentine to cutting wood because this is even more exhausting. Every time he raises the ax to lop off another branch, pain shoots through his shoulders and beads of sweat scatter. His hamstrings and butt are sore, too, from bending over to pick up the heavy sections of wood he's cut and carrying them to the central pile.

By evening, he's beat. Clarence rests for a breath before every swing of the ax. Every section of wood he picks up, he walks numbly to where he drops it on the pile. He barely sees the other men and hasn't spoken in hours. Too much effort.

Finally, it's dark and time to stop. "Can't have no more clumsy fools cuttin' themselves tonight," one guard jokes while the men shuffle back to their cells on the railroad cars.

When Clarence arrives, he sees Bill Baker, or, rather, what used to be Bill Baker, hanging from a tree, noose around his neck. Bill's body dangles there, arms hanging limply at his sides, eyes shut, slowly swaying back and forth in the gentle breeze. He's missing three of the fingers on his left hand. Bloody stumps are all that's left, oozing blood from where someone severed them just above the knuckle.

Bill is another of the men who'd been very sick and vomited in recent days. He was very skinny and frail even when he arrived at the camp. *Now we're down to twenty*, Clarence thinks to himself. He doesn't know if the guards murdered Bill, or if he'd died from his sickness first and then the guards had hung him up after he died just to send all the prisoners a message. As if that is necessary at this point. Either is equally possible.

Before long, Clarence sits chained alongside Elijah and Matthew like usual. "How was cutting timber?" Elijah asks.

"Bad. If they give you the choice, just pass," Clarence replies. "How did Matthew do today?"

"Poorly. He got some lashes because he was too sick and kept falling. So did some of the other sick men. The guards taunted him when he cried. At least he couldn't hear them."

"Tell him I'm sorry."

"He knows that already, but I'll tell him."

Elijah begins signing to Matthew, who smiles at Clarence as best he can through the haze of pain. Just like he did with Clarence several weeks back, Elijah tries to clean his brother's back the best he can.

"A guy I was working with lost his foot today," Clarence whispers to Elijah.

"The guards cut it off?"

"No. His partner did."

"On purpose?"

"Yeah. The guy told his partner to cut his foot off. He hoped he'd get excused from working without his foot."

"Did he?"

"For today. I don't know if he'll even live, he lost so much blood."

"How do you tell someone to cut off your own foot, Clarence?"

"You get in a spot like we're in, that's how."

Elijah only shakes his head. "What is this place doing to us, Clarence? I should be horrified, but I barely feel anything. It's like, with everything we've seen, something that bad barely even registers anymore."

"None of the woodcutters even said a word after it happened. I think everyone is too exhausted to feel empathy."

"That's what I mean. If the guards don't kill us, or the heat, or the insects, or the snakes, or the lack of food, this type of work destroys a person from the inside out. It takes away your ability to even feel bad for other people or worry about anyone besides yourself."

"We got to stick together, Elijah, or we're all going to die separately."

"You're right. And we need to look out for Tom even more, somehow. I don't know how much longer he'll last."

The guards have locked all the men in place by now, so they call for quiet.

Elijah just gives Clarence the look meaning they'll talk again tomorrow.

Clarence lies down to sleep like the others, but for once, he doesn't sleep right away. Fighting the blackness of sleep and exhaustion with every ounce of willpower he can muster, he waits until everyone is asleep and then sits up and pulls out the metal spike he garnered today. He doubts anyone will wake up by this point; Clarence hasn't woken during the night in weeks. As quietly as he can, he puts the tip of the metal spike to the bottom of the pin that serves as the hinge of his foot shackles. Gently at first, he taps the spike and pin together, the spike braced on the floor of the railroad car. The tapping sounds unbelievably loud in the quiet of the forest, but no one wakes. The pin doesn't budge, however. It's slightly rusted from the rain and humidity. Clarence realizes he needs more force.

Deciding he may as well risk it, Clarence slams the manacle onto the spike. The clanging echoes fill the night air. Instantly, the German shepherd leaps up, barking furiously at the prisoners.

Clarence drops down just as instantly, pretending to be asleep, but then sits up like he's just awakened. After a couple minutes, he sees some lantern lights approach as several guards come running. The dog howls away, presumably scaring off every creature within five miles.

Soon the guards arrive, lanterns ablaze and shotguns pointed. "What's going on here?" one asks.

"I don't see anything wrong," another replies.

"Give me a count!" the first man barks.

A couple guards board the train car, pointing fingers while they count heads. "We both get twenty, sir," one of them says. "That's the right number, isn't it?"

"Yeah, twenty is right. Must be a false alarm. All right, men, that's it. False alarms are the price you pay for having a good guard dog."

After a while and a little grumbling about the dog waking them again, the prisoners settle down and return to sleep. But not Clarence. Enough moonlight shines into the train car to see the result of his effort. The pin holding his manacles together popped up so that he can grab it. Gently, ever so gently, he slides it out and then puts it back in place.

Clarence smiles for the first time in weeks. He's learned two things. First, he now has the means to free himself. Second, he knows it took the guards nearly six minutes to respond to an alarm.

21

Joining Forces

"You look like you barely slept last night," Alannah Walker says to Sam Johnstone.

"That's because I didn't," he replies. It's true. Johnstone's eyes have that irritated feeling one gets after a short night of sleep, and his head buzzes a bit, too. Not a headache, just the fatigue of too much thinking.

She pours him some coffee, but he waves it away.

"That bad?" Alannah asks, standing with the coffee cup in her hand, faint curls of steam wafting upward.

"How did Ben's meeting with the lawyer go?"

"Well."

"He's going to look into the peonage on Winston's farm?"

"Ben said so."

"I'll take a glass of bourbon, Alannah."

"At eight in the morning? How bad was last night, Sam?"

"I just lay in bed all night, thinking of possibilities."

"Our plans are in that much trouble already?"

"No. I apologize, Alannah, I should have told you from the beginning of this conversation. It's just that I've been so busy thinking things through, I forgot I need to explain. I had an unusual visitor last evening after you went home for the night."

"Who was it?"

"Emily Winston."

Alannah Walker's mouth forms an "O" even as she drops the coffee cup. The delicate porcelain shatters all over Johnstone's hardwood floor, the steaming liquid splashing everywhere.

"My goodness!" she gasps. "I'm so sorry, Mr. Johnstone, so very sorry. It's just that of all the names you could have said, that was about the last one I expected to hear."

Even though he now has a couple of light brown stains on his white pants leg, Sam waves away her apology. "No need to apologize, I should have told you to set everything down before I spoke. Here, let me help you clean up a bit."

"Oh my, oh dear," Alannah continues fussing even as she runs to get a broom and rags to clean things up.

Once the two have the spill taken care of, Sam says, "Okay, now, let's try sitting down this time, shall we? I couldn't believe it, either, but last night Emily Winston came to the house."

"To threaten you?"

"No."

"To try to bribe you on her father's behalf?"

"No."

"What for, then, Sam?"

"She wants my help."

Alannah just stares at him. If she had another cup of coffee in her hands, she probably would drop that one, too, Sam thinks.

"Now I can see why you didn't sleep last night," she says after several seconds.

"Indeed. She is, shall we say, worried that the presence of Eric Hoffman in Athens may result in some unfortunate things coming to pass and asked my help in trying to prevent them."

"Why ask you? Her father can do almost anything he wants to."

"Not when he's involved in the middle of things like he is this time."

"Do you think she's lying to set you up? Draw you out and get you to show your plans before they're complete?"

Sam looks down at the floor, closes his weary eyes a moment, kneads his brow with his fingers, and gives a deep sigh. "I don't think so. I could be wrong, of course, and it wouldn't be the first time, but I didn't get that sense from her when we talked. Even though she showed great composure, I sensed genuine fear about what to do. A little bit like some of the men I fought with in Mexico, just before they went into battle the first time. They tried to look confident on the outside, but their tone and eyes told me whatever was about to happen frightened them and they didn't know what to expect. Emily had that look in her eyes. I thought she was sincere in what she said."

"I know you spoke to her and I didn't, but I still find that hard to believe."

"Maybe it is. Have you ever met Emily, Alannah?"

"No. I've seen her around town once or twice while running errands for you, but I've never spoken to her beyond saying hello."

"I've met her a few times in the past. Mostly at the formal local events that I attend out of duty because of being a prosperous landowner in a not-so-prosperous place like Athens. And we attend the same church in town."

"Why do you stay at First United Methodist? You know Winston runs the affairs of that church in almost the same way he runs the courts."

"You know my stubborn side. I'm not going to back down and switch churches just because of him."

Alannah smiles.

Continuing, Sam says, "I don't doubt Emily's loyalty to her father, but she also has an independent side to her, and I believe she's much smarter than most give her credit for."

"You're going to trust her, then?"

"I'm thinking about it. I need to get more information."

"I know I don't need to remind you of the risks."

"I'm quite aware that trusting her might be dangerous. However, if she is sincere, think of all it would mean, Alannah. Bringing

Winston down would justify the last twenty-five years of my life's work and undo at least a little of the damage he's done to lives in Limestone County."

"Well, you know I'll go along with whatever you decide, Sam."

"I also think I owe it to Elijah and Matthew Maxwell. They are good people. You know as well as I that they didn't commit any crimes and never should have been in court."

"True. Matthew is the gentlest man I know."

"If I have to take a risk to help them see justice, maybe it's time to take some risks."

Alannah gets up and hugs Sam. "I suppose I should get back to my work now."

Sam nods. "Tell Ben to contact Hoffman this evening. It may be time to talk with him again tomorrow."

After ending the conversation with Alannah, Sam remains hopeful. Although about forty years younger than he, Alannah has been his housemaid for over a decade. Her grandmother had been among the people Sam owned but manumitted from slavery in 1857. The grandmother had been his housemaid as a slave, but because Sam always treated her well and offered her good pay after freeing her, she'd stayed on. Alannah's mother had done the same until she died about ten years ago, at which time Alannah took over her mother's job.

She's learned well and been a faithful friend since she was a young girl. Alannah is tall, which Sam attributes to her mother's excellent cooking, and has lustrous long, dark hair, although usually she keeps her hair up, so it doesn't interfere with her work. Still, Sam thinks, if Alannah ever got a chance to dress up in the formal evening gowns he saw women wear at social gatherings in Athens, she'd impress anyone who could look past her skin color with her grace, manners, and beauty. He thinks of her almost like his own granddaughter. It feels good to Sam to have younger people nearby, people to remind him of the vigor and spontaneity of life that he'd once had himself. Because he's never married, it's as close to having his own family as he'll get in his waning years.

Sam also feels a little sorry for the woman. Her husband, Ben, is a good man, but between them, they've been unable to conceive any children of their own. Their friends are their family, and when one of Winston's thuggish overseers shot Ben's friend Walter while Walter supposedly trespassed onto Winston's property, Ben was devastated and wouldn't leave his house for more than a week.

He puts his head in his hands, elbows on knees, and rubs his temples again. Perhaps this is the time for a showdown, the final series of moves on the chessboard.

Eric Hoffman sits at the bar in the local drinking establishment creatively known as Ted's Saloon. It isn't far from the Commercial Hotel, just a walk north on Monroe Street, across the Louisville & Nashville railroad tracks and then left on Market Street. On the way, Eric passed the railroad depot and turned west onto Market before reaching the cotton and guano warehouse. Guano. Eric never imagined that solidified bird waste might have value, but it does. He isn't sure what the magic ingredient is in guano that makes it so useful for fertilizer, but he knows that's what farmers use it for.

Before reaching the saloon, Eric finds the 500 block of Market Street features a barbershop, butcher, tin shop, law office, two groceries, and a bank, most of the buildings of solid brick construction. About half of the buildings are one story while others, like the saloon, are two.

The beer isn't anything to speak of, at least not to speak well of, but it's his first drink in days and Eric is thirsty. Well, make that his first four drinks in days. He'd spent the morning writing out his cables and then sending them. The first, as planned, went to Washington. Eric cabled that he'd run into a situation that could be big, that might involve violations of federal peonage laws, and that he'd report back when he had more evidence and ask for more resources and manpower at that time, should he find it necessary.

He also suggested the Southern Pineland Company might be involved and the department should consider preparing an investigation into its activities.

The second telegraph went to John Ward in New York City. Hoffman informed Ward that Clarence Duval is not in Athens but that Duval's case is alive and well. He also told Ward that it is time to bring a mutual friend into the investigation and that he'd meet that friend in two days in Nashville, as everyone involved had prearranged.

Feeling satisfied with himself and suddenly hopeful about his investigation, Eric asks for one more beer, drinks it, and departs for his hotel room. When he gets to the front desk of the hotel, he sees the same man he met on the day of his arrival. He still doesn't know the young man's name, so Eric simply says, "Hello, my friend."

"Hello, suh, how's your stay been?"

"Just fine, so far, just fine. This is a superb establishment you help run."

"Why, thank you, suh. You's sure friendly and polite for a Yankee."

"I'm going to have to leave town on business for about two days, but I'd like to keep my room for when I return. I've yet to finish my work here. It may be several more days, in fact. You Southerners can drive a hard bargain on cotton sometimes."

"Cotton's what we do, suh."

"Indeed. Can I arrange to continue paying you for my time here, just to be sure? I really do like my room."

"Of course."

"Thank you, my good man. Evening." Eric tips his derby hat to the young man and strides away.

"Good evening to you, too, suh."

Eric's almost to his door when he sees a woman exit a room on the other side of the hallway. "Evening, miss," he says, doffing his hat again.

"And good evening to you."

The woman starts to walk by, then turns back and purrs to Hoffman in a deep Southern drawl, "Say, are you from up North somewhere? You don't talk like you's from the South."

"New York, ma'am, by way of Washington."

"New York! The city or the state?"

"New York state."

"Ah don't believe Ah've ever met a man from New York. What's it like there?"

"How much time do you have?"

"All the time in the world, sugar. You see, Ah'm supposed to meet my cousin and her husband, and we're going to Hot Springs, in Arkansas, to try out the waters there, but they won't get here until tomorrow afternoon, so Ah'm stuck waiting for them in this nothin' town."

"Well, I'm leaving town tomorrow, too. Maybe I'll see them when the train comes through."

"So, you've got time to kill, just like Ah do?" The words drip from her mouth like molasses.

"I'm afraid so."

"Care to join me for a drink, then? It's been ever so hot today, and Ah think Ah could use one."

Eric gives the woman a closer look. She's a few years younger than he and dressed in a rather attractive light blue summer dress. It's cut low across the chest. Not scandalously low, like a prostitute might wear, but low enough to give a hint of what's underneath. Her hair is blond and medium length, pinned in the back, and she's wearing light makeup to emphasize the paleness of her skin. The woman's face reminds Eric of his deceased wife ever so slightly, right down to the clear blue eyes.

"That's a nice offer, miss, but I think I've had my limit for today."

"Already, honey? The sun's not even down yet. Surely you can handle one more? Ah've always heard that y'all Northerners can handle liquor almost as well as Southern boys can."

"You sure it's not the other way around?" Eric doesn't know why he said that. Although his family is German, and thus supposedly prone to beer drinking, he's never bought into the idea that certain nationalities lean toward certain behaviors more than others.

"Why don't you show me, sugar? You look like a big, rugged man who can handle his liquor." The woman says this with her hands at her waist and with her hips pushed forward just a bit. It's a challenge, he realizes, but a challenge with the sweetest smile Eric's seen in years.

"No. Like I said, I've had enough," he says with a little smile of his own.

"Aww," she says with a pouting frown that Eric knows is fake because it's followed immediately by another seductively sweet smile. "Can Ah at least come in and sit down? These small Southern towns are dreadfully boring places, and Ah don't have anyone to pass the time with."

"I suppose. The room has two chairs. What's your name, by the way?"

Once seated, the woman says, "Louella. Louella Glennon. And yours?"

"Eric Hoffman." Seated across the table, he can smell her lovely perfume clearly. The scent, vaguely floral, isn't overpowering. More like pleasantly noticeable.

"You have any family, Mr. Hoffman?"

"Not anymore. I was married once, but my wife died before we ever had children. Here's a picture of her." He unclasps the locket he wears around his neck and shows Louella the tiny photograph.

"Why, she's just the prettiest, sweetest little thing. Can Ah ask how it happened?" Now Louella's face is sad as can be, her big, blue eyes capturing Hoffman's own gaze.

"Typhoid fever," he says before glancing down and putting the locket back around his neck.

"And you never remarried? Surely you must have had your share of chances?"

Such pretty blue eyes, Eric thinks again. "Never wanted to."

"Maybe you just haven't found the right person? Ah bet women would chase after you if you'd let them, sugar."

Eric realizes he's the one answering all the questions, which doesn't seem quite right to him. He tries to turn the tables. "And how about you? I think I could say the same about you, and yet here you are, on your own."

"Oh, Ah've had some suitors, sure enough. But, you know how Southern men can be. They all want me to just stay at home all the time, cooking, cleaning, watching the house. Ah'm not ready for that life yet. Ah love adventure, and taking risks, and doing unexpected things. Everyone tells me it's not right for a woman to think like that, but it's my life, right?"

She's so much like his former wife, Eric thinks to himself. Louise Hoffman was training to be a nurse with the Red Cross right before the typhoid killed her. He says to Louella, "I'm only speaking for myself, but I don't think that's a bad thing. My wife wanted to be a nurse, even though some of her family said she was wasting her time learning a profession."

"Well, that's something we have in common. We like adventurous people. Ah'm sure she was the perfect woman for you. But, Ah know other people like that in the world, too. Ah'll bet you could find another one if you looked around a bit."

To Eric, Louella just sounds so sad and sympathetic as she leans across the table slowly, folded arms resting on the table beneath her chest, giving Eric a peek at the tops of her breasts.

"I don't know about that," Eric says, looking down at the table again while leaning over his own folded arms.

"Sure there are, darling, you just have to open your eyes, so you can see them when they're right in front of you." She drawls the words like honey.

When Eric looks up again, she caresses his cheek with her left hand and leans in closer, her right arm reaching behind her back.

Then comes the knock at the door.

"Mr. Hoffman? Mr. Hoffman, suh?"

Louella's hands return to the table while Eric looks up with a start. It's the voice of the young man from the front desk.

"Yes?" Eric calls out.

"There's a colored boy says he here to see you, suh. Name of Ben Walker. He says you knows him, and it's important."

"Tell him I'll be out to meet him in a moment," Eric replies. "I'll meet him at your desk."

"Okay, right away, suh. I'll tell him."

Eric looks over at Louella Glennon. "Business. Sorry."

She makes the cutest disappointed face he can imagine. "You sure it can't wait? Ah meant what I told you just now."

Eric closes his eyes a moment, sighs deeply, and then opens them with a smile. "No, I'm afraid it can't wait. I need to go. It's a shame the evening must end this way, but I think you've given me some good advice. When I get back to Washington, I'll remember it."

"Whoever you meet will be a very lucky woman."

"I apologize again for ending things so quickly. Enjoy your trip to Arkansas tomorrow. I hear the baths in Hot Springs are wonderful," Eric says while looking in the mirror and straightening his tie. He adjusts his vest and checks his cufflinks. Perfect.

"Ah'll leave first," Louella says.

"Right."

She stands up, goes to the door, and peers down the hallway. "All clear. Good luck, sugar."

Eric watches while she walks back to her hotel room and goes inside, and then he strides to the front desk to meet Ben Walker. There's another man at the desk checking in.

"Evening, Mr. Hoffman," Ben says to him.

"You have something new for me, Ben?"

"Yessir. Mr. Johnstone wants to talk with you again, sir."

"Lead the way," Eric says while placing his derby on his head.

After Hoffman leaves, the other man finishes checking in and walks down the hallway. After thanking the desk clerk and leaving his suitcase in his room, he goes next door and enters Louella Glennon's room.

"Didn't work, did it, Rose?"

"No."

"What happened?" he asks while he takes two wedding rings from his pocket, placing one on his left hand and handing the other to her.

"I couldn't get him to go for drinks."

"I noticed. I had ol' Petey all ready to drug his drink, so you could bring him back here and we could plant the evidence on him after he passed out. What happened after that?"

"Plan B, of course. I tried to seduce him, and would have, but then that stupid desk clerk interrupted."

"Damn, I was wonderin' what happened with that. I was checkin' in, like we planned, and I was going to sit in my room with the door ajar. When you two got goin', you was gonna yell, and I was gonna burst in and save you from him. But that colored boy showed up and ruined the plans."

"Yeah, that about says it. Damn. It sure would've been nice to pull this off. Judge Winston offered us a nice sum of money to frame that Yankee."

"I just wish you coulda made the plan go faster, Rose."

"What was I supposed to do? Walk up to him and say, 'Take me to bed you handsome Yankee?' It's not like I'm some loose woman who does this every night."

"Woulda worked on me, 'cept without the Yankee part," he says with a smile as he leans in for a kiss.

"Well, we gotta make ourselves scarce for a while now. Can't let that lawyer see me again since I told him I was on my way to Arkansas."

"Yeah, well, I ain't spent much time in Huntsville, so I guess we'll see what it's like over there while we lay low for a bit. You go check out. I'll toss my bags out the window, and we'll get goin'."

Jefferson Winston closes the brass clasps on his brown leather briefcase and sighs. It was a long day. Between routine business, a couple mundane court cases, and this whole business with the Justice Department, there's plenty to worry about. It's late, past dark, and he's hungry.

He supposes he'll have to wait until morning to hear the results of his plot to compromise the lawyer. Rosie Bates and her husband had helped him under similar circumstances a couple years earlier, so he knew she was capable. In return, he'd found in their favor when a small fire started on their property and burned down a neighbor's tool shed. The neighbor sued for damages from the fire, but Winston ruled the fire started on the neighbor's property instead.

Just when Winston grabs his fedora and turns to leave, an excited knock comes at his door. "Judge Winston, it's me, Albert Dunlap! I have news for you, sir."

"Come in, Albert, come in. What can you tell me?"

Dunlap comes inside Winston's office, panting hard, his enormous belly heaving up and down. He wipes some sweat from his brow as he gasps out his news.

"Well, you see, Judge Winston, that lawyer from Washington came in today and sent some telegrams. I don't know all that they said, but I know he sent one to Washington and another to New York."

Winston nods. Checking with his superiors to inform them how the case was going and then probably checking in with John Ward, whoever that was, in New York City. All Winston knows about John Ward is what Seth Dean told him—that Ward used to play professional baseball and now is a lawyer. Winston doesn't know much about baseball and doesn't care if he ever does. Following baseball isn't going to sell any cotton or buy any new pieces of land. "Thank you, Albert, that's good to know."

"But there's more, Judge. A telegram came for you, as well. That's why I ran right over to tell you."

"From Thomas Brown in Boston, I take it?"

"No, from Pittsburgh."

Interesting. He didn't expect any communications today and doesn't know anyone in Pittsburgh.

"Well, here you are, Judge. I guess I'll be going now," Albert says.

"Not without this first, my friend," Winston says while reaching into his pants pocket, extracting two quarters, and placing them in Dunlap's meaty hand.

"Why, thank you, Judge. I'll report back again if anything else happens down at the telegraph office, sir."

"I appreciate that, Albert, I truly do. Thank you for your help."

As Dunlap hustles back down the corridor, his wrinkled suit bulging from his extra weight and sweat stains showing through the fabric on his back, Winston takes his fedora back off and decides to sit down and read the telegram.

22

Hoffman's Trap

"Thanks for meeting on such short notice, John," Eric Hoffman says to the tall man seated across from him in the Nashville, Tennessee, café on Friday, June 2, 1899. The man wears a classic dark suit coat with a white collared shirt beneath, set off by a navy-blue tie with white dots. Clean-shaven, his hair has thinned just a bit on top, but most of it is still there. The man's eyes are intense, but not in a threatening way, Eric notes.

"My pleasure. I never spoke much with Clarence at John Healy's funeral like I meant to, but when John Ward and Sally Healy told me about what Clarence did in Montana, I decided he'd earned whatever help I could give him."

"You're on board with my plan, then? All of it? It may take some time for everything to play out."

"Absolutely. Running a bank really isn't that exciting of a job, anyway. In fact, I'm thinking of starting a bridge construction company, too, just to try something new, but that can wait until this is over."

"It will be easy enough for you to get the funding to start your company, I'd imagine."

"Yes, I have a feeling that John Tener, president of the Charleroi Savings & Trust Company, will get along very well with John Tener, president of the Mercantile Bridge Company," the tall man says with a laugh.

"You've earned quite a reputation for your skill with money over the years. Didn't Al Spalding make you the treasurer for his tour back in '88? How old were you at the time?"

"I was twenty-five when the tour began. Somehow, I just seem to have a knack for finance."

"I'm so glad you're here. It's perfect. You don't even have to act to play this role in the investigation. Just be who you are: a bank president who's interested in investing in Southern agriculture."

"Hopefully, I can help. If something's happened to Clarence, I'm pleased to do my part. And, from what you've told me, it sounds like he's not the only one who may be in trouble."

"Winston agreed to meet with you?"

"Yeah. I sent him a telegram the same day you contacted me. Yesterday afternoon he sent a telegram back agreeing to meet. Perfect timing. I'll arrive in Athens tomorrow, one day before you, so we won't be on the same train. From what you tell me, this judge is a smart man, so it's best no one suspects that we're working together until we have the information we need. I told him I was visiting various places in the South, looking for investment opportunities and businesses to partner with to expand my bank's portfolio, so it'll look like Athens is just one stop on my tour. What plans have you made with Sam Johnstone?"

"So much hinges on the judge's daughter. If she's willing to testify in our investigation, or, even if not, if she can just get Seth Dean to testify for us, we may crack this thing open. I've also got a friend in Washington looking into the Southern Pineland Company and its role in everything that's happening. If either the company, or Winston, gets enough pressure, maybe one will sell out the other and cooperate with our investigation."

"Well, I'll see what I can do for you, Eric. If Winston wants to talk business, I'll ask to tour the properties, of course, so I can gauge their potential. That way, I'll be able to testify about the conditions I see there. I'll see if I can get him to share any other information about how he makes his money, too, but I rather doubt he'll share all of that with someone he just met."

"Then what?"

"I'll look for Clarence under the cover of continuing my Southern business tour. Thanks for locating the camp in Florida for me. I'll wire anything I learn, either at Winston's or in Florida, to the Justice Department and appraise them of the situation whenever the opportunity arises."

"Finding the camp's location was easy, John. It's a matter of public record."

"How could all these things be going on, and no one outside the South ever hears about it?"

"Do you think anyone cares what happens to colored folks in the South? Do people anywhere in the whole country really care? I probably wouldn't be here, either, if it wasn't for Roosevelt's influence."

"It's an open question, whether anyone in the country even cares, isn't it, Eric? Well, I care what happens to a particular colored person in the South, and I plan to do what I can to help him. It may not be much, but I plan to try."

"Any help you can give us is welcome. Oh, say, I just thought of something else you might find interesting."

"What's that?"

"Well, John, when I first got to Athens, I read a local newspaper, and one obituary mentioned the death of a William Duval. Do you think this individual might have any relation to Clarence? Maybe Clarence learned he was in Athens and that's why he went there in the first place?"

"When I traveled with him, Clarence never talked about his parents. They were dead already in his mind, I think, regardless of whether they were dead in reality. Still, I suppose it's plausible. Why else would he travel to Alabama in the first place? Maybe he had another reason, but given our lack of other information, I wouldn't discount the idea completely. With luck, I'll find Clarence and ask him myself."

"Oh, one last thing, John."

"What's that?"

"Don't mention the name Sam Johnstone around Winston. If anyone asks, you've never heard of him. But, if you can find either of his renters whom Winston and the Southern Pineland Company sent to Florida, the Maxwell brothers, see what you can do for them as well."

"Maxwell, right. Got it."

"Good luck, John."

"You too, Eric. I hope you can get the young woman or the local lawyer to come clean about everything. If we can show that the authorities arrested the convicts improperly, or that a conspiracy exists and that the convicts didn't break any laws, we ought to be able to set them free."

"Yes. We just need to hope we can get all this through the courts quickly enough to help the convict laborers. At least the peonage laws in question are federal laws, not state ones, so any peonage case will be in federal court where an Alabama judge can't block the proceedings."

The two men shake hands and leave the café, John Tener for the train station to journey to Athens, Eric Hoffman for one more evening at his Nashville hotel.

"You're sure of this?" Jefferson Winston asks his older son, Robert Lee Winston, while seated in the upholstered armchair of his study on Friday afternoon. A bit of bourbon remains in the glass resting at his elbow.

"Yes, father. I saw Ben Walker and the Yankee lawyer walk out of the Commercial Hotel together just before the lawyer left town," Robert replies while leaning forward in his armchair, elbows on knees, cigar clenched between his teeth.

"Father, Ben Walker is a friend of Dale Warren's family. Warren is the father of the one who got shot on one of your farm plots outside of town," James Longstreet Winston adds.

"If that's true, it's a good bet he's heard about the peonage," Winston tells his sons. "And I'm afraid that's not our only problem. The plan to set up the lawyer and plant evidence of immoral behavior on him failed. Plus, this morning I got a telegram from Thomas Brown up in Boston, stating that someone from the Justice Department has made inquiries into the Southern Pineland Company's actions."

"What do we do, then?" James asks, stroking his beard as he folds his wiry right leg over the left while leaning back in his chair. He blows smoke from his cigar into the still air of the study. In the pause that follows his question, it takes him a moment to realize his leg shakes a bit. He puts his right foot back on the floor.

Cupping his chin in his hand and then raising his head and looking at each of his sons for a moment, Winston says, "This is what I propose. Inform the overseers at each of our farms to make one of our peons disappear. Piney Creek has plenty of good spots where no one will ever find a body. That ought to send the proper message to everyone else about speaking with any outsiders, I'd say."

"What if the overseers get cold feet?" Robert asks.

"They won't."

"You sure, Pops? Askin' them to kill someone is a little beyond their job, isn't it?"

"Arrest them on the spot if they hesitate. I'm sure I can find a bookkeeping irregularity of some kind to charge them with defrauding me. Then make the peon disappear yourselves. I assume I can count on you?"

"To kill a nigger if I have to? Nothing makes me prouder," Robert says.

James simply nods his assent, then says, "It's a good move, involving the overseers in things this way. They know that if we go down, it'll ruin them, too. Gives them incentive to keep their own mouths shut about everything."

"Exactly. I can even claim they acted without my knowledge if worst comes to worst. Which is another part of my plan. I have valid work contracts with each person. If that lawyer accuses me of brutal treatment of the farmers, or peonage, which he may well do, my first defense is to deny any knowledge of it and claim the overseers acted on their own, without my permission, and exceeded my orders."

"That's a good move, too," Robert says.

Winston adds, "You should give them unmistakable hints to that effect if the situation calls for it. Make sure they're aware that I'm watching their performance, shall we say, intently. However, also be sure they realize that faithful performance deserves a handsome reward."

"I'll start by visiting Ed Hill first. I think he's the strongest link in that chain," James says.

"I think so, too," the judge replies. "Remember when he got in that fistfight with Jonah Morris? I think all the other overseers became terrified of him from that day forward. Once he moves, I think the rest will follow without question."

"I'm on my way," James tells his father while standing up and grabbing his hat.

"Wait a minute, James," Robert says as his younger brother gets up and heads for the door. "Father, what did you learn from Boston?"

"The Company's directors will countersue any legal action from the Justice Department. Thomas Brown assures me he has access to certain members of the relevant District Court, should that be necessary. In the meantime, Brown says his company will eliminate any incriminating evidence should the existence of such evidence prove a liability."

"Just like we're about to eliminate anyone who might be a liability?" James asks his father.

"Precisely. I've also wired Senator Pettus to put pressure on the Justice Department to stand down, or at least back off, in its investigation. He says he'll do what he can. The senator is from here in Limestone County. Athens, in fact, as you boys know. He would like to avoid his home town becoming embroiled in scandal. It's unlikely to damage his political reputation too severely, but all the same, politicians prefer to avoid negative press whenever possible, and Pettus is no different."

"Does he have enough clout to counter Roosevelt?" James asks.

"That remains to be seen. With any luck, Governor Roosevelt's aspirations toward higher office, and his need for as much support as possible to obtain that office, will cause him to reconsider his stance on sticking his nose where it doesn't belong in Alabama."

23

Clarence's Plan

Clarence knows it's Friday because the guards allow the prisoners the chance to bathe on Sunday, and it's now five days since his last bath in the small creek that runs near the camp. He stinks from body odor. The air in the camp stinks of turpentine and the burning pine wood necessary for extracting it. Bill Baker's body, still hanging from a tree in plain view of all the prisoners, stinks while decomposing, which doesn't take long in the Florida heat. Maggots writhe and crawl all over the corpse, occasionally falling off and dropping to the barren earth below. When the breeze blows in the right direction, everyone in the prison railroad car smells Bill's putrid, decaying flesh. It rained a bit again the previous evening, but the heat of each day only accelerates the decomposition of his body.

Although he knows it's Friday, Clarence doesn't know what day of the month it is. He guesses it must be June by now, but, really, he isn't certain. Days blur together here; when every day is a nightmare, what's the point of trying to draw distinctions between them?

The only thing looking up is that, whatever illness or disease Matthew had, it seems to be over. He's been having sweats, fevers, chills, and vomiting every second day for several weeks, but now it's been three days since the last episode. Not all the other sick men are better, however; whatever afflicts them, Matthew pulled out of it first. Clarence wonders if that's because of Matthew's size and strength. He hopes Matthew is better for good, and when he sees Matthew's improvement, he decides to share his escape plan with Elijah.

After another slow, grim, plodding, monotonous, hopeless march into the forest, Clarence summons up a bit of strength to speak with Elijah once the nearest guard is some distance off. "Elijah, I think I have half a plan to get us out of here," he says in a loud whisper.

Elijah keeps working but raises an eyebrow. "Half a plan? That won't be enough, Clarence."

"Well, better than half. I have a whole plan, but I've only figured out how to make half of it happen."

"Go on," Elijah says, although in such a dull monotone Clarence wonders if his friend believes him.

"I've got a way to get out of our shackles at night."

Elijah's weary, unshaven, sweat-soaked face looks Clarence in the eyes. "Now I'm listening."

"A while back, when I was on woodcutting duty, a guy had his partner cut his own foot off."

"Yeah, you told me that. How's that gonna help us? I'm not going to do that to anyone."

"When one guard went over to pick him up, the injured prisoner fell into the guard and knocked the guard into the woodpile. A metal spike fell out of his belt when that happened."

"Go on, Clarence."

"I picked it up in the confusion, and I discovered that I can knock loose the pin that holds our leg shackles together with it. I can get us free."

Elijah stops just for a moment, arms resting on his ax while he looks at Clarence. Now, however, there's a spark in his eyes Clarence hasn't seen in weeks. Instead of slouching like always, now Elijah stands straight and tall.

"That's a start, for sure. What else?"

"I've been experimenting at night. Every other night, I make a loud noise to wake up the guard dog and time how long it takes the guards to come check on us."

"It's *you* who keeps waking us up? I've been cursing whoever does that for a week. I guess I won't curse you anymore, though, now that I know the point."

"Here's what I've learned, Elijah. The first night, the guards' response time was a bit under six minutes. Last night, it was nearly eight-and-a-half. They're getting slower because they assume it's always a false alarm."

"The boy who cried wolf."

"Exactly."

"But, there's still the dog to worry about. Even if we get free of the shackles, how will we get past that dog?" Elijah asks.

"That's the part of the plan that needs work. We've got to find some way to silence the dog, or kill it, or something. If we can do that, we might be able to get a big start before the guards ever notice we're gone."

"We're going to need a big start, too, Clarence. A very big start. I don't know about you, but I feel so weak now, I don't know how far or fast I can run even if we get free."

"It's not you who I'm most worried about. It's Tom. I won't leave him behind. We agreed we need to stick together."

"What if we found a way to get everyone free of their chains? The dog can't chase twenty men."

"True, but that would mean one or two of us would have to sacrifice for the rest. How can we ask anyone to do that after everything we've suffered already?"

"Whatever we decide, Clarence, I think we need to do it soon. The weather's only gonna get warmer, and we're only gonna get weaker the longer we wait."

Clarence nods.

Before either man speaks again, a prisoner working about eighty or ninety feet away loses consciousness and falls over. He hits the ground with a dull thud and lies there momentarily. As always, a nearby guard rides over to investigate.

Right about the time the guard arrives and prepares to shout something at the poor man, the prisoner leaps up, screaming hysterically, bouncing from one foot to the other and patting and brushing all parts of his body. "Ants! Ants! They're biting me everywhere!"

The man runs in circles, or as close to a circle as he can while chained to his fellows, flapping his arms and brushing his legs frantically. After a few minutes, he finally calms down and looks around.

"Damn, boy," the guard chuckles at the poor man. "You done fell on top of a termite nest. Those ain't ants. They's termites. You can tell by the color."

"Did they poison me?" the poor man asks. "I don't know nothin' 'bout termites."

"Nah, you's fine. They bite some, like you just found out, but they ain't no threat to people. Jus' go work at the next tree until they calm down a bit. And be more careful. You's slowin' down the work."

Elijah turns back and resumes working himself. "Clarence, is Emory gonna make it?"

"Looks like it. Barely."

"Do you think we should bring him into our plan?"

"Don't know. He *is* a hothead. He might give it away before we're ready, even if just on accident."

"True, Clarence, but I want to help him. After spending five hours in that tin sweatbox, just sitting out in the sun while the heat inside the box blistered his skin and almost boiled him alive, that's the worst thing I've ever seen done to a person."

"And to think, it was all because he wanted to do the decent thing and bury Ezra. How about this. We won't tell him our plans now, but when we make our escape, he's the first one we'll help if the chance presents itself."

"Agreed. Unless we think of something better in the meantime."

The pair go back to working, but it isn't long before Elijah looks over at Clarence again. He gives Clarence a weary smile. "I just thought of something that might work, something that might stop the dog," he says out of the corner of his mouth.

"What's that?"

"Remember when Ezra got bit by that rattlesnake and died?"

"Of course."

"What if we could poison the dog somehow? We got nothing to kill it with because the guards lock up our tools in the equipment shed each night, but what if we poisoned the dog and it died? Then, it might take hours for the guards to learn we were gone."

"That's a great idea, Elijah, except one thing."

"Yeah, I know. Where we gonna get poison for the dog, right?"

Both men ponder this thought for some time before Clarence says, "Maybe Tom could do it. Next time he works at boiling the turpentine like he is today, maybe he can find something. I don't know if the dogs eat turpentine or if it's bad for them, but maybe he can find some other kind of substance there that might help us."

"How would he hide it and smuggle it back to our railroad car without the guards noticing him, though?"

"I'll ask him tonight when we see him."

The day is as horrible and exhausting as any. Clarence guesses the temperature reaches the upper eighties, and God only knows what the humidity is. Once again, he stumbles into the camp soaked in sweat, arms aching from work and stinging from insect bites, and eyes so heavy he knows he'll sleep instantly if he closes them. Tom is already there. Good. Clarence knows he'd never keep awake if he had to wait for Tom to arrive. Also fortunately, Clarence's work crew is the first to reach the railroad car this evening, so he can talk to Tom a bit without anyone but Elijah overhearing.

After his friends assume their places and relieve themselves for the night in the communal bucket, Clarence whispers to Tom, "Tom, how are you holding up?"

Tom whispers back something incoherent.

"Tom?"

Tom falls forward, but luckily, Clarence is right there and catches him.

Clarence hoists him back to his feet and gently slaps his cheek. "Tom, come back to me."

Tom's eyes flutter open. "Clarence," he manages to whisper. "I'm sorry. I think I've reached the end."

"Now, Tom, listen here. I can help us get out of here. Elijah and I made a plan, but we need your help."

"Get out of what?" Tom mumbles before falling forward again.

Clarence keeps hold of him and doesn't let him fall. "Stay with me, Tom. We need you if we're going to get out of here." He shakes the poor boy gently.

"Okay, I think I hear you, Clarence. You need me."

Clarence looks in Tom's half-shut eyes. It's hard to tell whether he sees more sadness or despair.

"Forgive me, Tom," Clarence says to him.

"For what?" Tom replies groggily.

Clarence slaps Tom's face. Hard. His eyes come open fully.

"What'd you hit me for? I thought you was my friend."

"Sorry, but I need you fully awake for a couple minutes, so you can listen to me."

"Well, I'm awake now."

"You'll thank me later, Tom."

"What do you need, then? You said you needed my help. I think I remember that, anyway."

From what seems like one hundred years ago, a thought returns to Clarence's mind. "Tom, when we were locked up in Athens after our trial, didn't you say you studied chemistry?"

"Yeah, a little. I've read a couple books."

"When you work at distilling the turpentine, do you add anything to the mixture?"

"No, you just boil the stuff."

"Nothing's left over that might be toxic or poisonous?"

"Wait, one thing comes to mind. You boil the water out of the turpentine to make it purer. When the water's gone, there's salt left behind."

"But salt isn't poisonous."

"This salt might be. It burns a bit if it gets on your skin. One prisoner rubbed his eye on accident after handling it, and he said he could barely see the rest of the day."

"If we got the dog to ingest it, maybe the stuff would burn the dog's throat, so it couldn't bark."

"Yeah, that's good, Clarence. Or, if we could find a way to get just a little in its eyes, that could work, too."

"What does it smell like? Will the dog notice if we drop some in its water bowl it drinks from?"

"Nothin'. It don't smell like nothin', but like I said, it'll burn your skin. The guards always warn us about that. I'm not sure how concentrated it has to be to hurt the dog."

"We need you to get us some, Tom. As much as you can."

"But how do I get it here?"

"Can you find a container and hide it inside your ring-arounds? They're so baggy I think you could get away with it if you could only find a container."

"I'll see what I can do next time I'm assigned there. When do you want it?"

"As soon as you can manage. Everything else is in place."

24

Emily's Move

Because it's Saturday, June 3, Emily Winston sits in her classroom, going over her Sunday School lesson for the young boys and girls tomorrow. She likes to come in and work on her plans early in the morning. If she waits until midday, all the gossiping society women come by to chat, and she never gets anything done. It isn't that she doesn't like the church women; they are nice enough and mean well, and they always treat her with great kindness, presumably because of who her father is. But Emily dislikes interruptions, and when she begins a task, she likes to finish it quickly. Consequently, she's gotten a key to her basement classroom, so she can arrive early Saturday morning and perfect her lessons. Emily has been doing so for nearly two years now, so it's nothing special to anyone involved with Athens' First United Methodist Church to find her working away when they arrive in the morning.

Since she usually is the first person at the church on Saturday and often works by herself for an hour or more before anyone else arrives, normally, the sound of footsteps coming down the stairs and echoing down the hallway toward her classroom would startle Emily. But not this morning. When she hears them, she walks calmly to her door and sees Sam Johnstone ambling toward her.

"Good morning, Mr. Johnstone." Emily sounds friendly, yet weary, as she brushes a lock of hair out of her face. She has on a peach-colored Sunday dress.

"Good morning, Miss Emily," he responds. "You're sure this is a safe place to speak for a while?"

"It should be. Usually, I'm the only one here for an hour or so this early in the morning."

"Let's hope so. I've given some thought to what you told me at my house. Do you still feel the same about things?"

"For the most part, yes. I know that the other members of my family have done things they shouldn't have done. I also believe that Seth is in danger. Maybe more danger than he knows. I care about Seth and don't want to see any harm come to him, even if he's done some of the same awful things."

"The best way to protect him is to get him to tell what he knows to a jury."

"I'm not sure he'll do it."

"Why is that?"

"We spoke last night. I didn't mention anything about your part in what's going on right now, but I asked him why the Justice Department is here in Athens so suddenly and if it has anything to do with all those arrests back in March. I told him I'm worried about him, which isn't a lie because I *am* worried about him, even if he's not the person I thought he is."

"What did Seth tell you, Miss Emily?"

"Not much of anything. He said it's all nonsense, that everything is fine, and that I shouldn't worry about it."

"Do you think that's what he believes, or what your father told him to believe?"

"I can't say for sure. Probably the second, but I just don't know. If it's the first, then he's truly in grave danger. Either way, I'm very scared, Sam. Even more so, after last night."

"What happened last night?"

"I asked our housemaid, Susan, to tell me if she heard my father or my brothers talking about business. She said that yesterday afternoon they all went into my father's study and closed the door. She listened and overheard them talking about making people on my father's farms disappear. I'm so scared at what's happening." With that, Emily drops her head into her hands for a moment, sniffles and heaves like she's about to start sobbing, but only does so for a few seconds before she steadies herself and looks Sam in the eyes again.

Sam already knows this look, although it has been decades since he's seen it regularly. It's similar to the look some soldiers get when they see a friend die in battle for the first time. Denial, shock, then sadness, and finally, regret. Carefully, he extracts a fresh silk handkerchief from his pocket and offers it to Emily. "Here, my dear, take this if you need it. It's clean, just washed and pressed yesterday."

"Thank you," Emily dabs around her eyes for a moment with the soft fabric before handing it back to Sam.

Sam sees the resolve and composure return to her face. *Impressive*, Sam says to himself, *for a young lady who has lived the sheltered life she has. Perhaps she has even more inner strength than I thought.*

Emily tells Sam, "I'm sorry for that. It's just that, I've always known my father was a stern man, but I always thought he was a fair one, too. Whenever he has guests to our house, he always treats them so politely, and they're always so kind and gracious toward me. I never realized that some of them were really awful people. Until now. It's all a bit hard for me to understand and deal with. I always thought my father was a self-made man, too, who earned all the nice things we have through being smart at business and law, but now I know some of that isn't true, either."

"How would you like me to help, Miss Emily?"

"I just don't want any people to die or get arrested just so someone can make money from their labor. How can I teach a Sunday School class and tell the children to love their neighbors and

213

be their brother's keeper when my own family acts like that?" Emily sniffles a bit this time and is one the edge of tears again. She starts crying for the briefest moment but then looks Sam straight in the eye once more. "How can I sleep at night knowing all that?"

"Miss Emily, if I told you some of the things I watched men do in the war in Mexico, you'd know that sometimes the better angels of our nature do not come out on top. I know it may not help much to make you feel better right now, but I've seen young children bayonetted while they tried to run from soldiers attacking their village. I've seen soldiers mutilate the bodies of men they'd killed only ten minutes prior, just to get back at their opponent for shooting a friend. The world is a hard place at times."

"How do you sleep at night, then, when you've seen all of that?"

"It's different for every person. Even though I didn't do those things myself, I've tried to make up for the wrongs of my fellow man by trying to do good in the world when I get a chance. Like you're doing right now."

"It's just that, I know my father loves me, and he's always looked after me. How can I betray him?"

"That's something you must work out for yourself, Miss Emily. It's just that . . ."

Sam stops for a moment. Here he is, a chance to defeat his old enemy and right a host of wrongs in the process within his grasp, and he's advising his most valuable witness to decide for herself what to do. If he convinces her to testify in front of a jury, his chances of winning rise dramatically.

Yet, at the same time, he knows it's a betrayal of trust if he does so by coercion or threats. If he plays things wrong now, the regrets will probably haunt Emily Winston for the rest of her life. She might be the daughter of Jefferson Winston, but she doesn't share his history. Sam doesn't want to penalize her for crimes she didn't commit. No, he can only truly defeat Jefferson Winston if Emily Winston agrees to help of her own free will.

"Yes?" Emily asks after a lengthy pause, eyes on Sam expectantly.

"Well, Miss Emily, if you'll indulge an old man another story, I'd like to share one with you."

"Go ahead."

"Did your father ever tell you how my family used to own slaves before the War of Secession?"

"Yes, and he told me how you set them all free and that you were a damn fool for it," she says with a brief laugh. Then, "My goodness, I've forgotten where I am. Pardon my language!"

Sam smiles an easy smile. "It's true. I set them all free. More than forty men, women, and children. Young, old, and in-between. All of them. It's why I never fought in the War of Secession, either. No one in Alabama wanted my services after that, I'm afraid."

"I guess not."

"But here's the point of the story. I've never regretted doing that. At the time I thought it was the right thing to do, and I still do. That was forty-two years ago, and I've had forty-two years of sleeping with a clear conscience because of it. When the biggest decision of my life forced me to choose sides, I chose the right one. At least for me. Money and success have come in time, but you can't put a price on going to bed at night knowing you did right by your fellow man."

Emily gives him a little smile. "I think I get your point, but I'm still not sure what I should do."

"I know you'll come to the right decision for you."

He's about to go on when he and Emily hear more footsteps coming down the stairs into the basement. Momentarily, Pastor Evans, clad in a black cotton shirt with a white collar, pokes his head into Emily Winston's classroom. His face is almost circular, it's so round, and his puffy cheeks and quickly receding hairline only accent the fact.

"Miss Winston. Mr. Johnstone. Interesting to find the two of you here together on a Saturday morning."

"Yes, Pastor Evans, I came to church this morning to drop off some flowers. You'll find them in the sanctuary, right in front of the altar," Sam tells him.

"That's very Christian of you, Sam. I've seen them. Lovely."

"You know, former military man, always up with the sun. I was on my way out when I noted the door to the basement stairway was open. I decided to see who else could be here so early but, on my way down the stairs, took a bad step and injured my ankle. Miss Emily here came to my rescue."

"That's funny, I decided to come down here myself when I heard some crying, but it sounded like Miss Winston."

"It was me that you heard, it's true," Emily puts in. "After I got Mr. Johnstone to sit down and rest a moment, he started telling me stories about going to war in Mexico. I got a little emotional about one of them, I'm afraid."

"War stories in church! Why, Mr. Johnstone!" Pastor Evans says with mock astonishment, sausage-like fingers going to his rounded cheeks momentarily. Then, the "o" formed by his mouth turns into a smile and a hearty laugh.

Sam grins. "I'm afraid so, Pastor. I wasn't thinking clearly, so my mind just fell back on what it knew."

"Miss Winston, did Sam tell you the story about how one time, when he went to strap on his boots, a scorpion fell out and almost stung his toe? That's one of my favorites."

"No, this one was sad, not funny. Mr. Johnstone talked about seeing a friend shot in the ankle, and how he had to walk with a limp forever after that. It just hurt me to think what it would be like to walk with a limp the rest of your life."

"I don't believe I've ever heard that one, Sam."

"I was in Mexico for nearly eighteen months, Pastor. There were a few things that happened in that time I've never told you about. Someday I'll give you the story of how I had a shot at Santa Anna but missed."

"A true story?"

216

"Maybe," Sam replies with a wide grin. He braces his arms on the wooden chair and tries to stand up, wincing as he does so. "Well, best be moving. The pain's gone down some, but it'll go back up again if my ankle gets stiff. Plus, I suppose Miss Emily would like to get back to her Sunday school lessons now that someone else is here to help an old man." Gingerly placing weight on his right ankle, Sam hobbles toward the hallway and the stair. "Thank you ever so much, Miss Emily. Pastor Evans, could you assist me up the stairs, my friend?"

As Pastor Evans leaves, Emily looks down at the plain, unadorned wooden table in front of her. Part of her knows that Johnstone is right. The other part wonders how she'll ever look her family in the eye if she helps him the way he wants her to.

25

Tener's Arrival

"Mr. Tener, I trust you've had an easy ride to Athens?" Jefferson Winston says while shaking the tall man's hand. "It's not every day we get Northern visitors in our town."

"Very much so, yes. I've not spent a great deal of time in your section of the country, but the Charleroi Savings and Trust Company has asked me to meet with certain Southern businessmen and examine the possibilities for investment in the region. We are an investment bank as well as a savings bank and, although we're based in the Pittsburgh area, the market for steel is already well-capitalized, so we're searching for other ways to support industrial and agricultural development throughout the country."

While Tener speaks, Winston ushers him inside his home. They sit across the finely polished table in his study, Winston's various books of law and Southern history filling the bookshelves that line the walls. Winston ties back the curtain billowing out from one window to let in more light and fresh air.

"And how did my cotton farm come to your attention?" he says when he finishes at the window.

"We're involved in the cotton mills of Massachusetts and Connecticut. Some of our depositors own or invest in mills in those states, and we've loaned money to others to build new mills and supply machinery. One mentioned your name as someone who supplied them with quality cotton at a very reasonable cost. I decided it merited contacting you."

"It's true that we ship a modest number of bales north each year. It hardly seems the amount that would attract a respectable Northern financial institution's attention, however."

"I'm flattered you'd think of us in that way," Tener says with an easy laugh. "If only the bank's board of directors shared your positive outlook. Typical banking types, I'm afraid. Very frugal and very uptight when it comes to spending money, even on looking for ways to make more money."

"So, what did you have in mind to talk about when it comes to cotton, Mr. Tener?"

"How do you transport your cotton for ginning, Mr. Winston?"

"Horse and wagon, same way as always. I own my own gin, so there's no need to send the raw cotton by rail somewhere else for ginning. Once it's processed into bales, I cart the bales by wagon to the rail depot here in town, and I ship things by rail from there."

"Have you ever considered using motorcars instead of horses?"

"I have, but not seriously. They're barely faster and still very expensive."

"It's true they aren't much faster than horses today, but I doubt that the current design of the internal combustion engine is the limit of the technology. We're likely to see dramatic improvements in horsepower before long. How much money would it save you to be able to move your raw cotton and cotton bales around twice as fast as you do now? And how much would it save you, in men and money, to not have to upkeep wagons and feed horses for that purpose?"

"It would save money, certainly, but like I just said, that's not possible right now. Motorcars are not yet powerful enough."

"You have various landholdings around the county, do you not?" Tener asks next.

"Certainly."

"What interest do you have in acquiring more?"

"I'm always interested, but it's a tricky business. You see, Mr. Tener, here in northern Alabama, we have some areas of good land, but we're also in the foothills. The Appalachian Plateau, I believe some call it. This isn't the Black Belt where you just buy a farm in some fertile river valley and wait for the cotton profits to pile up. We have some quality cotton land here in Limestone County, it's true, but someone bought it long ago. Acquiring those pieces of land today costs dearly."

"But the acquisitions would prove valuable if you had the money and would pay back a reasonable investment?"

"Yes, in time. Cotton prices fluctuate, as I'm sure you know, but in time it would pay, given the labor situation here in Athens."

"Could you describe the labor situation for me, Mr. Winston? I've wondered what it is that allows folks in this region to produce cotton at the price my friends tell me you sell it for."

"You've heard of sharecropping?"

"I've heard the term, yes, although it's not a practice that's prevalent in Pennsylvania, so if you'd like to offer a primer on its workings, I'm sure I'd learn something new."

"It's not a complex system. People farm on land that I own. It's a bit like renting, except that the farmers pay me in farm products in exchange for living on the land and working it. When the crop comes in at harvest, one-third of the revenue from its sale goes to the farmer, one-third to the landowner, and one-third to the person who provides the tools and equipment needed to farm."

"Excellent symmetry in that arrangement."

"Indeed, Mr. Tener. During the good years, everyone involved does well."

"Why don't the farmers buy their own land after the good years, then?"

"Most of the best land in these parts, someone already owns it, like I told you before. Besides, if you treat your sharecroppers well like I do, you'll find them to be loyal, just as is true in most lines of business."

"For certain, Mr. Winston. Honest treatment of an associate lies at the heart of sound business principles."

"Quite true. Furthermore, I provide my croppers with certain incentives to proper behavior and exertion and disincentives to laziness. I find this approach especially useful toward the Negros who crop for me, although the whites benefit from it as well."

"You have both races as sharecroppers?"

"Absolutely. No one is a greater friend to uplifting the poor, be they white or colored, than I am, Mr. Tener."

"Sounds like a fine arrangement. You know, Mr. Winston, you here in the South sometimes get poor press up in Pennsylvania, but I've enjoyed my trip immensely so far. I fear that the facts of life in your section are not always what we in the North have been led to believe."

"An all-too-common misunderstanding, I'm afraid. We Southerners of responsibility and intelligence have only the good of all our people at heart. No one is a truer friend to the Negro than those now governing in the South."

"Might I look at how sharecropping works in person? Regardless of whether you'd like to associate in business, I'd like to see sharecropping in practice. Perhaps, upon my return to Pennsylvania, I can use such modest influence as I possess to correct some of the misconceptions regarding life here in the South."

"I'd love to show you how it works. I'll call for my driver, Henry, and we can take a tour of one of the nearby properties I own. This family has cropped for me for nearly two decades, in fact. They're a bit on the quiet side, however, so forgive them if they harbor some suspicion toward a Northerner like yourself."

Before long, Tener and Winston clop along a dirt path toward a cotton field, Winston pointing out the glories of cotton agriculture to his guest.

A few miles away, Ed Hill speaks with James Winston. Like usual, James has a cigar clenched between his teeth while he speaks to Hill from horseback. A bit of mud flecks his riding boots after a light rain last night.

Winston says, "Eddie, I have orders from my father. He believes our peonage operations are in danger. I don't know if you've heard, but a Yankee lawyer from the Justice Department is here. We think he knows about what's going on at the farm you oversee."

Ed nods gravely, takes off his slouch hat, and fingers the brim with his calloused index finger. The hat is gray, just like his farm overalls and, Ed thinks ruefully, a bit too much of his hair. One consequence of a lifetime spent outdoors, he thinks to himself. Or, maybe, a lifetime spent worrying too much about what other people are up to. "I see. I've not heard anything about this lawyer. Too busy farming and keeping the niggers in order around here. They just won't work unless you keep your foot on their necks all the time and make them toe the line."

"You're the best at doing that, too, Eddie. My family values your services immensely. That's why you get a better salary than any of the other men who work for us."

"Yeah, I know that. I'm proud of it, too. Whatever the Judge wants done, I'm your man. Does he want me to rough up the niggers a bit? Maybe use the lash on 'em to scare 'em, so they won't talk?"

"No, Eddie, my father thinks something sterner may be in order."

"What's sterner than a whuppin'?"

"He wants you to make one of your croppers disappear, if you know what I mean."

"That so? Well, that's serious business, but you know I'm happy to oblige. One less nigger, one less varmint to worry about down the line. That's how I always looks at it, least ways. Which one?"

"He said to leave that up to your judgment. You work over these people each day. You know which one is most likely to talk and which ones will clam up if we set the proper example."

"Indeed, I do. I think I knows just the one. The uppity buck nigger who I had to beat last week. I don't know if he's all the way whupped yet, so it's less problems for me tomorrow, way I see it."

"After you do the deed, find a deep pool somewhere in Piney Creek and sink the body there. You ought to be able to find a good spot; the damn creek flows all the way to the Tennessee River."

"When does Judge Winston want it done by?"

"Tomorrow. Report to him at our home when you're finished."

"My pleasure, Mr. Winston. Expect to hear from me the day after tomorrow. This'll take a bit of doing, and I gotta make sure it's done right to set the proper example for all the other niggers. Hidin' the body will take a bit of time, too. Can't just carry around a dead body in broad daylight and expect no one to notice, you know. But I'll report in when it's over."

"You're our man, Eddie. We trust you to execute the plan properly."

"My pleasure." With that, Ed Hill resettles his hat on his head, turns, and walks off, heavy boots tromping down the still-damp grass. Short and stocky, but strong and fearless, he knows what he needs to do. The time has arrived to earn his real money.

26

The Piney Creek Shooting

"How did the meeting with the Yankee banker go yesterday, father?" James Winston asks after extracting his cigar from his mouth. The men have just returned from attending Sunday services at First United Methodist Church and have their Sunday suits on while they talk in Jefferson Winston's study. "I meant to ask last night but got in late from riding to all our farms and relaying your instructions to our overseers."

"Inconclusively. We discussed a loan to buy more land and improve our transportation of the cotton, but I don't think much will come of it. The time just isn't right. Even if all our current troubles weren't complicating things, I still don't deem it the right time," Winston answers his son.

"He thinks we should use automobiles?" Robert Winston says incredulously.

"Yes. He may be correct that they are the coming thing. He may not. But today they remain a toy for the wealthy more than a practical means to move goods or people. I told him as much after we toured one of our farms."

"How'd he learn about us, again?" Robert asks.

"One of the cotton merchants we've sold to gave my name to him."

"Seems legitimate, although the timing is interesting, given that there's a Yankee here investigating us; then, out of the blue, another one turns up wanting to know about our business," says James.

"I thought of that, certainly," Winston tells his son. "But I haven't found a connection. I sent a telegram to our cotton merchant to check the man's background, of course, and he assures me that John Tener is a respected bank president in the Pittsburgh area. He's never held any political office."

"He didn't drop any hints or do anything suspicious?" James inquires.

"No. If it wasn't for our present circumstances, I would have found Tener a most agreeable person to associate with. He has an easy manner and is rather outgoing and open for a Yankee. Tener asked about how cotton farming worked, I showed him one of our safe farms, and we talked business for a while after that but, like I said, the interview ended inconclusively."

"Where is he now?"

"He said he planned to tour some other large farms in the South to gauge their interest in acquiring more land and modernizing. Atlanta was his next stop, as I recall."

James states, "Probably better we work things out before taking on more business concerns, anyway. Speaking of, I talked to Eddie Hill and the rest of our overseers yesterday. Everything will be taken care of."

Winston nods, looking down at his shiny, newly-polished hardwood floors. It hurts just a bit to think of what "taken care of" means, but it's a necessary loss. Not because he cares about the lives of colored peons, of course, but because of the financial loss it entails. Still, better safe than sorry. One can always make small mistakes, but one must avoid the large mistakes at any cost.

Slowly, Winston raises his head. "We have one more concern I learned about today, boys."

Both men look their father in the face expectantly.

"I spoke with Pastor Evans after the services today, like I always do. He said that yesterday morning he came across Sam Johnstone talking to Emily in her classroom in the basement. Both claimed it was a chance meeting and said that the old fool hurt his foot going down the stairs and Emily just happened to be there to help him, but he decided to mention it just in case."

"I did notice Johnstone had a bit of a limp today at services and walked with a cane. I've never seen him with a cane before," James says. "Did you ask Emily about it?"

"Not yet, but I will. We may need to keep a closer eye on her. For her own protection, of course. No telling what Johnstone's plans might include or how deep they go, but if they involve doing anything to my daughter, I'll bury him myself."

Early Sunday morning, June 4, Ed Hill drops to one knee. He's tired from walking all night. Setting down his burden, Hill pulls out his canteen and drinks. Standing amongst a stand of hickories and chestnuts, Hill fingers his shotgun nervously while looking across Piney Creek to the field beyond. Hopefully, whoever owns the field is at church this morning. A bit of haze hangs in the air, but not enough to hide him from anyone's sight. However, nothing moves that he can see.

Hill sighs in relief. He doesn't want anyone from Athens to notice what he's about to do, for damn sure.

Shouldering his pack again, he says to the four colored people with him, "If we make it across those fields and over that ridge, we'll be in Tennessee, and out of the reach of the Winstons. A few more miles after that, ten, maybe, is the town of Pulaski. From there, we buy railroad tickets for Canada."

"How long we got to stay in Canada again?" one of his companions, Jed Thomas, asks.

"Can't say for sure, Jed. Hopefully, not long. If Winston goes down, and all his wrongs come into the light, we can come back soon. If they don't, well, it may be a while. It may be for good."

"Mr. Johnstone told you it was time to move out?"

"Yes. I just hope he's right and can build a good enough case against Winston, Jed."

"We trust you, Mr. Eddie. You've never done us wrong before," says Willie Allen. "You've always been good to us and said you'd get us out of Alabama and away from that awful Mr. Winston someday. You had to slap me around that one time, but I know you were just putting on a show for that evil Robert."

Hill winces. "I'm still sorry I did that. It was the only thing I could think of at the time to appear mean and ruthless. I should have just cursed you out, but those slaps sure impressed Robert."

"Can we have just another moment? My foot's still real sore," Larry Tucker says to the group. "I took a bad fall two days back when I stepped on that ground wasp nest and had to run away. I don't think I sprained my ankle, but I sure did twist it good."

"Yeah, but let's make it quick." Eddie tells him. "I want to go while things are clear. The Winstons will be at church this morning, and I told them I'd report back in a day or two, but if they come to check on me and find we aren't there, they'll be after us right quick. We'd best be on that train going north before they find us."

"Can I ask you something, Mr. Eddie?" says Tommy Taylor.

Tommy is the largest person in the group but also the quietest. In fact, he's downright shy, Ed thinks. If he ever tried to be mean and intimidating he'd be a sight to see. "Sure, Tommy, what is it?"

"Well, I've done some thinking. Ever since Mr. Winston's sons arrested me and forced me to work on his farm, you've been nothing but nice to me. You helped teach all of us to read, at night, when you could've been sleeping, and sometimes you spend a bit of your own money to get us more food to eat. Now, you're about to spend all your extra pay for the last eight months, and risk your neck besides, to help us escape from peonage. I've never seen a white person treat colored people that way in Alabama. But you've never told us why you do it. We've all been wondering about that."

Ed looks down, then slowly raises his head to look all four colored faces in the eye, one by one. He looks down again. "Because I owe it to you."

"But you'd never met us before the last eight months," Willie says.

"I owe it to your people, after what I've done to you."

"I still don't see," Larry tells him.

"I'm getting older now, but I was young once, like you all are. Young and stupid. When I was a teenager I lived in Louisiana, and it was a rough time. The Civil War was still fresh, colored people were trying to get their rights, and white folks were real angry about that. In 1873, we had a standoff in Grant Parish, Louisiana, between the colored people and the whites over the results of an election at a town named Colfax. The colored militia occupied the county courthouse, but the whites surrounded them and made them surrender eventually. The whites were a combination of war veterans and young people. You see, we had something called the White League for anyone who hated colored people, and I was in it. We drilled around and pretended like we were real soldiers, there to protect white folks from colored people."

"You?" Jed asks.

"Like I said, I was young and stupid. A bunch of my friends joined, so I did, too. Well, we made the colored militia surrender, like I said. We had a cannon, after all. After they did, the whites turned into a mob and just killed people left and right. Some of them we shot in cold blood, others we hung."

"And they never went to court for murder?" Willie asks Ed.

"Oh, a trial took place, all right. The district court indicted ninety-seven people for conspiracy, but only nine men ever faced charges, and the Supreme Court overturned their convictions in the lower courts. Said the law only protected people from actions by the states, not actions from individual people, so the Enforcement Acts of 1870 and 1871 didn't apply to what happened in Colfax. More than one hundred colored people died that day, and the courts said the law didn't protect them from getting murdered."

"But what did you do?" Jed asks him.

"I was part of the mob that hanged one of the men. And, when his tiny young daughter tried to run to her father, I was part of the mob that hanged her, too."

Hill's four auditors just stare at him.

A tear shows in Ed's eye. "At the time I thought I was some great hero, standing up for Southern civilization. But soon, I had nightmares. Still do, sometimes. I've never forgotten the face of that young girl. That's part of why I offered to help you all learn to read at night. Some nights I barely sleep at all because I still see those visions, so if I can't sleep anyway, I might as well do something useful at night.

"After a year or so, I felt bad about being part of the whole thing. Always will. Not a day goes by I don't think about it, even now, twenty-six years later. For a time, I tried drinking to see if the memories would go away, but they didn't. But because I drank too much, I wasn't any good for anything. I failed at everything I did and just got more miserable. No woman would look at me because I drank all the time, so I never got married."

"Then why did you go to work for the Winstons?" Willie says.

"I finally vowed to myself I had to try and make up for what I'd done wrong. I was aware that prison labor existed, for sure. For a while, I mined coal alongside prisoners outside Birmingham. Prison labor is no secret there. I finally decided the best thing would be to try to protect innocent people or save them from prison labor if I could. So, after I finally sobered up, I talked my way into a job in Athens with the Winstons and vowed that when my chance came to do something right by colored people, I'd take it. At this point, I don't care how much money it takes. I just want to make up for what I did twenty-six years ago if I can. Maybe I can rest easy finally if, just for once, I hear people say that old Ed Hill did one thing right in his life."

"Well, I'll be darned," Tommy says.

"Yeah, me too," Jed puts in.

Hill rises to his feet and shoulders his pack. It's still rather heavy because he stowed quite a bit of food for their journey, bread especially. "Sorry for the melodrama, my friends. I think I spent too much time talking. We'd better go now. Just remember our plan when we get to Pulaski. You all work for me as tenants, and I'm taking you north by railroad to look at new farm equipment and test it for use on our farm. Let's go."

Slowly, the group winds its way through the open field. No one notices, and before long, Ed is sure they've reached the Tennessee state line and crossed it.

Hours later, they're near Pulaski, but the going is slow. "It sure would be nice to take the roads," Jed says to the group.

"I know I'm slowing us down. A road sure would be easier for me," Larry Tucker says.

"I know that, too, but I want us out of sight until we get to town. The less anyone knows about what we're doing, the better," Ed tells everyone.

"I think I see some buildings up ahead. Look, over there," Tommy, who walks a short distance ahead of the group, reports to everyone.

"Yeah, just a few more fields to cross. Let's move," Ed says in exhortation.

They don't get much farther, however, before hearing the sound they're all dreading. "You there! What're you niggers doing in my field!" Before anyone can say anything, a gun blast follows.

An instant later, the bullet thunks into an old chestnut tree off to their left. "Run! Go!" Ed shouts, but it's unnecessary because everyone already has. They make for the tree line at the edge of the field.

Except Larry. He limps along, practically hopping on his good leg. Ed runs back to help him. Just as he reaches Larry, the gun fires again, and the shot hits Ed in the chest. He staggers momentarily and then falls backward while blood gushes from the wound.

Larry limps to where Ed fell and looks down at him. Already a bloodstain spreads across Ed's chest, and he's gasping and spasming. "Mr. Eddie, what now?" Larry asks, his voice breaking in panic.

"Take my pack and run. Carry out our plan. Get to Canada," Hill gasps between ragged breaths. "I'm not going to make it with you. But tell your children someday that Ed Hill did something good, finally."

Just as Ed finishes, another bullet strikes the ground about two feet from where Larry Tucker kneels. Ed Hill's body relaxes in Larry's arms, and Larry knows he's dead. He steals a glance and sees the angry farmer with the rifle continue advancing toward them while putting another bullet into his weapon. Larry wrestles Eddie's pack off his back and resumes hopping toward the line of trees just as his companions scurry back and grab him to help. A fourth gunshot goes over their heads, missing by a few feet.

Going as fast as they can, the group passes the line of trees marking the boundary to the field. They leap over a small creek and scramble up the bank on the other side. After crossing another field and hearing no more shooting, they slow their pace when they come to the outskirts of Pulaski.

"What now?" Tommy asks everyone. He's gasping for breath, sweating hard, and shaking.

Larry answers, "We've got to keep to the plan. Pretend we're going north on business. And make sure we never forget what Mr. Eddie done for us when we get there."

Meanwhile, the farmer approaches the man in his field whom he's shot. The man's worn, patched overalls are so threadbare that his legs feel the cooling breeze as it sighs through the trees on the edge of his property. As he walks, he hums a tune through his cracked lips, rubbing his sunburnt neck with his left hand while keeping his rifle steady in his right. Approaching the body, the farmer runs his left hand through the graying stubble on his face. "I shot me a nigger. I shot me a nigger," he says out loud while prancing around in a quick circle.

Finally, he finds the place where the man fell amongst the growing stalks of wheat in his field. The farmers steps back a pace when he sees the body. It's a white man.

"Well, serves him right for helping the niggers," the farmer says while kicking the body to make sure the man is dead.

27

Tom Morton's Mission

Late in the afternoon of Monday, June 5, John Tener steps down from his train into the muggy, oppressive Florida heat. Even the strong breeze wafting off the St. John's River onto the train platform in Palatka, Florida, does little to alleviate the punishing, stifling heat. He can only imagine what the place feels like in August.

That isn't the only thing Tener wonders about, however. He's learned from Eric Hoffman that the turpentine camp where Clarence serves his so-called sentence is inland from St. Augustine and north from Palatka, near the border of St. John's and Putnam counties on the west bank of the St. John's River. So, he'd taken this train to Palatka, planning to ride to somewhere near the camp on horseback tomorrow, and then investigate in person on Wednesday.

He'd tried to arrange to visit the camp by railroad. Tener knows that's how the Southern Pineland Company got the men to the camp in the first place, but, mysteriously, rail service inland to the camp's location no longer exists.

Furthermore, riding with him on the southbound train were scores of heavily armed men. Not in his car, but he'd seen them at every stop along the way to Palatka from Jacksonville. They weren't military men in uniform, and while Tener doesn't know with certainty what they were on the train for, he doubts it's good. His best guess is that the Justice Department's cursory investigation of the Southern Pineland Company has rattled the company's directors, and these men are going to the same place he is with the intent of destroying or erasing evidence.

Tener looks down and bites his lip. He can only hope that the evidence doesn't include the prisoners themselves.

Now, however, he isn't sure if arriving in two days is the best plan. The number of armed men on the train makes him think the sooner he gets to the camp, the better.

Palatka isn't a large town; Tener guesses about three thousand people live there, but after arriving in the evening, it takes him time to find a hotel and rent a room for a few days and then purchase the horse, gear, and food he'll need. It is dark before he can accomplish everything. He'll have to start for the turpentine camp tomorrow.

Sitting in his hotel room, Tener has more time to think. What will he do even if he finds Clarence and the Maxwell brothers? He can't just take them away like a parent picking up their children from school. Unless Hoffman has made an enormous breakthrough at lightning speed since their meeting, the prisoners are here legally. Tener supposes about the best he can do is to look at the place and be ready to provide expert testimony regarding conditions there.

Tener doubts he is in much personal danger from snooping around. At least, he hopes not. He is a bank president, after all, and he can claim any number of legitimate reasons for visiting the area. Looking to purchase land for timber or for a turpentine operation of his own, just to name two.

After washing up for bed, Tener strides to the window of his two-story hotel room and draws back the billowing white curtains for a last look at Palatka. When he does so, a train whistle reaches him through his open window. Looking out, John Tener sees a train leave the Palatka station. It's heading north. On the track where official service no longer exists.

Tom Morton doesn't know it's Monday, June 5. Tom just knows it's Monday and that on Monday he works at the large still where he helps boil turpentine.

Tom can barely stand. Just for a moment, he pulls up his baggy sleeve and looks at his arm. It has about as many insect bites and sores as everyone else in the camp, meaning that they nearly cover his entire arm. He curls the middle finger of his left hand around his right bicep and makes a circle around his arm with his left thumb and middle finger. They touch. That hadn't happened a few days ago, the last time he tried it.

It's almost quitting time. The sun has just gone down, and the gloaming deepens around him. As usual, the guards cursed and taunted him today for being scrawny and weak. One kicked him and screamed to work faster. Well, he *is* scrawny and weak, Tom knows. But his brain still works. Just barely. All the work, every day nearly collapsing from pain and exhaustion, has turned him into a listless creature, a broken work animal doing things by rote and trying to do enough to avoid pain. Clarence's news, however, gave Tom the faint spark of hope he needs for one final effort. He's waited all day for his chance at getting his hands on some salt. Now, that chance is here.

The man he works with today is new. He'd told Tom he got this duty because someone in his train car of prisoners died during the night. The new prisoner doesn't know what killed the dead man, although in this place, the list of possibilities seems limitless.

Tom feels a little sorry for the new man. He made many mistakes and received several punches and kicks from the guards because of it. Well, Tom thinks, he's going to have to make one more. Silently, he asks the new man's forgiveness for what might happen.

In the graying, dying light, Tom walks over to the man. "I need you to help me, friend," he says in a quiet whisper.

"How's that?" the man answers cautiously.

"Just give me a little nudge with your shoulder."

"Why?"

"Just do it. Please."

"I suppose," the man says, stepping forward and bumping Tom's body as requested.

Tom gives a little cry and then stumbles on purpose, toppling off the wooden platform used for dumping more raw turpentine into the large still. He drops about ten feet, landing on his back in the soft dirt near where all the pans for collecting salt lie on the ground. To himself, he breathes a sigh of relief that the fall didn't break anything.

"What you do that for?" the guard yells down at him. "You is clumsy, all right." *Good*, Tom thinks, *the guard isn't going to blame the other man for bumping me.*

"Sorry, sir, I just lost my balance because I got so tired," Tom calls up.

"Tha don' surprise me. You's right puny, you little monkey. Now, come on, I's ready for chow," the guard calls with a big yawn.

"I'll be right out, sir. Just got to walk off my bruises." In so doing, Tom wanders underneath the platform above, where the guard can't see him momentarily, and finds a flat pan well-stocked with crusted salt. He hides it under his ring-arounds behind his back and then cinches his belt as tightly as he can, so the pan won't fall to the ground while he walks.

"Come on down there," the guard shouts. "Time to go. I's tired, but not too tired to get the strap tonight."

"No need, sir, I'm ready now," Tom calls out while reemerging from under the platform. He stumbles off in the direction of his prison railroad car, trying to stumble forward with his normal exhausted and faltering gait. He's sure the outline of the pan probably sticks out but hopes the gathering darkness and the fatigue of the guard will help him escape notice. The wind, which has blown strong all day, seems to be picking up. Maybe that will be a distraction, too.

In the process, some of the salt gets on Tom's right hand and on his back. It sears his skin. Tom just closes his eyes, sets his jaw, and grits his teeth, so he won't cry out. All through the time where the guards lock the prisoners into place for the night, he sits down waiting, wincing, pleading to himself for the time to pass. Typically, this takes five to ten minutes, but the burning of having the salt on his skin and the excitement of what will happen next makes it seem like five hours.

At last, the guards are gone, the men are sleeping, and Tom can extract the pins from his leg shackles and slip out of them. He, Clarence, Elijah, and Matthew have already prepared for their escape the last two nights. Their noise knocking the pins out of their shackles had sent up so many false alarms with the guard dog that now only a few of the guards come out when the dog's fiendish howling wakens everyone.

Tom looks over the clearing while removing the salt pan from behind his back. He needs water to wash the salt off. That's what the men working the turpentine still always do when they get salt on them. When the guards let them, that is. Sometimes, if a man was new at the work and didn't know how much the salt burned, the guards made the new man handle the stuff and then laughed at him when it burned his skin, all the while refusing to let him wash it away. If a prisoner was properly submissive, however, they let the men clean themselves off after handling the salt pans. It was still another way the guards tried to condition the prisoners to proper behavior.

Using his baggy clothing like a glove to keep his hands from getting more salt on them, Tom begins chipping off chunks of the salt, still gritting his teeth all the while and trying not to cry out because of the burning sensation on his back. As gently as he can, he takes a few of the chunks and grinds them into powder by rubbing them on the floor of the train car, leaving four larger pieces for later. Scooping as much of the powder as he dares between his shirt-covered palms, Tom leans to the edge of the train car and tosses the powder toward the guard dog's crude wooden water bowl. Some of it splashes silently in the water. Tom tosses another scoop, and another, and continues until he's out of powder. He hopes it will be enough. The stiff wind blows some of the salt grains off course, but most of them land in the dog's water bowl.

Next, he jostles Clarence who, after slowly wakening, does the same to Elijah, who wakes Matthew in turn.

Each person takes one of the remaining salt chunks and tosses it at the German shepherd. All four pieces plop in the sparse grass near the ferocious animal. Instantly, it wakens and bellows its trademark howl, straining at its chain while it snaps and bites at the prisoners just a few feet from the reach of its jaws.

Predictably, a handful of guards come out to investigate. Clarence times them. Nearly twelve minutes by now. When they retreat after yet another false alarm, all four prisoners hear them grumble about the dog and how they just want to sleep.

After the guards depart, the dog notices the salt chunks near where it rests. It walks over to one, sniffs it a moment, and then gives it a lick. Recoiling instantly, it runs over to its bowl. Without hesitation, the dog dips its face into the water and laps up several mouthfuls. Then, it starts whimpering and pawing at its tongue. It drinks more water.

While the rest of the prisoners lie down again and return to sleeping like the corpses they almost are, Clarence, Tom, Elijah, and Matthew watch the dog. After what they judge to be about two hours, the brutal creature vomits for the first time and begins limping around weakly while it whines, all four legs spasming.

Clarence looks at Elijah. Elijah nods. This is it.

28

Check

Susan Anderson wakes and dresses quickly in her worn calico dress. It is very early, about three in the morning, but she knows she needs to complete her errand and return before six o'clock comes. No one else in the Winston home is awake yet, she notes, as she hurries away from her one-room shanty on the edge of Winston's property. Last night, Sunday evening, Emily had given her a letter and instructed her to give it to Sam Johnstone by hand.

"Why must I deliver it by hand?" Susan asked.

"Because my father controls the post office, and he must not know about this, and the letter must arrive as early as possible tomorrow morning. Time is important."

"Does this have to do with what I overheard the other day?"

"It does. I won't tell you more than that, though. The less you know about this business, the better for you, I think."

"I think you is right, Miss Emily. I only done it because you is so nice to me, and your brothers are so mean. I still reckon it might end badly for me, but I's gonna help you one more time and trust in the Lawd."

Eyes welling, Emily had given Susan a hug and slowly walked away. Susan understands why she must deliver the letter. Yesterday afternoon, Judge Winston gathered all the family's servants and told them he suspected Sam Johnstone might be up to something and that he was worried Johnstone might try threatening Emily with his plot.

She can't leave the house alone anymore. Not until this trouble blows over, anyway. So, Susan must go instead.

She doesn't need long to dress. It's warm, had never cooled off that much last night, in fact, so after donning her dress and tying her shoes, Susan begins her trek. It's a fair distance out to the Johnstone house; that's why she's up at three in the morning. She needs to finish this and then report to work by six and have coffee ready for Judge Winston and his sons before they go off to work in the morning.

At least Susan can enjoy a cool breeze while she strides along. She hopes that will keep up throughout the day. The town is so quiet this time in the morning before the sun comes up. Not even any hogs nosing through the trash and mud in the streets.

Finally, Anderson reaches Johnstone's porch. She slides the letter underneath the front door and walks away, her pace confident and brisk. No one has seen her yet, and now the evidence is gone. It's rare for a colored woman to be on the streets of Athens at this hour, for sure, but she can claim she's running any number of errands for Judge Winston. No one will question her about that.

The sun is up, barely, when Anderson returns to the Winston house and prepares to enter by the back door, through the kitchen, like she always does. Susan lets out a little gasp when she finds Robert and James waiting for her as she walks in.

Robert has a twisted grin. "And where've you been already this morning, up and about so early, Miss Susan?"

As the two men close in on her, all Susan Anderson can think of is to wonder who among her fellow servants sold her out.

Eric Hoffman sits in Sam Johnstone's library. Sam brings him a cup of coffee. Eric went straight to Johnstone's house instead of back to the Commercial Hotel once the train from Nashville dropped him off at the Athens station. He wants to keep a low profile this morning because he knows that any number of people around Athens report to Winston. Hell, Winston probably knows he's at

Johnstone's by now, anyway, but Eric wants to at least make him work to get that information.

"Let's go over the list of witnesses we have again, Sam," he says. "You'll testify about Winston's conflict of interest as a judge sentencing convicts and making them pay off their court costs by working on his farm. We have Ben Walker and Dale Warren willing to testify that they witnessed the murder of Dale's son, Earl, by one of Winston's overseers, to disguise the fact Winston holds prisoners in peonage. And, you say, Sam, that Emily Winston will testify about the plot between her father, her brothers, and Seth Dean to arrest Negros by design and sell their services to the Southern Pineland Company."

"Yes," Sam replies with the weary nod of a man's who's slept far too little for several nights in a row. His eyes sting a bit whether open or closed, a faint buzzing feeling won't leave his head, and his ears ring most of the time, but his energy remains undiminished and his heart undaunted. "I wasn't sure she'd agree to help until the very end, but I got a letter from her this morning stating she would testify. All she requested of me in return is to go light on whatever penalties her father and brothers get. Seth Dean, too."

Eric shakes his head slowly and then mutters, "Seth Dean. She couldn't persuade him to take the stand? We can offer him a reduced sentence if he'll give the court details about the plot. Did you ever mention that to her?"

"Yes, of course," Sam says. "It came up in one of our discussions. Her letter said she was scared to mention it to him, but she planned to try if she judged the time was right. Emily's note also mentioned that one of the maids in her father's house, Susan Anderson, had also overheard things and would take the stand. Her testimony might not help much in an Alabama courthouse because she's colored, but in federal court her word might count."

"Well, I hope she can persuade Dean to testify. I visited him a second time before going to Nashville, and he stuck to his original story. Still, that's a good list of witnesses to work with. Emily is the key, of course, and if the housemaid backs what she says, that can't hurt, either. In a federal court, Judge Winston won't be able to bribe half the town to lie on his behalf. Well, he can still try, but there will be penalties if they do lie to the jury."

Sam nods. "One further question. We have two main charges to bring against Winston. Conspiracy to arrest and convict people without cause and holding people in peonage. Will you get as many of the peons into court as possible, so they can testify about conditions on Winston's farms?"

"Of course, I plan to do that."

"Do you think they'll testify?"

"It's a federal court. We can make them testify."

"Yes, we can get them into the courthouse and put them on the witness stand, but that doesn't mean they'll talk. I'll bet those peons are so scared of Winston it'll be hard to get them to open up and tell anyone what things are like here."

"But we can protect them in federal court, Sam. They won't have to worry about retribution, especially if we get a conviction."

"Try telling that to a sharecropper or peon who has been terrorized by white folks all his life. I don't think it'll be that easy, and I doubt we'll convince them there won't be retribution. Even if it doesn't come from Judge Winston, it'll come from someone."

Eric nods, acknowledging that all this may be true, but says, "We'll cross that bridge when we get to it. Is there anything else we need to go over before I leave for Washington and make my report to the Justice Department?"

"I think we've covered the situation."

"I can't promise what will happen, Sam, but we've got as strong a case as most. I'll do all I can in Washington."

"It's a risk for me, yes, but all life is a risk. This is the best shot I'll ever get to take down Winston and bring his crimes to light. It's time to take it."

"I'll telegraph you from Washington when the Justice Department is ready to move on this. We know the telegraph operator reports to Winston, but there's no other way."

"Thank you, Eric. Godspeed, my friend," Sam says. He stands crisply as if to salute and shakes the lawyer's hand.

Jefferson Winston returns home as the evening deepens. While his driver, Henry, stables the horses and returns his carriage to the barn where Winston keeps it, he sits on the veranda to his home in his old rocking chair, just looking out at the venerable oaks lining the driveway to his front porch and enjoying the shade. It's been a very long day. He'd been up even before first light and had been at the courthouse by five-thirty, so sitting down for a moment to catch his breath feels soothing. Looking over the fields he owns, Winston can still remember climbing and playing in those trees as a young boy, chasing the old family hounds while his father sat where he sits now, talking business with older men in dark suits, sipping alcohol while laughing comfortably, stroking his beard and furrowing his brow in concentration when the business got serious.

Winston also remembers his two older sisters laughing at him when the thunderstorms came and he splashed in the mud puddles. They are much older than he, almost a decade, and after they turned twenty, each had married and moved to Birmingham, where they still lived. They'd looked so pretty in their lace dresses at their weddings, their hair made up so exquisitely, while his father's friends showered them with compliments. At the time, he hadn't gotten any compliments from the men in the dark suits.

Now, most of those men are dead, and so is his father. His sisters visit from time to time, and he's on friendly terms with them, but saying the family is close would stretch the truth. What matters most to Winston is that he's finally done his father proud. The empire he's built in Limestone County might not compare with the fortunes of the great industrialists of the day, but he's made a name for himself.

If his father's old friends came back to life and saw what he's built, maybe now he'd get a compliment.

After looking out across his land for some time, Winston closes his eyes, and the fear and depression return. It isn't the trouble with the Justice Department. He'll win that battle. It's James and Robert.

That his sons are unswervingly loyal to him, he has no doubt. But what will happen to the empire when he dies? At age forty-nine, he hopes his death isn't imminent for some time yet, but life is uncertain. His wife's sudden death nearly six years ago is proof of that. Winston knows, however, that neither James nor Robert can follow in his footsteps. They are ruthless and willing to be cruel when circumstances demand it, it's true, but they don't understand subtlety. Information is power, but neither of them care enough to even read a damn book, let alone master the fundamentals of running a large farm and making contacts with cotton buyers. James is the better of the two, but Winston doubts he's up to the task.

That leaves Emily. She's smart enough to run the family business, far smarter than James or Robert, but she's a woman. He can't leave the family in her hands after he's gone. Her suitor, Seth, is a decent fellow, and he seems to make her happy, but he's a mediocre lawyer, and he isn't blood. *If only this were ancient Rome*, Winston thinks for a moment. *Then I could adopt an heir and die knowing things would not fall apart the moment I was gone.*

The darkness clouding Winston's thoughts brightens when he sees Emily come through the front door of his home and onto the porch. Something isn't right, though. Her eyes barely meet his, and she stands opposite him instead of sitting down beside him like usual.

"Father, I have something I need to talk to you about."

"What's happened? I hate seeing my daughter looking blue."

"It's about this trouble with the lawyer from Washington."

"Did he try to talk to you today while I was at the courthouse?"

"No, Father. I've never met him."

"What's the matter, then?"

"Father, I . . ."

Before Emily can say anything more, her brothers burst onto the porch.

"Father, you're home," James shouts out.

"Boys, I'm speaking with Emily. What can be so important you must run out here to interrupt us?"

"Father, we caught the rat whose been talking with Sam Johnstone," Robert says excitedly.

"Excuse us, Emily, but I think I'd better see what's happened," Winston says, standing and walking inside his home.

29

The Breakout

Clarence nods back at Elijah, who signs to Matthew. Hoping they've neutralized the dog, they jump down from the railroad car.

It hasn't worked completely. The creature tries growling and barking, but all that comes out is a throaty sound that would have been pitiful had the prisoners had any love for the animal. That doesn't stop it from bounding toward them, however, even though its legs spasm at the same time. The sight is so unusual that Clarence pauses just a moment, giving the dog time to get close to him and jump toward his left arm when Clarence raises it to protect himself.

Whack! The dog falls to the ground, whimpering after Tom Morton smacks it in the face with the salt pan. Tears streaming down his face, Tom scoops the last of the pulverized salt dust from the edge of the railroad car and, when the dog scrambles back to its feet and prepares to lunge again, tosses the salt dust into the beast's eyes. It falls back to the ground, pawing at its face.

By now, all the other prisoners in the train car are awake and watching, staring in disbelief. Clarence turns to speak to everyone.

"Quickly, everyone, here's how to get free. Emory, hold out your foot," he says while limping over to where Emory Wilson lies in the railroad car. Clarence extracts his metal spike, holds it in place with one hand, and helps Emory swing his foot down with the other. It takes Emory three tries because he doesn't want to spike his foot, but he finally pops out the metal pin that holds the shackles together.

Clarence hands over the pin to Emory. "You deserve this, my friend. You go free first." To everyone else in the railroad car, he says, "Try to get loose and escape as quietly as you can. What you do when you escape is up to you, but try to scatter, so at least some of us will get away. I'm not waiting here to die."

There's another pop as Emory frees his other leg. "I's going with you," he says. "I came from Athens with you, and I's leaving here with you."

Emory hands the spike to the man next to him, a man named Solomon whom Clarence has barely spoken with. Solomon is one of the men who's been the sickest over the past couple weeks. He is scrawny, even more emaciated than Tom, and most of his hair has fallen out. Solomon fell the day before yesterday, and from how swollen his ankle is, Clarence suspects it's sprained or broken. The poor man says, "Get me free next. I can't run away; I's too weak and my ankle's bad. But I'll make a distraction when the guards come out and buy y'all time. Please, it's the only way I'll ever help. I can't make it out, but I's gonna help you if I can."

As if to underscore the importance of what Solomon says, thunder booms as soon as he finishes speaking. The wind grows stronger. Emory hands over the metal spike to Solomon and says to Clarence, "Let's go while we can, Clarence."

The five of them set off through the dark pine forest in the direction they believe is north. As they depart, they hear the remaining fourteen prisoners all clamoring to be set loose next in hoarse, loud whispers. After half-running, half-stumbling for about fifteen minutes, they pause at the first creek they come to, and Tom Morton jumps in. He pulls off the top of his ring-arounds when he gets out, and everyone sees his entire back is the bright red of inflamed and burned skin.

"What happened, Tom?" Emory asks him.

"I had to hide the salt pan behind my back, and it's been burning my skin ever since," he says, finally able to speak as the pain subsides slightly. "It was the only way." He starts to put his shirt back on but cries out from the fabric rubbing on his raw skin. "I'll carry it," he says through his set jaw.

At that moment, on the edge of sight back toward the camp, Elijah sees an orange light go up. "What's that?" Emory asks.

"I'll bet Solomon started a fire over at the turpentine still to distract some of the guards," Elijah replies. "Good idea. Let's take advantage of his help and get farther away."

Boom! Another roll of thunder, louder and closer than the last. A swirl of pine needles brushes Clarence's legs when the wind gusts again. Not only is the wind stronger than ever, it's become nearly constant. The trees sigh and bend above them. Then, the men hear a sound no one expected. A harsh whistle.

"What's that?" Tom asks the group. "It sounds like a train's coming."

"Why now?" Elijah says while signaling this new information to Matthew.

"Sometimes, the train comes to the camp to take the turpentine away after we've boiled the impurities out of it," says Tom.

"Do they ever come at night, though?" Clarence asks Tom. "I don't remember a train whistle ever waking me up at night."

"No, always in the daytime. Unless it's really behind schedule tonight?"

"So, what else would a train come to the camp now for?" Clarence wonders aloud.

"I'm guessing it isn't good. I think we should move out," Elijah tells everyone.

Matthew signs something to his brother. "Matthew thinks we should keep going, too. Right away."

The escapees continue heading the direction they hope is north, even though it's tough to tell for certain on a cloudy night like this one. They don't get much farther before the gunfire begins. Everyone looks back. The light from the fire glows brighter, even at this distance.

"Solomon must have really lit the place up," Elijah says.

"I just hope more people got away," Clarence puts in. "I wish we could have helped more of the prisoners get loose before tonight, but there just wasn't time."

"Some of them might have tried to escape prematurely," Elijah says wistfully. "Or, heaven help us, given us away to try to curry favor with the guards. You just never know. I hope we did right. Let's keep going."

"I think we have a good guess now who was on the train," Tom adds. "More guards, it sounds like. We got out just in time."

As soon as Tom finishes, the skies open and the rain begins pouring down. It's not a light rain or a steady rain, but a hard, drenching rain that flies sideways into everyone's faces because of the wind.

The group stumbles onward, but before half an hour is over, each man begins slipping and falling while the earth gets muddier. They try to keep running regardless, but the conditions of the camp have weakened everyone so badly their pace is no better than a plodding jog. They stop to rest often, so they can catch their breath.

After a time, the escapees come to their first big obstacle—a larger stream. No one knows how deep it is for sure because it's still dark, but it's about ten feet wide, although the water flows languidly.

Clarence thanks the stars that he finally learned to swim after almost drowning in the Marias River in Montana. He's about to jump in and test the waters when the men hear the sound they've been dreading. A dog, barking furiously, followed by gruff voices, loud enough to hear through the pouring rain. Sounds like two men.

"Quick! Hide," Clarence suggests, but he doesn't see many places to hide. He looks around frantically, but the longleaf pines and cypress trees bordering the creek won't help. Their branches are too high to climb. Clarence doesn't know if the other men can swim, and he refuses to abandon them by jumping in the water without them.

When the men hesitate just a moment looking around for shelter, it's too late. A few seconds later, another German shepherd comes into view, followed by a pair of men on horseback with rifles. One unveils a lantern, so he can see who he's caught. The dog growls viciously whenever one of the escapees takes a step, and in seconds the guards have all five prisoners covered with their rifles.

"Well, looka what we found," the first says.

"Some more escaped niggers," says the second. Clarence notes that he's the man with the long beard who whipped him.

"Should we shoot them, too? Set another example?" the first says.

"Nah. Least ways, not all of 'em," the second guard replies. "We done set plenty of examples already tonight. Maybe just the scrawny one. He ain't good for no real work anymore, anyways."

"Yeah, that sounds 'bout right. You wanna shoot him? Or can I?" the first guard says while taking aim at Tom.

"You take this one," the bearded guard holding up the lantern says. "All y'all showed up just in time to help put out the fire and recapture a bunch of the niggers, so I'll let you kill one as my way of sayin' thanks. We'll get most of 'em back before tonight's over."

"You sure?"

"Yeah, I'll get my fun with the whip tomorrow."

"Okay, fair 'nough," the first guard says while putting his eye to his gunsight.

From the corner of his eye, in the shaky lantern light, Clarence sees a large, dark blur shoot across the ground off to his right, heading for the dog. Just as the dog turns and notices, an enormous alligator opens its jaw and snaps them shut on the animal's neck, tackling it to the ground in the process.

At the same time, Clarence hears a weak scream on his left. Another alligator, almost as large, has Matthew by the left leg.

"What the hell?" says the guard who is about to shoot Tom. He turns his body and fires at the alligator biting the dog instead. The bullet strikes the earth with a dull sound.

Emory is the first of the prisoners to move. He runs for the guard who just fired and lunges at him. Emory isn't strong enough to knock the guard off his horse but does manage to get both hands on the man's gun before he can bring it around and fire again.

Seeing this example, Clarence and Elijah do the same for the other guard. It takes the bearded guard a moment to respond, and he drops the lantern in surprise at everything that's happening. It lands on the ground, breaks open, and the oil ignites and creates a small pool of fire where the oil leaks onto the wet earth.

Next, the bearded guard levels his rifle at Elijah and pulls the trigger.

Click. Nothing.

The water must have ruined the shot! Clarence barely has time to think to himself before leaping at the guard and grabbing the back of his shirt. At the same time, Elijah gets his hands on the rifle. They tug in opposite directions. The guard falls from horseback, landing on Clarence and knocking most of Clarence's wind out of him, while Elijah falls in the other direction, holding the rifle.

The bearded guard starts landing punches on Clarence's face. Weakened by his imprisonment and almost unable to breathe, Clarence just raises his right arm to try to fend off the blows, but it isn't helping. The guard strikes him in the face twice, and Clarence feels the blood spurt from his nose.

The first alligator, the one with the dog in its jaws, starts spinning around, thumping the animal on the ground, while making for the water. Whimpering and yowling, the German shepherd tries to claw and bite back but has trouble connecting before the alligator nears the stream and dives in. The two creatures disappear under the water.

Matthew, meanwhile, fares a bit better. The alligator took him by surprise, too, attacking from behind, but only bit one leg. With the other, Matthew kicks at the creature repeatedly, trying to get it to let go.

Emory is in trouble. After a brief struggle that Emory has little chance of winning, the guard wrests his gun from Emory's hands and kicks him in the chest. Emory falls to the ground. Quickly cocking the gun, the guard aims at Emory. Emory even sees the guard's trigger finger flex and shuts his eyes.

As Emory rolls to try and dodge, Tom throws his soggy, heavy work shirt at the mounted guard. It isn't much, but it hits the guard's face and arm just enough that his shot strikes about a foot from where Emory Wilson lies on the ground.

Knowing he has mere moments before the guard discards the soggy clothing and fires again, Emory jumps to his feet and makes another run at his mounted opponent. This time, however, instead of trying to wrest the weapon away, Emory notices the guard's right foot has slipped out of its stirrup. He grabs the guard's foot with both hands and pushes upward, just as the man swings his rifle down to take aim at Emory once more.

For the third time, the guard fires and misses, his bullet going over Emory's head while he slips off the horse, falling on his back in the mud.

Meanwhile, the bearded guard strikes Clarence in the face for the third time, and Clarence begins losing focus, tiny flashes of light exploding in his eyes while everything else blurs. Dimly, he sees the man draw back his arm for the fourth time when, from the side, Elijah clobbers the guard's face with the rifle butt, like a ballplayer hitting a fastball.

The guard falls off Clarence to the side, clutching his own face, even as Clarence blinks repeatedly and tries to clear his mind and sit up. Elijah whirls and strikes the bearded guard another devastating blow, bashing him over the head with the wooden butt of the gun. The guard falls to the ground, limp.

Tom pounces on the other downed guard. As the man sits up, Tom wraps his shirt around the guard's neck from behind and tries to squeeze his air. He doesn't have a good grip, however, and the guard swings his gun back, using the butt to give Tom a sharp blow in the ribs. Tom yelps in pain and falls on his side, clutching his ribcage and crying out.

It's enough, however, for Emory to tackle the guard and wrestle with him until Elijah can make it over and blindside the guard with another strong blow to the face. The remaining opponent goes limp in Emory's arms and slumps into the mud.

Just as the men finish off their opponents, they turn to check on Matthew. He sits on the ground, leg bleeding from several teeth puncture marks that shred his skin, but the alligator that bit him has retreated. Elijah looks just in time to see its tail disappear beneath the inky water of the stream.

Although the oil burned brightly at first when it spilled on the ground, now it's beginning to die down, and darkness descends on the escapees once again. Clarence sits up, having recovered his senses, and slowly rises to his feet. He wobbles a bit at first, but puts his palms on his knees, breathes deeply for several moments, and eventually stands straight.

Tom is the only one besides Matthew who hasn't gotten up. He lies on his back, both hands on his left ribcage, moaning. When everyone finally gets him to focus enough to speak with them, he pants out, "I can't. Breathe right. I think. My ribs. Are broken."

"What do we do with the bodies?" Elijah asks. "I don't know if more guards will come looking for them."

"Are they dead?" Clarence asks.

"They about to be," Emory says, grabbing the rifle that works and cocking the hammer.

"Wait, Emory, don't," Elijah says. "We might need those bullets if more guards come after us."

"Right, good point. What do we do with 'em, then? They don' deserve to live."

Clarence, Emory, and Elijah just stand for a moment, staring at each other. Clarence speaks first. "You're right. They don't. But, if we kill them now, doesn't that make us just as bad as they are? Killing helpless people? Fighting for our lives is one thing, but isn't killing someone who can't fight back another matter?"

"I don' see much difference," Emory replies.

"I think Clarence is right," Elijah puts in. "I don't like the thought of killing people to start with, even horrible ones like these two. Look, that one has rope hanging from his saddle. We can tie them up, gag them, and leave them here. That way, they can't chase us, and they won't be able to report us back at the camp, either. If they find a way to live after that, maybe the Lord has plans for them yet. If they don't, well, we gave them a chance."

"But Clarence," Emory says, "that one with the beard done whipped you. He could've killed you."

"I know. But I want to show there's a difference between me and them."

"If you asks me, I don' like it," Emory says to the group.

"I think we need to vote on it," Elijah offers. "There's five of us. Will that satisfy you, Emory?"

"I don' know about satisfy, but I'll live with whatever y'all decide. Y'all saved me, so I owes you, anyway."

Clarence turns to the other two escapees. "We know Elijah and I want to let them live and leave them here. Emory doesn't. Tom, what do you think?"

Tom still gasps for air, even though he's managed to sit up while everyone debates the fate of the unconscious men. "I'm tired. Of hurting. I'm tired. Of being in pain. And I don't want. To starve no more. These men are. The reason for. All of it. I vote. With Emory."

"It's up to Matthew, then," Clarence says after a heavy sigh. "Ask him, Elijah."

Elijah signs to Matthew for several moments, explaining everything the group just discussed. Matthew signs back quickly before lowering his head and closing his eyes. "He's thinking," Elijah reports.

Matthew remains with his head bowed for a long time. No one moves. The blood has slowed its oozing from the gash on his leg, but the alligator tore off a chunk of flesh before letting go, and no one doubts Matthew is in great pain, even though he doesn't show it. Finally, he looks up and signs a few words to Elijah. "He hates these men as much as anyone else, but he doesn't want them to die because of us."

No shout of exaltation comes from anyone, just weary nods by all. Then, Matthew signs something else to Elijah. It takes several seconds.

"What now?" Clarence asks.

"Matthew says he knew the one gun would misfire." Elijah replies with a nervous laugh.

"How did he know that?"

"It's a '97 Winchester. Matthew says you have to keep it well-oiled and dry, or else it won't work in hard rain like this."

"How does he know so much about guns?"

"Our dad bought one, back while he was still alive, and showed Matthew how to take care of it. But, Matthew doesn't like guns, so he sold it after our father died. I never even knew our family owned one."

Elijah looks back at his brother, who tries to smile through the pain. Everyone just stands for a moment, trying to let out the tension.

Finally, Emory speaks. "Who'll help me tie them up?"

"I will," Clarence says. "Elijah, I think you need to help your brother and see if he's able to walk. Tom, we'll find a way to get you and Matthew on horseback. Hopefully, that eases the pain a little. We've passed one obstacle, I hope. But we still need to find a way out of the forest and then find someone who'll help us."

<u>30</u>

Lost and Found

On Wednesday, June 7, John Tener sits eating dinner in the lobby of his hotel in Jacksonville, Florida. His mission to find Clarence and the Maxwell brothers is over. He never got anywhere near where he guesses the turpentine camp is. Armed guards intercepted him as soon as he'd tried to ride down the train tracks yesterday morning. Tener told them he was a bank president considering investing in Florida real estate, but his bluffs, threats, and demands didn't work. Tener faced several guards, and they had guns. He was by himself, unarmed, and that was that.

Tener plans to stay in Jacksonville for a while, a few days at least, so he's already booked a few more nights at the St. John's Hotel, which overlooks Forsythe Street. It's convenient; both the riverfront and the train depot are two blocks away. He'd sent a telegraph to Eric Hoffman in Washington that morning describing his failure to learn anything regarding Clarence, how the guards threatened to shoot him on sight if they ever saw him again, and how the city police ignored him when he protested his treatment to them. Tener hopes Hoffman will telegraph back with encouraging news in the next couple days. Failing that, he'll stop by and pay Hoffman a visit on his railroad trip back to Pittsburgh.

After he finishes dinner, Tener decides to stroll along the banks of the St. John's River. On the way, he passes a sign proudly proclaiming that Jacksonville is the seat of Duval County, Florida. The irony does not escape him.

As Tener walks south on Riverside Avenue, just one block from the river, he finds himself swatting at his arms and face over and over. How does anyone live with clouds of mosquitos like this? Yet, Jacksonville is a growing city. He isn't sure how many souls call the town home, but twenty-five thousand or thereabouts seems a reasonable guess. The dock district has both river and ocean steamboat traffic, a railroad bridge crosses the St. John's, and the town on the west bank has many blocks in neat, geometric squares. Both the St. James and Everett hotels have five stories. Nonetheless, after walking along for half an hour he approaches the outskirts of the city, and before long, Tener finds himself looking at fruit orchards, mostly oranges and peaches.

Being early June, it's not the height of fruit season. At least, it wouldn't be in Pennsylvania where Tener lives, but here in northern Florida, some of the peaches and oranges are ripe. In fact, it seems very tempting to pluck one, but Tener decides to just find a market in town on his way back to the hotel. Not that the orchard owner would ever miss just one, but somehow, taking someone else's fruit didn't seem becoming for a bank president.

With fruit now on his mind, Tener reverses course and strolls back toward Jacksonville. It's nearly dark, after all, and he is looking forward to reading a pamphlet he just purchased that morning at a bookstore owned by an elderly colored gentleman. He hadn't known the proprietor was a colored man when he'd gone in, but upon seeing that he was, Tener had asked the man for the most insightful work in his store written by Negros. Expecting something by Frederick Douglass, he'd been surprised when the owner offered him a short tract of about twenty-five pages by a man named William Edward Burghardt DuBois, titled "The Study of the Negro Problems." When Tener mentioned that he'd never heard of DuBois before, the bookstore's owner said DuBois was a professor at Atlanta

University and was the first colored person to earn a Doctorate in Philosophy from Harvard. Intrigued, Tener bought the pamphlet.

While thinking back on that experience, voices suddenly jar Tener from his reverie. At least, he thinks he hears voices. Somewhere off to the west. Louder than a whisper, but not much, as if the speakers don't want anyone to hear them. As he walks toward the sound, the voices get louder, but between the gathering dark and all the trees, Tener can't see where the speakers are with any certainty.

Shortly, he discovers why. There's a hedge across his path. Probably a boundary line between two orchards. The voices come from just on the other side. Approaching as quietly as he can, Tener kneels behind a peach tree about twenty-five feet from the hedge and listens.

"Go easy there, Emory. We haven't eaten much more than bread and beans for weeks, and this is our first food since yesterday afternoon. You'll get sick if you stuff yourself too much all at once," says the first voice.

"How's your back now, Tom?" says another person. He has a lower voice.

"It still screams at me and burns every time I move," Tom's voice replies in a painful whimper.

"Is it better, though?"

"I don't know. Between my back and my ribs, everything hurts all the time."

"What about Matthew?" the second, lower, voice asks. "How's his leg?"

Tener hears no sound for several moments until the first voice answers, "He says it isn't much better. His pants cover the bite marks, but the wound hurts a great deal. He won't be able to walk normal when we get to town."

"No one's going to think we're normal anyway. Look at us. We haven't had a haircut or a shave in about two months," says yet another person. "If I look as unkempt as the rest of you, and I'll wager I do, people are going to cross the street to stay away from us."

Tener strains his ears. It can't be. The voice sounds like . . .

"True 'nough, Clarence. What we gonna do when we get to town, anyways?" the lower voice says. "Where do we go? We gots some money when we traded our horses to that old farmer for a boat and some cash, but it ain't 'nough to take us that far. We're gonna need more money, somehow."

"I don't know. We'll have to do some odd jobs, or something, until we can scrape together some money. Still, I don't want to stay in Florida any longer than I must. We still aren't sure the authorities won't come looking for us."

"Where'll we sleep tonight?" the pathetic voice belonging to Tom asks the group. "It was nice for that farmer to let us sleep in his barn last night, but I don't think we'll have any such luck tonight. It's a bit late to go knocking on folks' doors."

"I guess we'll have to find a quiet, out of the way place to sleep on the ground," Clarence's voice tells the group. "Let's get moving and see what we can find."

Tener decides this is his moment. "Clarence Duval," he says in a clear voice but without shouting, "step over here. No friend of mine will sleep on the ground if I can help it."

A moment later, a bedraggled head looks over the top of the hedge. Tener can just see the face in the gathering twilight. It's Clarence, but it isn't. The face Tener remembers is gone, replaced by a grizzled face with a scraggly beard and hair so matted and tangled Tener probably wouldn't have known it was Clarence without the voice to help him.

"Who's there?" Clarence says. Tener notes with alarm that Clarence has a gun, and he's scanning the orchard.

"Clarence, it's John Tener. If you promise to put down your gun and not shoot an old friend, I promise you won't have to sleep on the ground tonight."

"John Tener? I don't believe it's you. He's not in Florida. He lives in Pennsylvania."

"Yes, I do, and I'm the president of a bank there. But I've come south to try to find you and two brothers named Maxwell. Now, if you'll hold off from shooting me, I'll help get you out of here." With that, Tener steps out from the shadows of the tree he's been hiding behind and slowly walks forward.

"John!" Clarence says at last. "It is you! What in the world are you doing here? How'd you find me? Come on, everyone, this is John Tener. He's a friend of mine."

One by one, five weary, fetid, limping, filthy, and shockingly thin men wriggle through the hedge and stand in a semicircle around John Tener.

"I sense you have quite a story to tell me," Tener says to Clarence.

Clarence doesn't respond. Instead, he drops to one knee and begins crying.

Tener puts a hand on Clarence's shoulder. "It's all right, lad, you can tell me all that's happened to you later. Can you stand, so we can get out of this orchard? I'll bring you to my hotel room, get you some food and a good shave, and you can explain everything you've been through."

Clarence nods slowly, rises, and he and his companions shuffle, limp, and stagger slowly behind John Tener while he leads the way back into Jacksonville.

Nearly three hours later, as the clock nears midnight, the six men sit in Tener's hotel room. No barber is available at this time of night, but Tener brings everyone some food and allows them to shave with his razor after each takes a bath.

"Tomorrow, I'll buy all of you some new clothes, too," Tener tells them once everyone finds a seat in the suddenly very cramped hotel room. "Now that we've introduced ourselves and you've had a chance to eat a bit, Clarence, tell me everything that's happened to you."

While Clarence recounts the ghastly stories of everything they endured in the Florida pine forests, now and then one of the others breaks in to add some details. Several times, Tener's mouth simply drops open.

"Tom, how old are you?" Tener asks the young man when Clarence finishes the story.

"Fifteen, sir."

To Tener's eyes, the kid can't weigh above eighty pounds. He looks like a skeleton with skin over the bones. Tom's eyes have sunk way back in their sockets, and Tener fights back his own tears when Tom shows him the burns on his hands and back. Especially his back. It's still one bright pink mess where blood oozes from damaged areas that haven't scarred over yet.

"And, Clarence, can I see your back, too?"

Taking off his shirt, Clarence shows the scars from his whipping. Tener can see the long, straight scars that crisscross Clarence's upper back and shoulders.

"Emory, what's a sweatbox? I've not heard of that before."

"Well, suh, they puts you in this box, like a coffin, but wid a hole for your nose, so you can breathe. It's dark inside, and you can't see nothin' 'cept the light comin' in through the hole. Then, they just leave the box out in the sun for hours. It gets so warm inside, your skin, it blisters, and you get sores and start bleedin'."

"My God," is all Tener can say.

"It hurts powerful much, it do. I couldn't even move or eat anything until two days later, suh."

"Why'd you end up in there?" Tener asks, his eyes watering again.

"Because Ezra died, and I tries to tell the guard we gots to bury him decent."

"Mr. Tener," Elijah asks, "is there any way we can ever go home? My mother is on our farm by herself now, and I reckon she's about died of fright that she'll never see us again. Matthew and I, we need to go home and see her."

"I hope that will happen soon, Elijah. But there's a problem."

All five of the men wait silently for Tener to explain. Tener almost loses it again seeing the hope drain from their faces so suddenly.

"The problem is this. The five of you are, so far as I know, still considered criminals in the eyes of the law. Now, the Justice Department in Washington has launched an investigation into your arrests. I'm expecting a telegraph from the lawyer assigned to the case, Eric Hoffman, any day now. If our plan works, the Justice Department will charge Jefferson Winston with wrongful arrests and the violation of federal peonage laws. If that happens, the five of you can testify against him. And, if I'm allowed to hazard a guess about such legal things, your injuries will make powerful testimony to the jury. But, until that happens, all of you remain fugitives. Therefore, I suggest we lay low here, and you all stay out of sight as much as possible. I don't know if the Southern Pineland Company and the guards running your turpentine camp have any relationship with the city authorities here in Jacksonville, but I suspect they do. Until I know for sure, I think you should stay here and keep quiet."

"Bless you, Mr. Tener, for all you've done to help us," Elijah tells him. "We're in your debt."

"Not at all. It's the least I can do, considering all you've been through. I think, my friends, I should go and see if any message from Eric Hoffman has arrived."

"I hope so. Finally, we can get out of here and go home where we belong," Tom says.

31

Down in Flames

Sam Johnstone sits in the telegraph office on Friday evening, June 9, savoring the taste of victory at last. Normally, he'd go home and read his telegram from Eric Hoffman there, but this one time, he just can't wait. His aged hands shaking, he opens the envelope and begins reading.

```
Samuel Johnstone, sir,

Investigation is over. Superiors in Justice
Department have instructed me to drop case. Will
be no trial or charges. Suspect backroom deal.
Am furious. Outraged. Have tried all channels
of protest. Am deeply sorry.

My deepest regrets,


Eric Hoffman


P.S. Have already resigned in protest over this
injustice.
```

Sam wanders listlessly into the streets of Athens, leaning heavily on his cane. He's taken to walking with one after pretending to hurt himself last Sunday, but today, for the first time in his life, he truly feels old and relieved to have one.

Now he knows why it took Hoffman all the way until Friday afternoon to reply with a telegram. He'd probably spent the past few days pleading with his superiors trying to keep the case open. Hoffman had the evidence, and the case would be big. How could the Justice Department not act? Someone with influence must've shut down the investigation or told the Justice Department to shut it down. A great deal of influence.

Sam stops walking for a moment, tears welling up. He hasn't cried in years. Maybe even decades. It doesn't seem fitting for a former military officer to cry, but today, he does. His dream of the past twenty years is over. Dead. Gone for good. He'd hoped to accomplish one more humane and worthwhile thing in life before his time was up, but he'd failed.

Arthur Walker, Alannah's husband and Sam's coach driver, comes over to give him a hand into the carriage to return to his farm. Sam waves him away. "Thank you, but not this time, Arthur. You go on. I'll walk."

"All that way?" Arthur inquires.

"Here, read this. It'll explain everything," Sam says while he hands the telegram to Arthur. By the time Arthur finishes reading the short message, he's crying, too. He just hands back the telegram before driving off.

Sam requires almost two hours to reach his home on the outskirts of Athens. Weeks of little sleep, stress, and failed planning have taken a toll, but he doesn't care. He has nothing to conserve his energy for now, anyway.

Approaching his property, Sam sees a light up ahead. An orange light. It's getting brighter. He walks closer to get a better look, but in his heart, he already knows.

Jefferson Winston sits back in his soft leather chair and closes his eyes, sighing with relief. He's finally put the whole troublesome business to rest. He'd instructed Albert Dunlap at the telegram office to withhold any telegram for Sam Johnstone until as late in the evening as possible when the next message came in for Johnstone, and to notify Winston first. As soon as Dunlap notified Winston he'd received a new telegram, Winston set the next part of his plan into motion.

Once Johnstone left his property, Winston's local contact in the Ku Klux Klan went into motion. Winston's instructions were simple: burn Johnstone's house to the ground, along with any other buildings on his property, but do not harm Johnstone under any circumstances. When the Klansman asked why not make his worst enemy disappear, again, Winston's answer was simple. He wanted Johnstone to live for a good many years yet. Winston wanted Johnstone to live the rest of his life knowing that Winston beat him, that his morally reprehensible plans to uplift the Negro were a failure, and that Winston had the power to control his fate. Killing him tonight would be too easy and not nearly satisfying enough. Winston wanted age, disappointment, and bitterness to do the job slowly instead.

Besides, Johnstone owes him for another reason. Of all the things anyone had ever done to Winston, Sam Johnstone's efforts to turn his own daughter against him cut the deepest. When Susan Anderson confessed everything she knew just before Robert and James sank her decapitated body in the Tennessee River, Winston realized how close he'd come to losing everything. No, Johnstone owes him, and Winston wants to take his time getting revenge. Tonight, it starts with the Klan, but this is only the beginning.

Normally, Winston doesn't approve of the Ku Klux Klan. Even though many of its leaders are friends and business associates of his, why go night riding and terrorizing people when you can do the same thing legally through the courts? Typically, combining power and the law is just as effective, if not more so, than raw violence. But, Winston must admit, the Klan does have its uses. Its violent activities and brutality made Northerners assume that all its members are ruffianly hardscrabble whites—the riffraff of society. Nothing is further from the truth. Oh, the Klan has plenty of scum in it, to be sure, but many business leaders and professionals, even a few churchmen, are members, too. Plus, Klansmen have energy and enthusiasm. They don't mind committing the occasional murder, arranging a lynching, or, in this case, burning someone's home to the ground in the name of sacred Southern civilization and white supremacy.

Winston looks over his telegram from Senator Pettus in Washington once more. It appears he neutralized the Justice Department, just as he said he would. Getting Theodore Roosevelt to back off had been easier than Winston expected. Pettus was a Democrat, and Democrats ran New York City's notorious political machine in Tammany Hall. Tammany was resisting certain reform judges Roosevelt wanted to appoint to state courts, and Pettus convinced them to ease their opposition in a couple cases in return for Roosevelt using his influence with President McKinley to get the Justice Department to back down on its Alabama investigation. What Pettus promised the leaders of Tammany in return for their cooperation, the senator didn't mention.

Does Pettus approve of Winston's methods for controlling things in Alabama? In all likelihood, yes, Winston thinks. A native of Athens himself, Pettus has deep Klan connections. Rumor says he'd been the Grand Dragon of the organization at one point, and although Pettus himself never admits as much, those rumors, combined with his election to the United States Senate, keep Pettus a force in Alabama politics.

His latest telegram from Thomas Brown in Boston also brings a smile. The courts in Massachusetts concluded there were no legitimate grounds for investigating the company's labor practices. Brown sent extra men to Florida just in case but had recalled them now that the trouble is over. Winston savors the feeling of complete victory.

No. Not complete.

A knock at the door. Robert pokes his head into his father's study. "Father, Seth Dean is here."

"Thank you, Robert. Show him in, please."

Dean comes in, flanked by Robert and James. "You wanted to see me, Judge Winston?"

"Absolutely, Seth. Please sit down. I'm sorry I couldn't meet you yesterday when you called to see Emily, but weighty matters required my undivided attention. I know you understand."

"I am so sorry about what happened to her, sir. You know I was, and am, very fond of your daughter and was devastated when I heard the news. I'm still devastated."

Winston has no trouble believing Seth when he says so. The bags under his eyes and his poor shave testify to his grief. "It can't be helped, and you are not responsible for what happened, Seth. You've been a great comfort to her in these recent trying times. I appreciate that more than I can say."

"Thank you, Judge Winston. I did all I could for Emily, sir."

"I know you have. She assured me you had nothing to do with her troubles, and I believe her. And, despite your mistakes early in our legal troubles with the Justice Department, you've performed admirably ever since. You stuck to your story, never wavered in your support, and, in consequence, we've pulled through. I've said it many times before, but I foresee you'll have a long and successful career in the legal profession here in Alabama."

"I'm deeply moved by your confidence, sir. I know the troubles partly stem from my actions, but I've done what I could to set things right ever since."

"That is true. My family and I thank you. I even mentioned your name in my latest communications with Senator Pettus in Washington. He's always on the lookout for bright legal minds to join his staff or to appoint to office should our treasured Democratic Party regain power in Washington during the next national elections."

"Me? In Washington? I'm flattered, sir."

"I believe in rewarding those who render great service."

"May I ask just one question?"

"Of course."

"May I see Emily again at some point? During our last conversation, she said certain things to me that seemed very strange at the time, and I wasn't sure why she said them, but now I think I understand."

"I'm afraid that's not possible right now, Seth. Her doctors at the Birmingham Asylum for the Mentally Ill tell me it may be some time before she is healthy enough to receive visitors."

32

Farewell, Clarence

While John Tener walks back to the St. John's Hotel carrying several loaves of bread for his guests, he shakes his head and curses under his breath. The telegram he's gotten from Eric Hoffman in Washington burns him. The five men he shelters were half dead when he'd found them. Tom Morton, more than half. In less than three months, they've gone from healthy adults to wraith-like beings and survived tortures too heinous for John to visualize. Now, with no legal help coming from Washington, John needs to figure out how to help five fugitives escape recapture and near-certain death while staying out of legal trouble himself.

When John walks into his hotel room all eyes are on him. "Friends, here's what I've found out from Washington," he says morosely while passing out some bread to each man. "There'll be no case against the Southern Pineland Company. The politicians sold you out in a backroom deal. Eric Hoffman, the lawyer I told you I met in Nashville, already quit because he's so furious. We're on our own if we're to get you out of here and go somewhere safer."

After the escaped prisoners voice various exclamations of surprise, anger, and despondency, John continues. "I also think we should move quickly. I don't know if anyone from the camp will come this far looking for escaped prisoners, but I think we should assume they will. So, here's the plan I came up with this morning. I'll buy train tickets for each of you. Anywhere you want to go, although I'd suggest somewhere outside the South. Once you get there, you can send word to your families that you're alive and make your plans at that point. I'll buy the tickets two at a time, so we won't attract the attention of the people selling tickets at the station. Hopefully, they won't pay attention to names or faces, and you can make a clean escape. We'll also have to hope the Southern Pineland Company hasn't bought them off, too, although, now that you men have had a shave and a wash, no one would recognize you as prisoners, anyway."

Again, everyone mutters a bit while they digest what Tener says. Tom Morton, who still looks frail beyond description, but who has regained a little color in his face and life in his step, says, "Thank you, Mr. Tener. I think Elijah and Matthew should go first. I owe them so much for helping me with the work drawing turpentine. They covered for me almost every day because I'm so weak. The guards would've whipped me to death long ago if it wasn't for them."

"Tom, please call me John," Tener replies.

"No, Tom should go first," Elijah counters. "He's suffered the most of any of us. The sooner he leaves here, the quicker he'll recover."

Elijah turns and signs to Matthew, so Matthew knows what they're talking about. Matthew signs back without hesitation. "Matthew agrees. Tom goes first. He needs real medical attention for his back."

"What about Clarence?" Tom asks. "He's the one who got us free of our chains, and if it wasn't for Clarence knowing Mr. Tener, I mean John, here, we'd still be wandering through the countryside trying to figure out where to go."

John says, "Clarence will go last. I'm taking him to New York to see some old friends. And to find out what happened in Washington along the way."

"You don't have a family, Clarence?" Elijah asks, eyebrows rising. "You never told us about that. I always figured you were trying to get home to your folks this whole time."

"Yeah, me, too." Emory puts in.

Clarence looks around. His gaze drops for a moment before he lifts his eyes back up and addresses his friends. "No, I guess I don't have a family. I came to Alabama looking for my father but didn't get to stay long enough to search. I haven't seen him in about fifteen years, anyway, so as far as I'm concerned, I don't have a family."

"What will you do then?" Tom asks.

"I don't know. The last couple months haven't allowed for much planning. Maybe I'll go back to St. Louis and stay with Sally Healy and Mary for a little while. Look for a job there. I'm not sure. It would be nice to settle down and live a less dramatic life for a while. My luck has never failed me, but I don't know that I can count on luck forever."

"Wherever Tom goes, I goes," Emory says after a brief pause. "He saved me from gettin' shot. He's my little brother now."

"That settles it. Emory and Tom go first, Matthew and I next, and John and Clarence last," Elijah says, bouncing up from his seat.

The following evening, with Tom, Emory, Matthew, and Elijah already gone, John and Clarence sit in the hotel dining room. They get a few stares from the people around them, but both men hardly notice. It's after eight, and they see the darkness gather outside the dining room window.

"You eat everything you can, Clarence. It'll do you good."

"I still can't believe you found us. That was some chance."

"Perhaps. However, after everything that's happened to you in Florida, your luck was bound to turn for the better at some point."

"Maybe. I don't know, John. For some of the prisoners, their luck never turned. Four of them died in under three months before I escaped, and that is just from the twenty-four who arrived in the same train car I did. I have no idea how many more died during the escape, but I suspect the number is high."

"I tried to go to the camp and look at things for myself, but I couldn't get close."

"So many people died just to get turpentine faster and cheaper, and I don't even know what turpentine is for."

"I think it's used in paints, oils, and other things involving chemistry. The chemical industry is growing fast, Clarence. It wouldn't surprise me if that's where most of the stuff you extracted ended up going."

Clarence just sits, chewing thoughtfully on his food for a while. The steak, potatoes, and strawberries are so tasty. Of course, after months of eating mostly biscuits and beans, anything would be tasty, but this is good food.

After a pause, John resumes speaking. "Clarence, can I ask why you went to Alabama in the first place? That's one part of this whole story no one's told me in full. You said you wanted to look for your father, but how did you know to look in Alabama?"

"I got a letter. From Fred Pfeffer, of all people."

"Pfeffer sent you a letter? I find that hard to believe. I've not talked with him in years, but I don't believe his views on the race question are any different than they've ever been."

"They aren't. He's the same bigoted man he was on our tour. But, in his letter, he said that an old friend of mine saw my father and told him about it. So, he wrote me to tell me my father was in Alabama. Looking back now, though, I think maybe he set me up. I suppose I'll never know; I was only in Athens for half a day before I got arrested, so I had no chance to look for him."

"It wasn't a setup, Clarence. Least ways, I don't think it was."

"Why do you say that?"

"When I met the Justice Department lawyer in Nashville, Eric Hoffman, he told me he saw an obituary in the local Athens paper for a man named William Duval. Was that your father's name?"

"Yes."

Clarence stops chewing and looks down at his plate for a long while, saying nothing. Finally, he lifts his head and asks Tener, "Did the obituary say how he died?"

"It claimed an accident in the sawmill where your father worked killed him."

Clarence bites one lip gently and looks down again. His cheek twitches a few times.

"Well, I guess that doesn't matter much, does it? I've been on my own for fifteen years. It's all I've ever known. My life isn't going to change."

"Still, I'm sorry, Clarence, now that I know the whole story. I know it must still hurt, at least a little bit."

"I suppose it does, yeah. I never thought about my parents much over the years, except to wonder why they left me. Now I'll never know. That's what bothers me the most, John."

"What if you turned that from a sad memory to a happy one?"

"How?"

"Well, since you don't know for sure, you can choose to believe anything, right? You can believe that something bad happened to them, and they didn't have a choice. Or that someone else made them do it. You don't have to go through life thinking they just abandoned you because you were a disappointment or a burden on them."

"I don't know about that, John."

"Just think of what happened to the Maxwell brothers and everyone else in the Florida work camp. Their families will wonder the same things until they find out the truth. If they ever do."

"I've always assumed my parents thought I was no good, or that they didn't love me, so they left."

"But you don't know the truth about that, Clarence. You can keep believing that and let it weigh you down the rest of your life or believe something else and feel less guilty about your past. Think about it, at least, will you?"

"Maybe. I think I'll need some time before I'm ready for that, though."

"I suppose it's a lot to throw at you considering everything you've just experienced. Do you really plan to go back to St. Louis for a while? I think it's a good move, for what that's worth."

"I think I'll start there, although being there will remind me of John Healy too often, I'm afraid."

"He was a fine man, Clarence. I miss him, too. Our grand tour was only ten years ago, and already Williamson, Crane, Fogarty, Sullivan, and now Healy are gone."

"The Order of the Howling Wolves is going to need some new recruits," Clarence says with half a smile.

"That's not all, either. Remember the ship that took us from Australia to Egypt? The *Salier*? It sank off the Spanish coast during a big storm in 1896, while you were in Montana. Everyone aboard, passengers and crew alike, went down with the ship. Nearly eight hundred people drowned."

"Captain Thalenhorst was so kind to me on that trip. I wonder if he was still the captain when the ship sank? I hope not."

"The newspapers didn't mention it, if he was."

"Well, since I don't know for sure, I'll choose to believe he wasn't, and that he's still alive today, happily raising his son in Germany."

Tener gives a big smile. "I think I will, too."

"Do you ever see any of the boys, John? Did the people on our tour ever get back together again?"

"Only once. In 1893, a Broadway play came out based on our adventures. William Gillette wrote it. You've heard of him, I'm sure."

"I remember that. I was in Montana in 1893, but when I joined Walker and Williams, I heard about the play *Ninety Days*. As I recall, an American maiden gets kidnapped by the Khedive of Egypt while she travels the world in search of a rich and handsome young man she's betrothed to but can't locate."

"Yeah, that's the one. The plot wasn't the most original, perhaps, but in act three, a bunch of us ballplayers helped storm the Khedive's palace and rescue fair Matilda Watkins. We vanquish a host of the Khedive's guards with our baseball bats."

Both men laugh at the absurdity. John goes on, "I was there, along with Ned Hanlon, Ed Crane, George Wood, and Ward, of course. Tom Burns, Tom Daly, and Bob Pettit represented the Chicagos. Spalding came as well, along with Harry Palmer and George Wright."

"Did Daly and Pettit howl like wolves?" Clarence inquires with another laugh.

"Nah, not this time. I'm sure the thought crossed their minds, though."

"It sounds like it was a fun evening."

"Yeah, it was. After the show, John Ward organized something he called the "Globe Trotters Club" for all the tour members who could make it. We had a great time and vowed the club would hold a reunion every year. Never happened, though. Without a big event to bring us together, we just couldn't all find a reason to be in the same place at the same time, I suppose."

After another short pause, Clarence raises his wine glass and clinks it with John's. "Here's to the Spalding Tourists, what's left of them, anyway, the Order of the Howling Wolves, may their voices never grow weaker, and most of all, to John Ward and John Tener, for looking after an old friend."

"You forgot one person in your toast, Clarence."

"Who?"

"And to the mascot, Clarence Duval. May his luck never run out."

Clarence clinks his glass with Tener's again and drinks. He hasn't had a glass of wine in months. Not since John Healy's funeral, in fact.

Just then, Clarence sees John look over Clarence's shoulder. Tener's brow furrows, and he presses his lips together.

"What is it, John?"

"Don't turn around, Clarence, but I see some policemen through the door. They're at the front desk of the hotel, asking the manager something."

Clarence feels his heart sink. "Do you think it's time for our emergency plan?"

"Yeah, I'd say so. Here's what we'll do. I'll get up first and walk to the doorway of the dining room. I'll stand in the doorway and block the view inside as best I can. Give me thirty seconds before you get up and walk upstairs to the room. You packed the extra clothes I bought you already, right?"

"Yeah, it's all ready, so we can leave on the train when it comes through tonight."

"Good. Go upstairs, get your bag, and mine, and then jump out the window into the alley behind the hotel. Our room is on the second floor. You should be safe jumping from that height."

"Right. Then, I meet you on Laura Street, and we walk together to the train depot."

"Yes. I'll leave through the front door of the hotel because I won't attract any suspicion. When I'm sure no one has followed me, I'll meet you on Laura Street."

"I'm ready, John."

"Good luck, Clarence."

"You, too."

With that, Tener rises and strides off toward the exit to the dining room. At six foot, three inches, Clarence hopes Tener's frame will be enough to impede unwanted eyes from watching him. After thirty seconds, he rises and heads for the stairway to the second floor. Walking quickly but calmly, so he won't attract more attention, Clarence strides up the stairs briskly, runs to the room, and goes inside.

The suitcases sit right where they left them. Opening the window sash, Clarence tosses them to the dirt alleyway below and leaps down, landing with a dull crunch in the dirt.

Meanwhile, after standing in the doorway for a bit, John Tener advances to the front desk to inquire about the situation.

"Evening, officers," he says.

"Evening, sir," one of the uniformed men drawls, briefly doffing his hat before resuming his talk with the desk clerk.

"Is there a problem I might assist you with, good sirs?" John inquires politely.

"Perhaps, my good man. You see, certain individuals, convicted criminals, in fact, recently escaped from a turpentine farm some miles south of here. Because they are criminals, we believe they may be both armed and dangerous."

"How many criminals escaped?"

"Some number, although we don't know for sure. We believe up to twenty may be at large. We want to warn the public to be on the lookout, both for the public safety and to help us return these dangerous individuals to where they belong."

"I see. I'll certainly relay any information I come across, officer. May I leave any information here at the front desk?"

"That would be splendid, yes. Or, if you please, one of the superintendents of the turpentine farm is at the train station right now. He's here to identify the escaped prisoners."

"And now, officers," the hotel manager says, "you have my full permission to search my hotel for fugitives. I expect our guests will cooperate with your search without hesitation once you tell them the nature of the threat."

"Good evening, gentlemen," John proclaims while stepping outside the hotel. He turns right on Forsythe Street, then right again onto Laura.

"Is it clear, John?" Clarence's voice whispers from the shadows.

"Yes. Let's go. The police were still in the lobby speaking to the hotel manager when I left. I hope they're still there."

Clarence steps out and follows John. The pair walk briskly toward the waterfront, turning right on Forsythe and then left on

Hogan Street. They cross Bay Street and the Florida Central Railroad Station comes into sight.

"We can't return to the hotel," John says. "The police are searching it. Even if they don't find you, it's possible another guest will. We've got to get you out of Jacksonville."

"Right," Clarence responds. "On to the train depot. It's just up ahead."

John stops up short and then resumes at a slower pace. "Look, Clarence," he says without pausing again. "The passenger depot is just ahead on our right. But I see several police. We can't leave that way without them asking questions. The officer in the hotel also mentioned that someone from the camp is at the depot to identify missing prisoners."

"Can we talk our way out of this?" Clarence asks. "You're a bank president. The police will listen to you if you vouch for me, won't they?"

"I don't know, Clarence. In Pittsburgh they would, but I don't know about Jacksonville. Besides, like I just said, the police at the hotel told me one of the prison camp's superintendents is at the train depot right now. We can't risk trying to get you on that train."

"I can't go back to that camp, John. They'll kill me, sure, for escaping. I can't risk it. We must try something else."

"Okay, Clarence," John tells him. "Go now!" he whispers while he pushes Clarence into an alley on the other side of the street.

From the dim, unlit alleyway, John and Clarence survey their options. Across the street is the passenger depot for the Florida Central Railway. A little to their left lies the railway freight depot. Clarence keeps looking.

"Look, John. What's that sign say? I can't read it very well in the gas streetlight, but I think it says, 'Clyde New York & Florida Steamship Lines.'"

"You're right, Clarence. You can't chance leaving here by rail, but if we can get you on a steamship, you've got a chance."

"I only see one at the dock. I wonder where it goes?"

"Anywhere is better than here, isn't it?"

"Yes. It'll have to do."

"I'll go and buy the ticket," John says. "You just wait here and stay out of sight."

Checking to make sure he has a clear path, John strides across Hogan Street and finds the ticket office for the steamship line. In about ten minutes, he returns.

"Bad news, Clarence."

"The office is closed, and you can't get a ticket?"

"No, I have a ticket. It's the destination that's the problem."

"Somewhere else in Florida?"

"No. The ship that's in port right now is a foreign ship. It's a steamer for Liverpool."

"In Great Britain?"

"Yeah, we went there on our tour together, remember?"

Clarence nods. Liverpool was where the ballplayers played rounders against a local British team.

"Here." John takes out his wallet and empties it save for a few dollar bills. "Take what I've got, take the ticket, and go. You can trade the money for British pounds when you get there. I hope this is enough to get another ticket back to America when you get to Liverpool. If you take this, it leaves me just enough to get home myself. Now, go, Clarence. I'll speak to the police at the train depot to distract them. You've only got about thirty minutes before the ship departs."

With that, John stoops over, gives Clarence a hug, and turns and walks toward the train depot without looking back. Clarence watches his friend cross to the other side of Hogan Street, enter the building, and then he's gone.

Clarence creeps to the steamship dock, walks to the boarding ramp, and presents his ticket. The man taking tickets lifts his black cap and looks Clarence up and down. His heavy red overcoat and thick black pants look almost comical in Florida in June. Clarence can see rivulets of sweat on his brow, even now, in the late evening after the sun's gone down. "Traveling alone this evening?" he asks in a heavy British accent.

"Yes, sir."

"Just one suitcase? On a trip to Her Majesty's kingdom?"

"My friends stowed my other luggage when they boarded earlier, sir."

"I see. Well, you have a ticket, so please board. Not my business if you choose to travel lightly."

Waving his right arm and bowing courteously, the man steps aside. Clarence strides up the gangplank.

A few minutes later, the ship's whistle blows, and for the second time in his life, Clarence watches the United States recede from his view. The last time, he'd been a young homeless boy. A baseball mascot. A good luck charm. This time, as an adult, Clarence departs as a fugitive and criminal. He isn't sure when he'll return. He isn't sure he wants to return.

Clarence's adventures continue in book five of the Clarence Duval Series, *Piercing the Heart of Darkness*.

Clarence's adventures continue in book 5 of the Clarence Duval Series, *Piercing the Heart of Darkness*. Go to my website at

robbauerbooks.com

to learn more. If you want updates on future books, please join my Reader's Club mailing list at Rob Bauer Books.

I'd like to thank everyone who purchases *Darkness in Dixie* for reading my book. If you enjoyed reading it, I would be grateful if you'd leave a short review of the book on whatever website you purchased it from. Favorable reader reviews are very important to authors like me. They help tremendously in attracting new readers and spreading the word about existing books that you think others will enjoy.

Thank you!

Author's Note

After reading *Darkness in Dixie*, the reader may wonder if the prison labor system of the South could really have been this bad, or if I've exaggerated the severity of things for the sake of a more dramatic story. Although I wish that were true, I have exaggerated very little in this book.

The prison labor system as practiced in the South at the turn of the twentieth century is one of the darkest chapters of US history. It's one people would prefer to forget about, and it rarely appears in the history textbooks we read in school.

Because people have sanitized this chapter of US history or forgotten it completely, it's even more important that someone keep the story alive. If the reader wants to know more about the heinous nature of the prison labor system, both David Oshinsky and Douglas Blackmon have written award-winning history books on the subject. I recommend them for readers who want more perspective about this topic.

About the Author

I'm Rob Bauer, author of historical fiction and nonfiction books and owner of Rob Bauer Books. I hold a PhD in American History and was a Distinguished Doctoral Fellow at the University of Arkansas.

My fiction has two purposes—entertaining readers and explaining historical injustice. Although I enjoy adventure and humorous books as much as the next reader, I'd like my books to stand for something a little bigger. All my studies in history put me in a position to do that. Whether I'm writing about how racism damages the individual psyche, the deportation of the Métis people of Montana, the South's prison labor system, or the utter terror of the Belgian Congo, with my books you'll find yourself in powerful historical stories.

I also write nonfiction about baseball history because I've always loved the game, its history, and its lore. I sometimes joke that baseball may be the one thing in life I truly understand. Although I love the statistical side of the game, if you don't, never fear because my histories go light on the statistics and heavy on what baseball was like in the past. They're stories about baseball, but stories with a point.

The history blog on my website offers posts on a variety of interesting historical figures and events. I'd love to have you follow along.

When I'm not working on my next story or writing project, I enjoy spending time at the beach. And, oh yeah, I still read a history book or two. When I'm not watching baseball.

Acknowledgments

I also want to thank the people who helped make this book possible, especially Jim Soular for his help with editing. Ali Holst gets the credit for the cover art and design. Thank you to Jennifer Lodine-Chaffey and Mary Asplund for reading and making suggestions.

Made in the USA
Columbia, SC
22 April 2021